The Real
MRS. TOBIAS

Also by Sally Koslow

The Real
MRS. TOBIAS

A Novel

Sally Koslow

HARPER

NEW YORK · LONDON · TORONTO · SYDNEY

HARPER

HarperCollins books may be purchased for educational, business, or sales promotional use. For information, please email the Special Markets Department at SPsales@harpercollins.com.

FIRST EDITION

Designed by Jamie Lynn Kerner

Library of Congress Cataloging-in-Publication Data has been applied for.

ISBN 978-0-06-322374-5 (pbk.)
ISBN 978-0-06-327235-4 (library edition)

22 23 24 25 26 LSC 10 9 8 7 6 5 4 3 2 1

For my mother, who loved to read, with thanks

You never meet your mother-in-law on the day that you are well-dressed.

—CREOLE PROVERB

CHAPTER 1

Mel

THE AROMA OF ROAST CHICKEN MINGLES WITH A TOP NOTE OF Diorissimo as potent as if lilies grew in the foyer. The scent of my in-laws' hospitality.

"Darling," my father-in-law says as we kiss on both cheeks. "Looking gorgeous."

He is a courtly throwback able to call a woman *darling* without being slapped with a sexual harassment suit. Only men born before 1950 have this ability. Once, David and his son—my husband, Jake—were both beyond six feet, though thanks to a herniated disc, my father-in-law is slightly stooped, on his way to becoming a leprechaun. If I wear heels, as I am tonight, we meet eye to eye. His are twinkly, and his headliner of a nose prominent. If David weren't such a natty dresser, he might have walked out of a folktale by Sholem Aleichem. I adore him, and the sentiment is returned. I have my issues with Veronika, my flinty mother-in-law. With David? Never.

"Come in, come in," he booms. There are kisses for Jake, too, to whom David says, "Your mother is in her cathedral." The kitchen.

"Are the kids here yet?" Jake asks.

"They texted—they'll be late." David hangs Jake's sports coat and I toss my denim jacket on a chair. "After you say hello to your mother, join your old man for a drink." My father-in-law and I may have a mutual admiration society, but the invitation is directed only at Jake. "We can watch the World Series later. You have to give it to the Red Sox. That team is the rat's pajamas."

I follow Jake as he pushes open a swinging door. On the other side it's 1992, when his parents installed white laminate cabinets. As my husband greets his mother, he says, "Loaded for bear?" This idiom, which Jake learned at an Adirondacks boys' camp along with a wicked butterfly stroke and a comprehensive off-color vocabulary, is their code-speak when he senses that Veronika, his mother, is in a mood.

"For the record, I'm not angry with your son," she scoffs, "just concerned."

"Who can tell the difference?"

I can. If a vein throbs above Veronika's left eyelid, she is in the full flower of fury. And there it is. "Hello, Mother," I say. "These are for you." I offer up a bouquet twice as big as her head. Cosmos, dahlias, freesia, hydrangeas, ranunculus.

"Thank you."

Veronika's split-second wince tells me she'd have preferred chocolates or wine. Her eyes scan my vest and choker. When I last wore this getup, scored at a craft show, she remarked that I looked like an escapee from a Renaissance Faire. I laughed as if it were a joke. It wasn't.

"Anything I can do to help?" I ask.

"Please find a vase for the flowers. First closet on the right. The taller Lalique is best."

I know where Veronika keeps her vases. I've visited this apartment for twenty-five years, and little changes beyond books, always hardcover, alphabetized by author. At my apartment, books are arranged by color; my mother-in-law has told me this is an insult to authors.

I walk through a hallway hung with family photos identically framed in black with wide ivory mats. Many document Veronika's beauty, which has evolved from dainty to dignified, as if she'd willed each feature to come into sharper focus. There is only one of her as the child it is hard to believe she ever could have been: 1947, when Veronika and her mama arrived in America. After the war her mother's hair had grown in silvered, though by the time I knew her she was a Marilyn blonde. In the picture, you can feel the day's elation as mother and daughter begin life in a new country. There are formal portraits of Jake; our twins, Jordan and Micah; and one from my wedding, taken at an angle that makes my nose look enormous.

My marriage didn't kick off to the most auspicious start. I was aware that my mother-in-law never quite saw the point of me when her son could choose from an urban sorority of intellectual spitfires and trust fund princesses—her friends' daughters or Jake's classmates—about whom Veronika would remark in my presence with convulsive admiration. "Meryl Grossman had a breast reduction—you'd never recognize her!" "Nicole Adelman got into dentistry school!" "Linda Moskowitz, Rita's daughter, said, 'Be sure to tell Jake hello from me,'" adding, "She's an actuary."

I felt sure Veronika saw me as a pebble on the beach you'd never bother to add to your collection and that Saint Paul, my hometown, was populated exclusively by big, pale people eating big, pale portions. During college I lived with my parents, commuting across the Mississippi to the state's vast university where students, overwhelmingly from Minnesota, cheered for Gophers. Only these many years later do I have sympathy for Veronika's viewpoint, because from day one my daughter-in-law, Birdie, struck me as an equally unlikely partner for Micah, my son.

Had I been Birdie's mother, I might have pointed out her folly in squandering a chance to enter an esteemed master's degree program in writing—a program even I knew about—in order to move from Iowa to New York City to be with a boy, because despite his chronological age, when they met, Micah wasn't quite a man. At first, in rare solidarity, Veronika and I considered Birdie to be no one to take seriously, if we considered her at all. For a brief interlude we bonded, agreeing that Birdie was too submissive. Too perfect a physical specimen. Too other. As tightly made as a hospital corner and not on brand, given that Micah's preceding girlfriends had rings dangling from their noses as well as, I'm betting, places we'd just as soon not see.

Birdie is a woman who, because she is an introvert, refuses to believe she can intimidate people. Now, as I look at an image of her with Micah, I understand the spell she cast, because my daughter-in-law, more than I suspect she realizes, shimmers with the ultimate superpower: sex appeal.

Soon after they met, Micah stammered that a baby was on the way. History was repeating itself, since this had been my story, too, though I'm not claiming I have Birdie's ooo-la-la-ness. Micah—like my husband, Jake—entered into fatherhood far too young. I imagine people must wonder if any of us ever learned the facts of life and how babies are made.

Alice, my granddaughter, changed everything. I hear her now, squealing and asking, "Can I ring?"

Jake and I greet her at the front door, with David a step behind. We hug and kiss in a mockery of normal while I wonder, Can Alice sniff out that something's off? Has Birdie been crying? Has Micah been shouting?

"Sorry we're late," he says.

"Accident on the bridge," Birdie adds, though every intuitive cell in my body tells me they got a late start because somebody had a tantrum, and it wasn't Alice.

When Veronika enters the foyer, Alice hands her a picture. I am sure I am not alone in my gratitude for the distraction generated by a three-year-old with an affection for Magic Markers.

"Oh my, it looks just like me," Veronika says, bending low, using her apron to wipe her hands, flawlessly manicured in the pink of poached salmon. "Thank you, Alice. Later, will you help me find a place to hang this lovely portrait? Now it's time to eat."

Veronika herds the family into the dining room. Resting on a carpet, valuable and Chinese, is a table set with Dansk dishes. My mother-in-law will have no Meissen or Rosenthal china—nothing German—in her home. A Chagall lithograph with its requisite dancing cow faces the table where white tapers stand in sterling-silver candlesticks next to David's father's elaborately embossed Kiddush cup.

The cutlery is Grande Baroque, and its legend is Tobias lore. Long before Veronika became a lionized psychoanalyst and David's simple haberdashery multiplied into a tiny kingdom, she picked a silver pattern after she visited Altman's eighth floor from ten to twenty times, depending on the telling. After she filled out service for eighteen, one utensil at a time bought with money she'd saved, Veronika moved on to pickle tongs, iced tea spoons, and vegetable forks that weigh more than the squash and broccoli they convey to plates. To this day, I know she takes pleasure in keeping each piece tarnish-free. Possessions complete her. They represent substance, abundance, tenacity. At least that's what I, Melanie Glazer, M.S.W., think.

Yes, I remain a Glazer. This was not a decision I overthought. It simply struck me as quaint to morph into "Mrs. Tobias" when Jake slipped a gold band on my finger. Though I am proud to be his wife, that is not my sole identity, nor is becoming a Tobias going to make me feel more married.

Tonight's preliminaries speed by. Dinner starts with Veronika kindling the Shabbos candles, where in Hebrew, you can hear her Eastern European roots. David, in a velvet yarmulke embroidered with BAR MITZVAH OF JACOB DOUGLAS TOBIAS, chants a quickie blessing over the wine. Veronika passes the platter with two challahs to Micah and, as if he were nine, insists he bless the bread. He plops the yarmulke by his place setting on his head and does what she asks. After his grandfather belts out "Amen," every Tobias but Veronika pounces on the bread like an aquarium seal jousting for feed. My mother-in-law serves lavishly, yet barely eats herself.

"Would you help me with the soup, please?" she asks David.

I spring up from my chair. "I'll do it."

"No, Melanie, you sit." I knew she'd say this. I asked anyway.

I turn to Alice. "How was Matilda's birthday party?" I pride myself on name-checking my granddaughter's buddies. Hazel, Emil, Piper, Madeline, Quentin, Sunny, Felix, William, Genevieve, Finn, and Matilda.

"Not Ma-til-da, Gran. *Tilda*."

"Tilda." I stand corrected. "Was her party fun?"

"I got a goodie bag with a wand! And stickers!"

"Did you wear your tutu?" Jake asks.

"Of course." Alice rolls her blue eyes. "Guess which—the pink or the purple?"

"Pink?"

"Purple!" Point, Alice.

I am all in favor of raising rowdy, confident girls. I inadvertently raised one of my own, the stout-hearted Jordan, who would be here if she weren't traveling for her business. But I confess to having given Alice armfuls of rhinestone bracelets, more than one tiara, and high-heeled plastic shoes. While I try to pacify mom-clients' fears of the Princess Industrial Complex, for me Alice is a novelty on whose behalf I ignore my cautionary advice about our nation's Pepto Bismol–pink ecosystem. It's simple. Pink is pretty. Why else would Eloise have wanted a pink, pink, pink room at the Plaza? I want Alice to feel pretty. As a child, I never did.

Birdie and Micah sit still, their daughter between them, a pigtailed Switzerland on whom the conversation refocuses, again and again.

"What's your teacher's name?"

"Your favorite part of preschool?"

"Do you think Kermit will ever marry Miss Piggy?"

"Who's Kermit and Miss Piggy?" Alice asks.

Perhaps Kermit and Miss Piggy have retired to Boca.

"Soup course coming through, choo choo choo," David says as he pushes a tea wagon. The family sips away their portions and moves on to entrées while Jake explains how cashmere is collected from Mongolian goats. (Carefully, we learn. Goats bite.) I long to report on a client, but know I can't. This is why we therapists come off as dull as dust; the interesting aspects of our work can never be shared.

"Has anyone seen the show at MoMA?" Veronika breaks in to ask. I have. There was much to look at but nothing to remember, so I'm relieved when she offers up a ten-minute analysis with sidebars. Birdie says conspicuously little. Micah, less. At least we aren't subjected to a PowerPoint about the real reason we've gathered. We know what's coming, and it isn't a cheese course.

Alice topples Birdie's red wine. "Uh-oh spaghetti-os!" she shouts. Rivulets shoot out onto the ivory damask tablecloth, with each adult scrambling to undo the damage. I proudly find club soda to mix with salt and blot the stain.

Veronika informs me that I'm wrong. "It's white wine that gets out red. It's all about the enzymes."

Enzymes never were my thing.

"I'll cut you more chicken," Jake tells Alice when the mess is largely obliterated.

"But none of that," Alice says, accusing the kugel. "It has *stuff* in it."

Birdie answers Alice with, "Honey, those are apples. You like apples."

"Show us all what you learned in ballet!" I goad Alice into performing a string of twirls that end with a curtsy and take the applause that follows as a sign to start the coffee—one of the few tasks Veronika allows me to perform—while others clear the plates and wrap leftovers. We work in silence as Veronika fills the dishwasher, because no one else knows how to do it right. I deliver milk and sugar to the table while David presents a cherry pie on Veronika's favorite cut-glass stand, a doily strategically covering its hairline fracture. She brings out green Majolica dessert plates, a pie server, and cake forks. I wait for her recitation on how cake forks are different than salad forks, but she claps and announces, "Time for dessert." Down to business.

Alice casts a skeptical eye on the pie. "No cookies?" she asks. When she visits our apartment a few blocks away, I stock up on black-and-whites.

"Try some, please," Birdie urges. Normally, neither she nor Micah force dessert on their daughter. Tonight, they'll do anything to stonewall.

"No, I want to watch TV," my granddaughter whines, acting uncharacteristically bratty. As sure as a bird fleeing an oncoming tsunami, she must sense that something's off.

"What do we say?" Veronika prompts, surely to Birdie's annoyance.

"May I watch, please?"

David ushers Alice into Jake's former bedroom, a shrine to boyhood with its well-preserved sports ephemera and Cornell pennant.

As if an interrogator has snapped on a spotlight, Micah shifts in his seat and squinches his eyes. Birdie displays her standard erect posture, but I hear her not-so-silent yoga breathing. Finally, after the pie has been cut and the coffee and tea poured, Veronika places her refolded monogrammed napkin to the left of her plate and begins. "Let's not pretend we don't know why we're here. Micah and Birdie, we're all family, which makes your problems our problems."

Like it or not, we will meddle.

My shrinking shrink mother-in-law sits as tall as her five-foot-one inches allow. In the mirror hanging over the burnished walnut buffet, with the chandelier too bright, every one of her almost seventy-five years show. I notice a droop in her chin that wasn't there the last time I looked. And yet, Veronika remains exquisite, her beauty rivaled only by her tenacity.

"Mother is right. It's time we talked about the issue at hand," I say.

Veronika, the self-appointed head of the family and possessor of the Tobias nuclear codes, offers me a look of withering disdain and grinds on. "There are few situations that can't be resolved, given love and determination. How can we help?" *This needle won't hurt a bit.*

Micah fidgets with a fork, glowering. David's index finger traces figure eights in the tablecloth. I suspect that Jake wants to hit the pause button on this discussion before it starts, but at forty-four he's not going to start telling his mommy what to do.

"Nana, Birdie and I appreciate your concern, but this is our business." Micah speaks quietly, though I hear an edge. I am proud of my son.

"You need to take control before this problem takes control of you," Veronika counters. "Think of how much better you'll feel if you go to the authorities and explain what happened."

Birdie chimes in with, "This is all we've been talking about." She brushes away her bangs. "We'll get everything straightened out." *Leave us the fuck alone.*

I wish I'd coached Birdie. She might have said, "Perhaps I've given the wrong impression—we're not looking for advice, especially not from you." Veronika would have been as startled as if her pie server had taken a bow.

"I'm sorry, sorrier than I've ever been in my life," Micah adds, "but no good can come from reporting an accident with no witnesses."

Jake plunges in. "The criminal attorney I've spoken to agrees. Micah's situation is like a tree no one hears topple in a forest. There's no reason to go running to the police."

"Except his ethical obligation," Veronika insists, talking over Micah as if he weren't sitting directly across the table. "How will he be able to live with himself if he doesn't turn himself in?"

"I don't know for sure if I hit a person. I might have hit a"—Micah grapples for a word—"a garbage can. And going to the police isn't going to help the person I hurt, if that's the case."

"There are two issues here, ethical and legal—possibly hitting someone and leaving the scene of the accident," Veronika says. "Neither is trivial."

Micah's voice rises. "But confessing to hitting a person—if it was a person—when there was no witness—not a one—why would anyone do that? My confession would hurt me, and by extension, Birdie and Alice. So, Nana, will you . . ."

Shut up?

"Will you stop?"

Does Micah realize he's shouting?

"No, I won't stop. Your accident is the tip of the iceberg, and you aren't working together." Veronika turns toward Birdie. "It takes two horses to pull a cart. You need to make your husband understand this."

Warrior Princess Birdie doesn't move.

"And where does my great-granddaughter fit into the picture? Have you considered Alice? You can't raise a child in a maelstrom. She'll act out. I guarantee it."

"Could you back off?" Micah says, quieter now.

I rake my son's face for a clue to what he's thinking and feeling, but someone has replaced him with an animatronic Micah, his heat and rage gone. I'm also pissed that by appointing herself both judge and jury, Veronika is usurping my role. Micah is my son. I, the Dynamic Opposition, decide to use my words.

"Young marriage is hard," I say as I note my mother-in-law's astonishment at being displaced. Because I listen to my clients rant and sputter all the live-long day, in civilian conversation Jake claims I interrupt and don't let others speak. Perhaps I drive him as bats as a woman who's invented her own religion, but I am compelled to say what's on my mind. "The first few years are the hardest, especially when you are no more prepared to be a husband and father than to govern a developing nation. You're working everything out, not just what you want from your relationship, but how to merge backgrounds while you're both still growing up."

So what if I sound like I'm ad-libbing a graduation address?

"Birdie, I imagine it hasn't been easy to live far away from your parents." Russ and Luanne Peterson have never visited from Iowa. She's told me her father refers to his daughter's borough as Crooklyn. "Jake and I want to remind you that we're here for you," I add as a garnish.

"Mel, I appreciate this," Birdie says, "but Micah and I are working things out on our own. We're talking about seeing a therapist."

"Excellent," I say, though my inner cynic has little belief in couples' counseling, my least favorite therapy to conduct. No matter how reflective two people might be, by the time they haul ass to a therapist's office, nine times out of ten the relationship is on its way to extinction, rendering the exercise little more than a time suck.

Yet Veronika says, "Good—because this incident could rear-end your marriage,"

"Is that a threat?" Micah asks.

"A prediction."

More questions, more toothless advice, more defensive posture from my son until Alice returns and announces, "I'm tired. Can we go home?" This is the get-out-of-jail-free card for which her parents have most likely prayed. Within minutes, the three of them have fled tonight's dinner-palooza.

My mother-in-law accepts my offer to help clean up. While she finishes loading the dishwasher and prepares the morning's coffee, I wipe down counters, Swiffer the floor, fold the damp dishtowel in thirds and hang it on the handle of the stove, sure that Veronika will refold it. We perform this choreography silently and efficiently. In the den, David is dozing in front of the ballgame he'd been watching with Jake. My husband and I wish Veronika good night.

Had this been an evening with friends, a postmortem would be our virtual after-dinner cognac, one of marriage's finest perks. But instead of "Can you believe that bitch's remark?" or "Did you see how much he drank?" all I say is, "I'll give it to Birdie—she didn't cry." In her place, I would have.

"Was I as big a baby as Micah when we got married?" Jake asks.

In truth, no. Jake grew up the moment Jordan and Micah arrived, twenty-three minutes apart, in that order. Like a penguin, he intuitively fulfilled his fatherly destiny while I had to teach myself motherhood as if it were Italian, memorizing parenting books and seeking advice from every mom I met, including strangers at playgrounds.

"Did your mother really say 'no one in the family has gotten a divorce'? What about my brother?" Fred's marriage lasted less than two years, but most likely, Veronika has forgotten I had a brother, may he rest in peace.

"And her own brother-in-law?" Jake asks. Uncle Ezra, David's older brother, died in the bed of a woman who wasn't his wife.

Though if there were only one spot in a lifeboat, I'd be a ninny to test Jake's loyalty, I savor the rare occasion when we are on the same page, aligned against Veronika. On the point of my mother-in-law's condescension, I am as resolute as Jake is defensive of her virtues, but squawking to him about Veronika guarantees the accusation that I am oversensitive. I'm willing to say I may be. Yet I can't resist asking, "Do you think your mom can spook Micah into going to the police?" As a therapist, I abhor that strategy. As a mother, I hope it might work.

Jake dodges the question and asks, "Do you think he and Birdie should stay together?"

"Absolutely."

The person I cannot lose is Alice. I love that child with a vengeance. Alice is my blood and my joy. Before she arrived, I never once had fantasized about becoming a grandmother. What woman turning forty does? But because I had kids insanely early, and Micah did the same, along came grandmotherhood, the Powerball of marriage. From the first time I held Alice, not only was I *that* grandma—gaga—I realized she offered a chance for a do-over where I could try to correct all the flubs I made in Motherhood 1.0.

I have a single grandchild, but the difference between one and none is infinite.

Losing Alice? Non-negotiable.

CHAPTER 2

Micah

TEN DAYS EARLIER

For Micah Tobias, tonight became both the end and the beginning. He'd activated the grin he reserved for seduction, and the air of the bar in which he'd spent the last few hours was swampy with desire, pheromones flying. He was sure that at least two women—three if he counted the redhead—would welcome him into their beds. Nonetheless, when Micah pictured the typical post-grad apartment to which he expected his conquest to conclude, its bathroom alive with female clutter, he put on the brakes. Believing he could get his married-but-looking card punched was sufficient.

After a lengthy pee, Micah paid his tab and headed outside. A streetlight shimmered in the evening haze like a glowstick seen through Vaseline, barely illuminating the rain-slicked road. He fumbled for his keys, reminding himself that he'd driven in far more inebriated conditions, and that despite a battleground of words exchanged with Birdie, he still attracted other women. Most important, he'd thought about a meeting that afternoon with a guy who knew a guy who might be willing to put a little skin in the game of his business. If Micah could turn a profit, maybe his mother would stop debriefing him every time they met. Maybe he'd see Birdie's perfect smile again.

As he drove away from the bar, Micah's truck huffed like the geezer it was. He turned, then turned again, confused now as to whether he was traveling east or west. A Brooklyn and Manhattan guy, he knew little of Queens. The borough's appeal began and ended with Citi Field and his grandfather's fables about Forest Hills Stadium, where David had once seen a Beatles concert.

He remembered he could check Waze and fumbled on the seat and floor to find his phone. His eyes strayed from the road just long enough to hear and feel a thud eclipsed by a thunderclap. Damn, not only could he not find his phone, he'd hit something solid—a bike, a motorcycle, a Smartcar? As he slammed his foot on the break he heard a short, spiky sound, like a squeegee scraping glass.

Micah shuddered, unlatched his seat belt, and leaned out the door. In the dark of the night, whatever was in front of the truck's right fender was alive, writhing and moaning. A big dog, he told himself. Yeah, that's what it was. Its howl was brief, followed by silence.

Micah's first impulse was the right one. Get out of the car. See what happened. Try to help. Call the cops. Were he in possession of his phone and not in the shallow end of common sense and sobriety, this is precisely what he would have done. But Micah's legs refused to budge, as paralyzed as if he'd suffered a stroke.

A minute passed. He found the nerve to walk in front of the car to see who or what he hit. Nothing was there.

Micah Tobias knew he should return to the bar and look for his phone, which he probably had left behind. Yet where the fuck was the place? Probably only a half mile away, but in what direction? Confusion began to fold around him like a blanket. His brain closed down.

Later on, after the accident curdled him with shame, Micah convinced himself that he drove away to look for help, a lie he revisited so often he believed it. If Micah had found the bar and his phone, he'd have sought assistance. If he'd seen a policeman, he'd have explained. But in a city of more than eight million people, Micah Tobias was alone, without an angel to lend a hand or lead the way. As he pulled out of the godforsaken grotto of outer-borough New York City, Micah didn't see another soul. He did, however, stumble on the major artery that took him to Manhattan.

Birdie would take no pleasure in seeing him seriously buzzed. This is why he headed to Jordan's.

CHAPTER 3

Mel

I COULD NEVER HAVE GOTTEN THROUGH IT WITHOUT YOU."
Chemo, divorce, job loss. Audrey is leaving my office stronger
than the facsimile of a woman who entered two years ago. Tears
mist her eyes. Mine, too.

It's our final session and I, proud mama bear, am sending
my client into the world confident that our work has teased her
anxiety into a steadier shape. "I'm here if you need me," I say.
"Only a phone call away."

"Okay if I hug you? Not protocol, I know."

We embrace. Audrey is an art critic who has kept me au
courant on gallery openings and cheap Greek restaurants in As-
toria. I'd pick Audrey as a friend if being her therapist didn't
preclude such a relationship.

I like to think of myself as a watchdog of the human condition, an annotator of emotional specimens. Am I a good therapist? How would I know? Clients appear to listen when I
sprinkle them with my penetrating pixie dust, I have received
only two one-star ratings on Yelp, and no one has gotten close to
committing suicide on my watch. In fairness, I do not treat the
world's maddest hatters. Psychopaths never kick in my door. The

Mel Glazer clientele is bewitched, bothered, and bewildered—stressed, depressed, narcissistic, sexually confused, lonely, rejected, and marginalized, but rarely malevolent or sociopathic.

As if I were listening to the rough draft of an audiobook, I hang on my clients' words, challenge with questions, and chime in with quotable sound bites. Just twice in fourteen years have I snoozed in a session, once when the air-conditioning went on the fritz, the other when I'd popped an allergy pill. Nondrowsy? Ya think?

I, Melanie Glazer, therapist to the neurotics next door, am a woman who loves her work and hopes she can do it forever. Damn smart of me to choose a field I can't age out of. Occasionally, I find it hard to focus, but what therapist doesn't? Actually, I can think of one, a full-fledged shrink, a woman I know well and to whom I am quasi-related.

After Audrey closes the door, I enter a termination summary in my laptop, gather my belongings, lock up, and briskly walk to a bistro blocks from my office. Jake will be waiting with a bottle of our favorite Pinot Noir. He usually greets me with a warm kiss. As the syncopation of my marriage has etched a pattern, some days—some years—I am more in love with my husband than others. This is such a day, such a year, though it hasn't been ever thus. There was that time I almost bailed.

Our routine in this restaurant is as predictable and comforting as a Japanese tea ceremony. I scan the Instagram-able room with its soft lighting that I hope takes a year or two off my face. Eating here makes me feel as if I am starring in a movie directed by Nancy Meyers.

There's Jake, waving. We kiss. I take a chair and lean toward him as we click glasses. "Hello, you," I say.

"Babe, how do you rate this week?"

"An eight. Audrey and I terminated."

"How does zat make you feel?" Jake wiggles his Groucho

brows. They remain black, though his hair is laced with entry-level silver strands.

"When a client finishes therapy, it feels as if I'm giving birth. I'm part mother, part obstetrician, and part God. And your week, husband?"

"Eight point five. Coats flying out of the store."

"What kind?" I picture scholastic Chesterfields, sailing in formation, velvet collars aligned like Canada geese.

"Italian cashmere, black, navy, and camel—three-buttons, notched lapels."

Right. Jake and his father own three high-end men's clothing stores. He has mentioned the upcoming promotion, but I am incapable of retaining the minutia of my husband's work. Jake is as reliable as sunrise and annoyingly sane; he will not crumple into craziness if I occasionally zone out when he speaks or fails to return a text. Fearing a segue to glove pockets and colorways, I ask, "What would you like to do tomorrow?"

"I'm driving up to the Greenwich store in the morning."

"In that case, I'll do a barre class"—even if the other women will be in their twenties and thirties and kick forty percent higher. To their kind, I'll be invisible. If you want to have your ego auto-corrected, try fishing for a compliment and remarking to the woman next to you in such a class that you're old enough to be her mother. The look you'll get in response will say, *Tell me something I don't know.* I try not to let in middle age, but like any woman who is almost forty-four, with her first reading glasses and mammogram appointment to prove it, who claims not to obsess about dimpling thighs and a libido at risk of going AWOL, I am lying.

"I'll be back by two," Jake says. "How about a movie marathon?"

"Fine. Go ahead and pick an inane blockbuster. I know what brooding, foreign film I want to see." My wingspan is sagas with whalebone stays, dysfunctional families, or anything set in Paris except crime thrillers, whose plots I fail to follow.

We leave the restaurant. Jake wraps his arm around my shoulder and as we walk, parking spaces gape open, as odd a Manhattan sight as nun's knees. I savor the drowsy calm of the October evening, and that our bed is only blocks away. It's not a small thing that my husband is a guy that other women would syndicate, were they aware of the lovemaking expertise possessed by this Adonis, if Adonis were a merchant prince with tortoiseshell glasses and a bald spot the size of a crocheted yarmulke. The dazzle that sex sprinkled on our early relationship glitters still, even if Jake tends to wax on about center vents.

Not that my life has been all moonlight and meatloaf. There was the regrettable sinkhole I fell into some years ago when I decided that while I loved my husband—who is not just good in the sack but loyal and kind—I suddenly couldn't stomach how he started humming at bedtime whenever he wanted a blow job or quoted his mother as if she were Eleanor Roosevelt. To my lasting regret, I let my attention wander, not a practice I endorse even if, to my knowledge, Jake never discovered my indiscretion. The memory of that breach will always be a fault line in my marriage, one I promise myself I will never cross again.

The wind kicks up. It starts to rain, hard.

Jake mentions a few movies that will be loud and long; the others, dystopian. His call, I tell him. I know I'll be paying only half attention to the screen as I wonder about the new client who will be filling Audrey's hour. What problems will she lay at my feet? Gender jumble? Incest? Profound loneliness? Perversely, I hope her issues will be juicy and that I'll be able to enrich her life as if I were rewriting a diary.

Jake has moved on to embroidered ties. "Are they expensive?" I ask.

"Top of the line. Each one takes two days to finish."

What a colossal waste. I'm stuck on how to respond. Why couldn't Jake be a theater critic? An oyster shucker? A bronco rider? Something interesting. Because the family business beckoned, rechristened David Tobias & Son after he joined it.

We reach our building, greet our doorman, and collect our mail. As we stand by the elevator, Jake says, as breezily as if he were telling the time, "By the way, we're all going to New Orleans this spring to celebrate my mom's seventy-fifth birthday."

The elevator door opens, but I'm frozen. "When was this decreed?"

"C'mon, Mel." Jake's voice is on the cusp of pleading. "I'm sure we talked about it."

"I'm sure we didn't."

"This won't be incarceration at Guantanamo. We're staying in a five-star French Quarter hotel that's been rehabbed since Katrina." His face flushes until two red spots appear on either cheek like clown makeup.

"You could have—should have—asked first." My father-in-law is a peach. It's Jake's mother, Veronika Tobias, M.D., marquee psychiatrist and eminent psychoanalyst, the third person in my marriage, with whom I'd rather not vacation. We get in the elevator and squabble all the way to the eighth floor.

This is not a fight I'm going to win tonight—or, most likely, ever. But on the virtual spread sheet hidden in my heart, Jake's sin has been duly noted.

CHAPTER 4

Birdie

"M ICAH, WHERE ARE YOU? I'M WORRIED."

It's the fourth message Birdie Peterson leaves, each going straight to voicemail. The previous night, her husband had bolted after they'd rumbled about money, their default battleground. Birdie was raised not to complain or to scold, behavior as foreign to her native Iowa as cactus. Now, she splits the difference between worry and fury. Micah has disappeared before, yet always trickled home by dawn. This time he's been gone for eighteen hours, and Birdie's dread displaces lesser emotions. Her husband is wrong about a lot of things, but what if he is dead wrong?

She doesn't know who to call. Micah has drifted away from his friends, who one by one have taken a turn toward serious, studying to be doctors, lawyers, or high flyers on Wall Street. He hasn't replaced them, as far as she knows. The obvious—phoning her in-laws or Jordan, Micah's twin sister—is bound to incite a stampede into her private life that will make everything worse. She sees no reason to suffer the indignity of the Tobias family getting a more intimate look at her marital dings and dents than they already have.

It seems premature to reach out to the police, and what would she tell them? The hubby and I had a spat and he split. Yes, he's done this before. Well, the other time he slept at his grandparents' apartment. No, I'm not sure if they gave him ice cream.

Birdie decides to wait a little longer.

The phone rings. "Wanted to touch base," her mother-in-law says in the low register that Birdie knows signals alarm. "Everything okay?" Mel Glazer isn't nearly as good an actress as she thinks she is, no better than Birdie is at lying.

"Fine. Busy. One of the other instructors sprained her ankle and I'm covering for her, doing double-shifts." She wishes. They could use the cash.

"Uh-huh." She senses that Mel knows something is amiss. "I hope my slug of a son is pitching in."

"No complaints." That she'd admit.

"Do you think something is wrong with Micah's phone?" Mel's nonchalance is as counterfeit as Birdie's cheer. "I've been leaving messages."

"Can't help you with that one."

"Can you put Alice on the phone, please?" Mel asks after a pause. "I miss my favorite granddaughter."

Her only grandchild. Mel worships Alice. Since she was born, her mother-in-law has posted an unrelenting jamboree of photos on social media. Birdie hopes none of Mel's clients or their daughters who suffer from infertility see this all-you-can-eat buffet of cuteness.

"Sorry, she's in the tub." Not much gets past Alice, and Birdie can't risk her repeating that Mommy and Daddy have been yelling, or that he's been sleeping on the couch. "In fact, I better check on her. Alice!" she calls out. "Sorry—got to go."

Birdie hangs up, disgusted by her lie and apologies when it's Micah who is at fault. The other night, he tormented her about whether she was sleeping with her boss at the studio. The absurdity of the accusation amuses her. For starters, Jagat (née

Darren) prefers men. In response, she teed off on how lazy Micah has been in trying to make a go of Mash, his company with its fleet—if two food trucks count as a fleet—that roves upper Brooklyn and lower Manhattan flogging mashed potato sundaes topped with gravy, cheese, caramelized onions, or tomatoes. She wondered aloud if Micah and Archie, his bungling assistant, even take the trucks out of the parking lot. From there, Birdie moved on to how her husband failed to pull his load with Alice. Not enough income, not enough incentive, not enough help. Sis, boom, bah. This was the percussion of their argument, followed by her saying, "I can't stand it anymore—I'm out of here. With Alice."

It wasn't the first time she'd threatened to crash the marriage, but the lifespan of her rage typically lasted only slightly longer than one episode of Alice's favorite TV show, which Birdie is letting her watch too often. As soon as Micah stormed out, she started to blame herself, because when she harps, Birdie knows she sounds like her father exploding at one of her brothers when they were young. *Better pick another line of work, son. Loafer like you'll never last a good goddamn Sunday on a farm, and, hell, that's the goddamn day of rest.* Like that. He is a good man, Russ Peterson—'til he takes a drink.

Alice wanders into the kitchen, her nearly platinum hair tangled. Yesterday's Play-Doh is stuck under her fingernails, which need cutting, and last week's sparkly lavender polish is chipped. Alice needs the bath Birdie lied about to Mel.

"What's for supper, Mommy?" she says. "I'm hungry."

"Good question." Birdie looks into the recyclable bag filled with the family's final farm-share delivery. Kohlrabi and Jerusalem artichokes. Micah doesn't know the name of either vegetable but loathes both. This might be a good reason to serve them, Birdie thinks, should he appear.

She takes the remains of last night's turkey meatloaf out of the fridge, sticks three sweet potatoes in the oven, rinses the red-leaf lettuce, peels and slices a cucumber and a tomato and adds them to a handful of elderly radishes in the big acacia salad bowl. If they split, who gets the bowl?

Birdie had hoped to have a marriage like her parents', minus her father's drinking and the mooing Jerseys whose cycle of ministrations Birdie's mother has accepted with relentless forbearance. Russ and Luanne Peterson are hard-working partners, raising cattle, pigs, and children—Russ Jr., Clark, and Birdie. They stopped short of lecturing as they watched their daughter forego the spot she'd worked off her tail to be offered in the Writers' Workshop at the University of Iowa—a program more competitive than Harvard, they'd heard—in order to move to New York City to be with a guy she'd met on an airplane only months earlier.

The Petersons consider their daughter to be mature and responsible, which Birdie demonstrated by teaching yoga to put herself through college. Being an adult, they believe, means living with the consequences of your decisions. Interfering? Not their style. *It's okay to make mistakes, just don't keep repeating the same one*, is her dad's favorite aphorism, unaware that somebody famous—Benjamin Franklin? General Patton? Ronald Reagan?—said it first.

"Where's Daddy?" Alice climbs into her booster seat and begins to scribble a picture with the crayons and paper Birdie keeps handy.

"He has to work, honey. We talked about this." Birdie will once again single-handedly perform the bedtime rituals—the books, the sweet-dreams to dolls and bunnies, the butterfly kisses, the good-nights to absent family. She'll tuck in Alice wondering where her husband has slept.

"Can I wear 'Punzel tonight?" squeaks Alice, a three-year-old soprano.

Alice loves the hideous garment, dripping with ruffles and

bows. Had it not been a birthday gift from Joy-Ellen, she'd have donated it to Goodwill.

"Remember?" Birdie says. "We're saving the nightgown for Halloween. It can be your costume."

The Peterson and Lindstrom women, potentates of DIY, worship at the shrine of Etsy. Any one of them—Birdie, too—can make a needle and thread dance into a costume. This year she wants an easy out. In Carroll Gardens, their corner of Brooklyn, Halloween trumps all other holidays. Homeowners decorate with towering wheat stalks, wryly carved jack-o'-lanterns, and webs of ghostly gauze, not an inflatable Casper in sight. Moms dress as witches, though not the slutty sort she imagines might haunt hard-partying lower Manhattan. The mommy-witches of brownstone Brooklyn wear their requisite clogs (Birdie has scored a gently used pair on eBay) and show only a sneak peek of cleavage in smock dresses, Dries Van Noten maxis, or their vintage, sister-wife equivalents. Half will be trailed by pets transformed into scandal-ridden politicians.

Last year they'd been invited to two Halloween parties. One featured a skull-shaped punch bowl and chili served in a hollowed pumpkin the size of a toddler. At the other, guests roamed through a backyard corn maze designed by a Broadway set decorator. Her Iowa reserve maligned the flamboyance, but Brooklyn Birdie didn't want Alice—and herself—to miss it. This year's invitations are pinned to a bulletin board. Parents are expected to come in costume, too. Double, double, toil and trouble.

Who are you dressed as, Birdie? A divorcée!

After nearly five years with Micah, regret has settled like silt. How many disappointments are they from separating? She's overheard Mel tell Micah not to worry, that his wife isn't bred for combat. But there is more than one way to end a marriage. Her mother-in-law has failed to factor in the limits of patience.

"Mommy, can I have a snack?"

"Apple?" Birdie ruffles Alice's curls. Physically, she is Mel all over again. Alice even likes to dress like her grandmother. Oddly. Her daughter has begun begging Birdie to buy her clothes at neighborhood stoop sales.

Birdie quarters a Granny Smith, cuts a wedge of cheddar, and herds Alice into the cramped living room. She tunes in to *Bluey* and stations her daughter in front of the screen, then returns to the kitchen, picturing Alice eating three meals a day of Cocoa Pebbles. What would Alice's grandmothers, both militant advocates of healthful food, think, or Nana Veronika, her high-minded great-grandmother? When the woman snaps her fingers, the other Tobiases form a conga line at her feet.

Birdie doesn't want to imagine her small, fragile family shattered. Micah may be angry with her and she with him, but he adores his daughter and Alice adores her daddy in a straight shot of reciprocal love. No intricate equation. But as her own grandmother, Joy-Ellen, often proclaims, sometimes you gotta fish and cut bait.

Damn it. Should she call the police? Yes. No. Tomorrow.

"How's my bumble bee?" Micah had asked Alice at their last dinner together. "What was the best thing that happened at day care?"

"Miss Melissa taught us how to make milk carton houses! Wanna see?" And she was off, skedaddling to the alcove they call a bedroom, where Birdie had perched her creation on a bookshelf salvaged from the street, repainted cherry red. Alice ferried her house into the kitchen and Birdie placed it in the middle of the pine table set for dinner. "Doesn't it look like Grandma and Grandpa's house?" Alice's pride lit her pink-hot face.

"Theirs is a little taller," Micah said. Mel and Jake live on the eighth floor of a stolid Manhattan building.

You bozo, Birdie thought. It looks exactly like the Petersons' house in Iowa: green shutters, two stories, and a chimney smack in the middle of the energy-efficient roof. Birdie snapped a picture. "I'm going to send this to Grandpa Russ and Grandma Luanne right after supper."

When Birdie sits down to dinner with Alice, she says grace. Silently. Bless us, Jesus . . . Bring my Micah back and let me work out the problems in my marriage. If I'm the cause, give me strength to own them. Just let my husband be safe, somewhere. I love him. Goddamn it.

CHAPTER 5

Mel

ARE NORAH AND I FROM THE SAME SPECIES? I SWIVEL TO GET a better fix on my long-standing eleven o'clock. Her cheeks suggest the soft, rosy fullness of a ripe peach while I am all angles—cheekbones like flying buttresses and a significant beak. As if added by a diabolical calligrapher, lines fan my hazel eyes. I've been coloring my hair for so long, I'm not sure what shade it used to be or what to call it now. Burnt Sienna if I'm being generous. Idaho Potato if I'm being truthful.

I do not look like the wife you'd expect of Jake, my aging preppy who, like his father, dresses as if it were eternally 1995. You have only to see me from the neck up to guess that my wrists will clank with bangles and fingers will flash rings that Frida Kahlo might have coveted.

"Just because you're a therapist you don't have to dress like a caricature of one," my mother-in-law has chided. "You'll distract your clients."

But Norah moves right along with a grave pronouncement. "Jealousy works opposite from the way you'd expect."

"How do you expect it to work?" When I'm jealous, I've been known to wish temporary misery—adult acne, identity theft, athlete's foot—on someone. The emotion behind my impulse clarifies how I feel about another person. Not that this makes me proud.

Norah shifts in my salvaged Louis XV armchair and unleashes a smile as big as a Panama hat, which she does often. She inhabits her well-proportioned body stiffly, as if it were on loan. "Jealousy makes me feel trivial and nasty," she says.

"When that happens, what helps?" A question, boring in both ways.

"I only know my jealousy reflects how little I like myself and I want to like myself more."

I could draw a Venn diagram of Norah's inner life. A mother lost to breast cancer, a hedge-fund-hero husband whose childhood sounds like a country western ballad, and the fact that she is turning fifty. Norah has been ruminating about this milestone since before she turned forty-nine.

Today I notice that Norah has acquired not just the athleisurewear in which she dresses for our sessions, but her alleged philosophy from a chain of shops whose bags feature psychological graffiti. Last Mother's Day Birdie gave me workout pants from one of the stores. *Friends are more important than money*, the gift bag preached. Easy to say if you've got the big bucks, I preached to the bag. *Creativity is maximized when you live in the moment.* But I wouldn't have a practice if excavating the past had no value. Half of my clients aspire to writing memoirs, thinking they'll fart out a book in six months. Most give up after chapter one.

"You've mentioned you're trying to do more things that scare you," I point out in a tone of interest without judgment, a voice I rehearsed with a tape recorder when I first hung out my shingle. "How's that coming?"

"Well, this morning I called my mother-in-law." It takes only for Norah to say the triggering term "mother-in-law" and Jake's mom's queenly status poisons the room like a virus. How many times has she stuck it to me that I have a mere fun-sized M.S.W., while her degree is M.D.? That not only is she a physician, she belongs to an esteemed analytical society for which my street cred falls so short I couldn't even make their B-team?

Still. Veronika may be Bergdorf's and I, T.J. Maxx, yet even if I'm part motivational coach, who is the better therapist? I suspect her of terrifying patients—she does not, like me, have clients—who stick around, year after year, prostrate on her suede chaise, as they chase their tails and pay high fees insurance rarely covers. Meanwhile, the good doctor murmurs, "Hmmm." Lucy van Pelt in pearls.

Once, for Mother's Day, a holiday Veronika celebrates with vigor, I gave her a sampler, scored at a thrift shop. It was embroidered with ABANDON HOPE ALL YE WHO COME HERE. I imagined Veronika hanging the gift in her office. She was not amused.

I dimly hear Norah say, "When I'm with my mother-in-law I start seeing myself through her eyes. She holds it against me that my life hasn't been as tough as hers."

Ditto Veronika, whose hard luck history is as tragic as it is dramatic. Veronika was born in Germany in 1941. Her parents were deported by Nazis, though able to hide their baby girl with a lion-hearted farm woman. Veronika's father didn't make it out of the camps, but her mother managed to survive and rescue her daughter in 1945—though at only four years old Veronika had no idea who the strange lady was who arrived to take her away. My mother-in-law's Brothers Grimm childhood, she told me once—with rare candor—still scripts the hellscape of her nightmares. Stormtroopers. Stomping boots. Thundering *achtung*s. Since she spent the war years safely disguised as a happy little Catholic, this terror comes not from recovered memory, but survivor guilt and a restless imagination.

I consider something I've said aloud only in my own therapy. At what point do trauma-induced scars become merit badges for astute judgment? Do they entitle my mother-in-law to constantly offer what she calls "loving assistance"—what I call battering boundaries?

"My husband insists I overreact," a faraway voice says. "Do you think he's right?"

"Excuse me?" I am surprised to find myself in my office.

"Am I oversensitive?" Norah says in an earth-to-Mel tone. "My mother-in-law wishes *le petit prince* had found someone more like her."

Veronika and I both know she'd have been happier if Jake had wed her frosty clone, a woman who favors cashmere in shades that flatter those with caramel hair and plays viola on Sunday afternoons in a quartet, making Mozart echo in Riverside Drive rooms stiff with Art Deco furniture as an audience of sycophants reverently nod as they wait for tea and babka.

Norah, Norah, Norah. I try to suppress my Veronika-animosity. "Have you and Brian discussed your feelings about his mom and how she treats you?" I've been known to utter a word or two or two hundred to Jake about how haughty his mother can be toward me.

"You can't be serious," Norah says. "To talk smack about her would be like nuking our marriage vows, and, here's the deal—" She lowers her voice and smiles bashfully. "I don't utterly loathe the woman. She can be exceedingly kind, just not to me."

Got it. This is why it's tricky for me, too: I admire Veronika as much as I resent her. She is as resilient as anyone I know—and brainy. She moves from English to Polish to French to Italian, and for amusement, recently added Arabic. She can also tell a joke. *Why do they bury mothers-in-law twelve feet under? Because deep down, they're really sweet.*

After years of my own therapy, I've realized I wish I could be loved more—or at all—by Veronika. My own mother's love was wool and flannel, providing constant warmth, but Veronika's love is sequins and satin. Her praise can make people feel ten pounds thinner. She elevates her favorites, and sees past their faults. If she'd had a daughter, that woman would undoubtedly be president.

"If only I didn't feel my mother-in-law was trying to outdo me all the time," Norah adds, leaving the thought bubbling in the air.

Veronika doesn't strive to best me in particular. She competes against every woman she meets—with perhaps the exception of my daughter-in-law, Birdie, and daughter, Jordan—and Veronika expects to win. Usually, she does. That she's no *jeune fille* doesn't stop her from wanting to be considered the most soigné woman in any room, though she's usually the only one who drops *soigné* into everyday speech.

"We're all supposed to go to the Galápagos together," Norah announces. "Ten days of togetherness on a ship the size of a studio apartment."

"Ah, the Galápagos. I know it well," I offer irrelevantly. "My husband's bag disappeared at the Quito airport, and he had to shop for clothes on the one island in the Galápagos with a store. Since Ecuadorian men are about a foot shorter than Jake, there weren't many choices in *muy grande*. He spent the week in a blue-footed-booby sweatshirt, shorts with a giant tortoise on his behind, and sneakers that lit up in the dark."

As Norah laughs, I say, "Cruise ships can be suffocating, so walk the deck, practice yoga, take a dance class, meditate, read." After each suggestion I lightly rap the arm of my leather chair. "You've got this."

"I hear you, Mel, but if I break away, you-know-who will say I'm anti-social, especially if I read, because the books I like put her to sleep. Brian's mother gobbles up either a whole romance novel a day, like a gooey hunk of supermarket birthday cake, or a book with so many brand names it may as well be a catalog."

Instead of digging for why Norah lets her mother-in-law's reading habits irritate her, I find myself reviewing Veronika's literary icons: Joan Didion, Penelope Lively, Toni Morrison. She has urged me to read their work, and I have enjoyed each author, though when I press my own favorites on her—Ann Patchett, Min Jin Lee, Elizabeth Strout—she never gets around to reading any of them.

Norah gulps for air. "Do we have time to talk about something Brian said?"

I glance at my brass clock, strategically placed to allow me to monitor the fifty minutes that count as a therapeutic hour that in Veronika's office lasts five minutes less. I've squandered much of the session stewing in my own mental juice, violating every rule of clinical training. "I'm afraid not," I say. "Until next week."

It's a wrap.

After a five-minute sabbatical, I open the door for another client, aware that my mind is wandering like a stray cat. Do I need to return to therapy myself? The person who might know the answer to this question is the last one I would ask: Veronika.

CHAPTER 6

Mel

A S I ENTER MY OFFICE, MY PHONE IS RINGING DEEP IN MY TOTE. Micah? Let's hope. Last night Birdie hurried me off the line as if I were trying to bamboozle her into buying a timeshare in the Ozarks. She and my son must be in the middle of something twisty and private and want me to butt out. Another mother might.

When I find my phone, Veronika bleats without preamble, "Why hasn't your son called me back?"

"I have no idea."

"I've left that boy message after message. Pulled strings to get him tickets for the Bong Joon ho screening. He could at least show some gratitude. Should I give the tickets away? We're committed to Mark Morris at BAM tonight."

Age hasn't slowed Veronika. She walks fast and speaks fast. Nor are my in-laws home much. Their calendar is clogged with dance, opera and Philharmonic subscriptions, gallery openings, lectures on history and current affairs, benefits connected to diseases or the arts, and movie nights followed by discussions with a circle of well-spoken, well-worn friends of which half are luminous eccentrics. She and David treat the city as it were a village, traversing Manhattan and Brooklyn by car, trying out trendy restaurants before they've even hit my radar.

Soon Veronika will turn seventy-five—hence the boondoggle Jake sprung on me. For my mother-in-law, I expect this to be prime time: whatever age she reaches strikes me as the revised ideal, as if she had a running start and is always twenty paces ahead of other women. She plants a flag for younger ones while intimidating the shit out of women her own age who'd like to retire their zippered pants along with half their responsibilities, let their hair go grey, toast their freedom with a glass of Chardonnay, take up pickleball, and inhale a crème brûlée.

David is four years older than Veronika, and getting forgetful. Given the chance, he naps like a toddler ragged from the playground. My father-in-law would surely be content to stay home on most evenings, shouting at sports telecasts or contentious news programs, but Veronika schlepps him along like Queen Elizabeth did Prince Philip.

"When you speak to your son, please give him a crash course in etiquette," Veronika snaps. She has conveniently forgotten that on my watch I did just that, forcing Micah and Jordan to write notes thanking her for the argyle cardigans, dictionaries, and monogrammed stationery that arrived on birthdays and Hanukkah. I hear Veronika grinding her teeth. Ignoring my in-laws' dental irregularities—which includes the faint smacking of David's dentures—can be a full-time job. "Let him know it's polite to respond to his grandmother when she provides a service." She speaks like a narrator for a PBS documentary.

Veronika finally takes a breath, allowing me to say, "I'm sorry, but I can't talk. A client is here."

"Ah, your *client*. I don't want to get in the way of your counseling. But please do call back as soon as you can."

Thanks to the viral quality of neuroses and phobias—and my reputation, I'd like to think—my practice has a waitlist. Because Audrey terminated, I have room for the woman who is outside my office door. I know only that Bambi Leander is an actress and twenty-five. She sashays in, her black curls stiff with hair gel, wearing so much perfume my office smells like a duty-free shop. Her physical charms are on display in a swishy top with a plunging neck. As she settles into a chair, a heart pendant vanishes into the cleavage of her rather motherly bosom.

We take our first step on the gentle, therapeutic on-ramp to what's beyond as I ask, "Bambi, what brings you here?"

The rare pragmatist lays out worries tidily, as if she is staging a yard sale, but most people reveal themselves at a languorous pace, followed by skittish smiles. They may as well be waiting for tips on how to crack a safe. *"Maybe you'll think I'm cat-lady crazy, but I might be OCD,"* a client may say as she neatly lines up her iPhone, pen, and notebook on the table beside her. Months may pass before a confession arrives. *"I revile my sister." "Starting when I was nine, every night my father . . ." "I come from a family of nurses, ministers, and teachers, but what I love most is money."* After these disclosures, I shout a silent *yippee* and the sympathetic chemistry begins. On my best days I think I'm an Old Testament sage only masquerading as a Manhattan therapist.

Occasionally people attack a problem straightaway, as if it were a Lancôme bonus ready to unwrap. "I can't stop thinking about sex," a client may say, as Bambi does.

"Uh-huh," I respond. With most clients, sooner or later sex comes up.

"I'm in love with a guy who isn't my husband and I feel as if my life is about to explode." She grabs a wad of tissues from the requisite box beside her and swabs her eyes. Before I have a chance to mine this rich ore of disclosure, she announces, "I love Joe—that's my husband. We just got married nine months ago, but now I'm not sure I'm *in* love with him. Clyde, on the other hand—he's directing my show—is like a narcotic I'm addicted to. I can't stop imagining us having sex." Bambi's face contorts, peeling off years, until I'm looking at a high school senior while I'm thinking how happy I am that my mother didn't name me Bambi. "Is it common to get attracted to someone else as soon as you say 'I do'?" Her words puddle at my feet, and my new patient goes from vanilla to salted caramel fudge with sprinkles.

I immediately think of the long-ago itchy patch in my own marriage. The twins were young and needy, and Jake and I usually too exhausted to have sex. When he regaled me with tales from David Tobias & Son, I tuned him out and defaulted to thinking about my grad school courses or how lonesome I felt as a mommy. Into this Mardi Gras of stress arrived the man I think of as Dr. Transference, my former supervisor, who, for a spell—a word I pick with care—was the first person I lusted about in the morning and the last I pictured at night. When we were together in public, we sat a bit too close, and looked at each other longingly. When we were apart, I listened to his favorite music, which ran the short, vapid distance from to ABBA to Beyoncé.

Dr. T and I had an affair. It lasted for five months I'd like to erase from my hard drive, five months when I was only halfway into my marriage. Then, by divine intervention, the good doctor got a job in Cleveland. We broke things off. I drowned ABBA and Beyoncé in the river and had the wherewithal to start a new round of therapy, deliberately selecting a female practitioner. Yet even after all these years, my sexcapade feels like a zombie in the basement freezer, waiting to defrost and ruin my life.

"Yes, marriage can be like this," I offer, speaking as much to myself as to Bambi. "If that's the case, you might try to walk a straight line even when—especially when—you're intoxicated with possibilities."

When Facebook suggests Dr. T as a friend, I resist. The closest I've gotten to him, I'm happy to report, is reading his work in a medical journal.

"We're still paying off our wedding," Bambi whimpers. "Every time I see Clyde I make myself promise I'll say no if he asks me to have a drink later, but when later comes and he puts his hand on my wrist—oh my God . . ." She closes her eyes and wriggles in her chair. Before I have a chance to respond she asks, "How do people stay faithful?"

It would be easier to define how many roads a man must walk down before you call him a man. How to hold a moonbeam in your hand. Who invents emojis.

"The point isn't how do 'people' stay faithful, but how *you* can stay faithful, if that's what you want." I stammer and indulge in air quotes that flutter like moths. "Weigh risk against reward. Recognize that when emotion runs high, logic runs low."

In a first session, a better therapist—honestly, any therapist—would start to delicately tease out the roots of her client's obsession rather than dispense bromides based on faulty reasoning and a mosh pit of emotions. But my new client is a wave washing away caution, getting me worked up, literally. Perspiration beads at my hairline as I hope I've done no harm.

I wonder why I'm unraveling. The same thing happened this morning, during Norah's session. Is this because Jake didn't bother to discuss the New Orleans trip before he committed to it? Prompted by whatever *mishegas* is going on with Micah and Birdie? Perimenopause?

"Dr. Glazer—" I don't correct Bambi when she honors me with a title I haven't earned. "Clyde is more than 'impulse.'" Her firmness hits me like an asteroid.

"Tell me about him."

"Clyde is a man. Joe is still a boy, klutzy in bed, no matter how many times I tell him where to put his hands or tongue."

Bambi, I am starting to realize, reminds me far too much of myself when I was in Dr. T's thrall. Clyde sounds like a schmuck, as Dr. T would have sounded to a friend, had I ever confided in one about him. Hand on the wrist, my fat fanny. I picture Bambi's grand thespian prolonging a glance before he sweeps the hair out of her eyes, into which he ogles soulfully. Telling her he loves her perfume. Black Orchid? His favorite. That he knows her pussy will feel like silk. Then the image shifts to Dr. T holding back my curls to nuzzle the back of my neck. He treated me not like a novice colleague and frantic, exhausted wife and mommy, but a nubile goddess immortalized in a torch song.

"Clyde gets me."

I was waiting for that one. Does Bambi think she's Emma Bovary?

I squelch the memory of Dr. T, and therapeutic Ping-Pong owns me for the next thirty-five minutes. I like Bambi. I want to help, think I can do just that, and hope she won't muck up her life with a Dr. T. I see my job as delicately guiding her back to her husband, as I wholeheartedly returned to Jake after I let Dr. T disrupt my life. If I'm to believe Bambi—a big if—she and Clyde haven't done the deed, and Joe is none the wiser about her fantasies. Perhaps I can help make it stay that way.

When the session ends, Bambi says, "I am going to love working with you!" She angles a beret over one dark, heavily fringed eye, and leaves.

For me, reclaiming my marriage was the inevitable right choice. I can't imagine anyone other than Jake with whom I'd like to go to bed or travel our long odyssey as a family. When we hit Jordan and Micah's adolescence, we couldn't make the rules up fast enough, which put our couple problems in perspective. I admit some snags persist: Jake is still in the pocket of his mother, whose interference and disdain I resent. But that's Mel Glazer's life. Should Bambi necessarily stay with Joe? I don't know her well enough to have a clue. Can I honestly say that our session was helpful when I let my attention hemorrhage for its first half?

Stay in your lane, Mel.

CHAPTER 7

Mel

I TRY MICAH AGAIN. STRAIGHT TO VOICEMAIL. NEXT, BIRDIE, who doesn't pick up. At least Jake answers. "Any word from the kids?" I ask. We know that means Micah or Birdie. Jordan calls far less, and this week she's playing catch-up after a trip to Morocco.

"I have a sick feeling," I admit. "Do you think there's something's wrong-wrong with Micah?"

Micah is the child who has always made me worry. By three he was a refusenik who wouldn't put away his toys as well as a dedicated hothead tossing rolls around restaurants. His temper tantrums had three flavors: mild, spicy, and thermonuclear, and though his IQ exceeded his twin sister's, at school he rarely sat still and her grades were far better. Was he on the spectrum, with an executive function disorder? In need of drugs? Experts never agreed. Two high schools—one public, one private—glossy pay-to-play summer school, a tough-love wilderness program whose most memorable feature was his lost virginity, and three colleges, six years to graduate, the usual drinking and smoking and enrolling in law school, which he quit after a semester. This became Micah's life and, by extension, mine.

All along, he had friends, because who doesn't want to hang

out with the sixth grader who persuaded the others to egg Fifth
Avenue buses on Halloween? The kid who busted out of a Bar
Mitzvah with a posse of thirteen-year-olds in order to get their
ears pierced? The freshman every frat wanted to rush?

And girls? Always girls. From the time he was twelve, Micah
was catnip to females not just because he was handsome and
bone-sweet, but because—following advice from his wise sister—he learned to listen when girls spoke. Seeing how effective
rapt attention was on the opposite sex, he polished this trait and
extended it to most everyone he met, appearing to be interested in
whatever they said while conveniently fending off questions about
himself. Win-win. He was also generous and kind, perhaps not at
the Mother Teresa level, but when a classmate got cancer during
his senior year of high school, it was Micah who first shaved his
head in solidarity, and convinced others to do the same. When he
passed his driver's test, he was happy to schlep friends—or grandparents—to the airport. A great guy, that Micah Tobias.

Micah took missteps, that I can't deny, but they weren't exactly Chernobyl. Still, like every mother, I blamed myself when
his peers began to build earnest careers and my son failed to do
the same. Did I pay Micah too much attention or not enough?
Expect too much or too little?

I'm not saying I considered motherhood a hobby, but neither did I steer my son toward friends who might be strategic
twenty years later while simultaneously seeing that he got into
essential AP classes with primo teachers, attended only the most
elite camps, and took every other blow-dried step to become a
superstar by twenty-seven. Which is ironic, since by default that
may happen to Jordan, who rejected even the gentlest maternal
direction.

My daughter is a rising genius at a move-fast-and-break-
things video-conferencing start-up called TogetherX, whose

work is measured in metrics, clicks, and user experiences. She votes in primaries and rarely loses keys or her temper. She, or possibly her assistant, sends Valentine's and birthday cards and, if she gains three pounds, doubles her gym time and sheds it in a week. My daughter manages an eighty-million-dollar budget with financial sonar so incisive that Jake and I have entrusted her with our modest investments and seen a handsome return.

As early as kindergarten, Jordan fell in line as the teacher's de facto assistant. This was a kid who always knew what she wanted. After watching the Thanksgiving Day parade, for example, she demanded baton lessons—I had to schlep her to Long Island—but when my daughter couldn't be the head majorette, she quit. The CEO, Jake began calling her. Veronika 2.0.

Nothing in my life has been as hard and humbling as raising children. Is my job done? On this point, Jake and I differ. He peeled off the college bumper sticker the summer Micah graduated, but I can't let go. "Time to allow yourself to be marginalized," therapist-me has advised bereft empty-nesters. "Immerse yourself in work or a cause—tutoring, docent-ing, fundraising." I was fine with that advice myself until Micah, at twenty, announced that he was getting married.

There was no mystery to Birdie's appeal. She is Aphrodite of the cornfields, as pale and wholesome as Micah is dark and Semitic, with a drink-of-water body and hair the color of freshly baked biscuits. For months after they started seeing each other, when her name came up, Jake would channel the Beach Boys, sotto voce: "Midwest farmers' daughters really make you feel alright." But beyond physical attraction, I never detected one thing they had in common, nor can I blame Micah's decision on being young. When he married, he was the same age Jake and I had been, with Birdie just as pregnant as I was. Still, the timing of Micah's marriage was early—for me. Had I done enough to teach him to become a man? Tough if I hadn't, since when Micah became Birdie's husband my official mothering ended.

"Whatever is going on between Micah and Birdie is none of our business," Jake lectures me now. His parenting guru is that Teutonic overachiever, Johann Wolfgang von Goethe, who said, "Too many parents make life hard for their children by trying, too zealously, to make it easy for them." "Them" includes Alice, whose giggles and grins form a Gulf Stream that warms my life. It scares the bejesus out of me to think that Micah and Birdie have problems that might damage her childhood.

As the kids grew, and demands galloped through our life, Jake and I were sleep-deprived and rushed, though with enough time to say *j'accuse* when the other forgot to buy milk or ran an extra loop around the reservoir in the morning. Conversations were child-centric. TV on weeknights or weekends only? Public school or private? Those were madhouse years, with Jake a human jungle gym dangling two toddlers while earning his MBA as I finished my own master's, handled the primary child-rearing, and, God forgive me, cheated on my husband.

Why don't more female clients rant that they have to crash every essential into two titanic decades—find a mate, earn a degree or two or three, pick and sculpt a work identity, make babies, and let them loose on the world? Instead, they eat their ambition when accomplishments fall short of triple axel standards. At least I settled on a profession with a long shelf life. As I get older, I'm counting on people seeing me not as a fossil, but an oracle. This is how it rolls for Veronika, empress of psychoanalysis, more in demand every year.

"Check in with you later," I say to Jake, because it's time for the day's last client, Hank, whom I've seen for years. I open the door and he plops down in his regular spot. "I had this dream," he says, as he does at the start of every session.

My phone, which I forgot to turn off, pings. Forgot? Really,

Mel? "I'm sorry," I say. "I have to look at this." I lack the restraint that would postpone reading the text for almost an hour. "Family emergency." It may be from Micah. But it's from Jordan.

Mommy dearest my bro is here. B in touch soon. No worries.

No worries? Not an option.

CHAPTER 8

Veronika

Veronika waits for David to pick her up outside their apartment building and drive to Brooklyn. She's made a reservation for dinner before their evening at the Brooklyn Academy of Music. Her husband is ten minutes late. She drums her fingers. Veronika considers the sought-after set of film screening tickets that Micah would apparently not be using; he'd failed to respond to messages, nor did she hear back from Birdie. There was also the conversation with Melanie. Veronika doesn't hold it against her daughter-in-law that she didn't know what her son was up to. That would be unreasonable, and in Veronika's own therapy she's worked on containing her tendency to demand perfection in others. But there is no excuse for Melanie's cheeky tone. Veronika expects the level of respect she feels almost seventy-five years have earned her.

In the dusty attic of her imagination, she'd set a higher bar for her only son's wife. Melanie Glazer, the daughter-in-law fate has dealt her, has a personality type you won't find in the *Diagnostic and Statistical Manual of Mental Disorders*. Veronika believes the technical term for her is, plain and simple, a flake. Melanie named the twins for her father, Mendel, and his mother, Yardena, both of whom were murdered in the gas chambers—though the decision about the names was probably her son's doing. But Melanie is a poseur, scattered and dizzy. When Veronika ruminates on the many years she trained to do the deep work of psychiatry and considers the brilliant analysts whose paths cross hers through their highly esteemed psycho-analytic society, it infuriates her to think Melanie also believes she is conducting "therapy," often of the Band-Aid variety.

In the abstract, Veronika has no truck with social workers, of which Melanie is one. They fulfill a purposeful role lining up, say, health care aides for patients discharging from hospitals, but social workers should steer clear of people's brains. They are a farm team to the psychiatric major leagues. Would you hire a house painter to execute a portrait?

Veronika harrumphs away, checking the time every two minutes. A text or phone call is pointless. David ignores both when he's driving. And then she sees him, loping down the sidewalk, slightly swinging the briefcase she gave him for his seventieth birthday.

When David spots Veronika, he whistles, grins, and shouts, "Hey, good-looking—aren't you a sight for sore eyes?" Veron-ika is wearing a fitted black velvet jacket over trim charcoal wool pants, and a silver crescent pendant. The BAM audience is artier than a Broadway crowd—last time they were there, Glenn Close was in the next row and on other occasions, Veronika spotted a few of her patients. She wants not to fit in, but to lead the pack, and has attempted to hit a mark of casual elegance.

"Where's the car?" she asks David after he plants a kiss on her cheek. They garage their six-year-old Lexus two blocks away.

"The car . . ." David squints in confusion.

Not again. Veronika struggles to control her rising voice as she feels her stomach churn. "Remember? We're going to

Brooklyn. Dinner at Osteria before Mark Morris. We went over this at breakfast."

David reddens and mutters, "Oh, shit."

"*Liebchen*, you must write these things down. I keep saying that."

"Yes, you do."

They lock eyes. Veronika silently counts to ten. This won't be the first time David has forgotten an important appointment or the first problem she's solved. "If we hurry we can still get there," she says with forced calm, linking her arm in David's. "I'll call an Uber."

Veronika does not think of either of them as old. When you're seventy-four and seventy-nine, *old* is ninety-four and ninety-nine. But no matter how shrewdly she tries to outsmart aging with the right jacket, procedure, or podcast, Father Time—that jackass—is a relentless pursuer. It appears that David, in particular, has a target on his back.

CHAPTER 9

Birdie

MICAH IS STANDING OUTSIDE BIRDIE'S YOGA STUDIO. HIS EYES beg for her pardon as he rambles on about a rainy night, a lost phone, and almost incidentally, a collision. Possibly with a bike. A motherfucker of a Great Dane. Maybe a person, he throws in, practically an afterthought.

"You may have hit a person?" Birdie asks, incredulous. Her bullshit detector activates. She waits for the part of the story when ducks and squirrels talk. "Why didn't you call the police and stay to find out what happened? Why Queens? Were you with someone? Were you wasted?"

"I was alone. I'd lost my phone. It was late. I didn't know how to get back to the bar where I'd had a few beers." Maybe more than a few. "There wasn't a public phone. I was tired . . ." Micah goes round and round like a toy train set, only now admitting to himself that even if he'd had his phone, he would have been afraid of getting a DWI had the police arrived.

"Are you serious?" Yet from the way she sees Micah hunch over and look anywhere but into her eyes, that's all he's got. "You could still get in touch with the police, to make sure no one was hurt."

His voice rises to full strength. "Is that what you'd do?"

Birdie wants to think her answer would be yes, but who is she to wave the red flag of the righteous? A sermon rumbles in her memory about how in haste, good people make bad choices, and how we should not only forgive them, the guilty should forgive themselves. Everyone knew why Pastor Paul had preached on that theme. Birdie's friend and prom date, Leif Nordbeck, had been roughhousing with friends in the lake while his seven-year-old brother, not much of a swimmer—and Leif's responsibility for the afternoon—had drowned fifty feet away. She'd forgiven Leif. The whole congregation had, even his parents, though she had no idea if Leif ever forgave himself. But Micah is no Leif, who stayed at the scene, trying and failing to revive his brother.

Birdie has heard nothing on local radio or television, or read about a hit-and-run in the newspapers, but this is New York City, where she imagines such accidents would be reported only on the slowest slow news day. Then again, because someone's misfortune isn't sufficiently sensational to merit media coverage doesn't mean it isn't a nightmare. Two truths surface: Micah hit something or someone and bolted before he learned if it was alive, and he was upset enough not to hurry home or even call her.

"If I come clean with the police and it's bad, this won't end well for us. You realize that." It isn't a question.

"Why did you run to your sister?"

"That's what bothers you?"

"I'm waiting for an answer."

"Did you forget we've been fighting?"

Birdie tosses her head and narrows her eyes. *Don't pin this on me.* Had they not been in public, she would protest.

"In case you forgot, you were threatening to leave with Alice."

Birdie comes from a line of repressors and seethers, Micah from shouters and debaters; it doesn't take much for the Family Tobias to go *Lord of the Flies*. When there is crossfire, Birdie feels her words become a skeet Micah shoots down with ease. This renders her incapable of digging for clarity without striking the bedrock of bigger confusion about how she feels and what her husband has done. "I'm glad you're back—and safe," Birdie says. She wraps her arms around herself and steps toward the studio. "But I'm done. I have to teach—I'll see you tonight." She stops. "You are coming home, aren't you?"

Micah extends his arm to block her path. "Bird, of course I'll be home, and I'm sorry for everything, especially running away." He speaks softly and pulls his wife toward him. "I was a jerk, but I'm not a monster." Birdie says nothing. "Hey. Can you just forget about this? I'm begging."

Though Birdie believes Micah would never intentionally hurt another person, she says, "We'll see," and enters the studio where her class is waiting. She slips on a mask of equanimity and sits in front of twenty-nine yoga practitioners who wish they could look like long, lean Birdie Peterson. They hope that ninety minutes from now their fears and misgivings will have vanished like dandelion fluff in the breeze. Elegant as an egret, Birdie tucks her legs beneath her and rests her hands on her thighs, palm ups in supplication, leading the charge toward serenity.

"Allow your eyes to close," Birdie murmurs. "Breathe in and out. Bring your awareness inward. Notice how your breath feels, and where it is in your body." Her breath is stuck next to the shrapnel of shock and anger. Tension in her neck is a steel brace. "Start to deepen your breath," she says, "deeper into your belly." She can tell her class to relax, though she cannot do so herself. "As you inhale, feel your belly expand like a balloon." This, she can do. "As you exhale, feel your navel draw toward your spine." This, too. "There should be no movement. Just feeling."

This she cannot do. Birdie cannot meditate away her resentment or regret. She bloats into a porcupine, each quill a sensation that pierces and poisons. "What we are doing now is breathing that replenishes the body and spirit," she says, wishing it were true for her.

An hour later she instructs the class to finish with a cycle of breaths, and counts them off. One. Two. Three. Four. Five. She wants not merely to slow time, but to walk it back to when life was simpler, when she and Micah didn't battle.

"Take one last deep inhale and open your eyes," Birdie says, and does the same. That means you, she repeats to herself.

CHAPTER 10

Mel

M ᴏᴍ."

I startle to a hand on my shoulder. It takes me a second to reconcile this manly hulk, solid as a side of beef, with the squirmy, peach-fuzzed twelve-year-old who refused to try cauliflower. Whenever I see Micah, I have the feeling that my son has had a recent growth spurt, though he's been six-three for seven years. As he bends to kiss me, his curls tickle my cheek. Our embrace lasts twice as long as usual.

"You need a haircut."

"Hello to you, too." He slides into the opposite side of the booth.

"Where's your sister?"

"She'll be here in a few minutes. You know Jordan—working a meeting. Told me to order for her."

"Does Birdie know why you ran off?" Because I don't.

"I stopped at the studio on the way here." Though this is our regular spot, Micah studies the menu—mostly pizzas, give or take some olives and sausage—as if it were the Constitution. "What'll we have? Marinara or salsiccia?"

"Whatever." My son has yet to remember that I have never

intentionally eaten a sausage. He has nothing to say for himself until the server takes his order.

"Beer?" he asks.

"Not for me." I want to be clear and unflinching, should there be a big reveal at this very restaurant table. Micah deliberates between the Irish Brown Ale and East India Pale as if the decision truly mattered, he was a functioning alcoholic, or both.

"I'm sorry about all this, Mother," Micah says as he arranges and rearranges the salt and pepper shakers on the table.

He has chosen the proper noun, though after he gave up "Mommy," he's never called me anything but Ma or Mom. Mother is what I call Veronika, her preference, though when I married Jake I still had a mother.

"How are you?" Micah asks as he begins to build a tower of sugar and sweetener packages.

"I'll be better when I know what's going on."

His face cracks into a cautious smile and my heart does a back tuck. Could his cryptic behavior indicate that something good is happening? After trawling in the real estate market, getting outbid, will he announce that he and Birdie want to borrow money for a down payment on an apartment? I've tried to pry them loose from overpriced Brooklyn, attempting to sell Queens—Every kind of ethnic eatery! One hundred and thirty-eight languages!—or Riverdale, where swimming pools, underground garages, and river views mitigate the blocky architecture of Soviet-style apartment complexes. But they adore their liberal arts ghetto in Brooklyn. Who am I to disparage a neighborhood where Micah and Birdie see themselves coming and going, one more aggressively casual couple fetching fair trade kale and coffee at farmer's markets?

I recently suggested to Jake that we move to Brooklyn ourselves. I'd be an old-fashioned granny, seeing Alice every day.

"You think Birdie wants her mother-in-law in her face?"

"*Moi?* A *mother-in-law?*" I tend to forget that to Birdie this is who I am.

I up the ante. Is Birdie pregnant? God only knows how they'd afford another baby, but I'd love a second grandchild and I'm not counting on Jordan, who acts as maternal as a Slinky, though this could change. I've worked with clients both straight and gay and everything between whose dormant urge for motherhood becomes an inferno as their years tick-tock. Along with half her class at Smith, Jordan declared her sexual fluidity during her freshman year. My daughter has a range of abilities that far exceed my bandwidth. She rock-climbs, does stand-up, and lavishes time on Shivers and Muldoon, her rescue dogs. Hers is a big life, but is it big enough to include children? No, I'm not investing in Jordan Tobias mommy futures. For another grandchild, the smart money's on Birdie.

I wait for my son to spill. But when I take a closer look, he is tight with apprehension. I let myself pipe dream with the most delusional of thinkers, but not for long.

"What's going on," Micah says, "is complicated."

He's seeing another woman. Birdie's seeing another man. His business is tanking. He's sick. God, please don't let him be sick. And then someone shouts, "Mel!"

Jordan stopped calling me "Mom" when she was eleven. I swivel to see a sunflower. My daughter has the Tobias height and the bright ginger hair of Veronika's youth.

"Sweetheart." I stand to hug, and know I am not the first woman to look at an adult and think, did I actually give birth to you? How can this imposing woman with spiky hair and oversized Harry Potter glasses be my baby girl?

Pregnant with twins, I remember the internal kickboxing, and the snug contentment of three bodies united. I was a Matryoshka doll craving grape Popsicles, waddling through a blistering city summer. I gained fifty-two pounds, twelve of which remain

as a testimonial to a maternity journey distinguished by acid re-
flux, Braxton Hicks contractions, a shadowy line that snaked up
my belly, and a hashtag of stretch marks that took years to fade.
Nor can I forget, after nineteen hours of hair-rising labor, the
doctor proclaiming, "It's a girl," then "and a boy!" An episiotomy
rendered me enthroned on a plastic donut for weeks. As for my
breasts, sadly, I own no sculpted memorial to their early splendor,
since thanks to nursing two famished infants, the days are long
gone when my halters seemed to be filled with helium.

Half the evidence of this distant pregnancy is the woman
grinning before me. Jordan's features are defined with lapidary
precision—a delicate declension of the Tobias schnozz, conspicuous eyebrows and cheekbones showcased by the severity of a
short haircut. While you wouldn't call Jordan beautiful, hers is
a face you recall. I predict that she will age well.

"Sit, honey. Your brother was just starting to tell me something."

She sits.

"Birdie and I are unraveling." Micah's words land like dice
on a table.

"You haven't been cheating, have you?" Bambi, my new
client, is parked in my cortex.

"No, and as far as I know, neither has Birdie, but she thinks
I'm immature. She's tired of waiting to see if my business takes
off, tired of struggling. All that. She thinks our marriage may
have been a mistake."

After Micah and Birdie's wedding, I hoped, for Alice's sake, that
their relationship would become a petri dish where they might
grow up together. I especially hoped I wouldn't be hearing this.

"And I fucked up." Micah is visibly sweating. "Big."

"May I jump in?" Jordan says. "Micah had an accident. It
could have happened to anyone."

And then he tells me.

CHAPTER 11

Mel

THERE IS LIFE BEFORE I KNEW. NOW THERE IS AFTER. WHAT kind of person leaves an accident when they might have hit a person, or even a dog?

I've waited until after dinner to tell Jake. My hands tremble as I try to balance two decafs on a tray. It soothes me just a bit to use mugs Alice and I painted; whenever she visits, a project awaits, since there are limits to how many times any grandmother can endure Candy Land.

"What the fuck," Jake says, after I spit out the story. "That schmucky kid!" He paces, a snorting bull in a ring. "Where, exactly, do you think we went wrong? Where? Tell me, where."

"Can we skip the recriminations?" I won't deny that as parents there were times when Jake and I papered over when we should have dug deep, splintered instead of unified, and pretended only other people's kids had sex at fourteen or stole money to buy weed. Still, love rushes down the Tobias family tree like rain in a tropical storm. I am unwilling to think of Micah as a bad seed. "Look at me," I insist. "The accident part could have happened to anyone."

"Any drunk or stoner, you mean?"

As if Jake hasn't gotten into a car when he had no business being behind the wheel. "It's how Micah reacted that—"

"Shows the most deplorable judgment." My husband shakes his head.

"He's young." I am working to keep a sob out of my voice.

"But old enough to be a husband and father."

"You're right. Looking for excuses is not our first priority." Though I've been doing exactly that for hours. "How can we help him?"

"Why didn't he come to me? I'm his father."

Because you're judgy. You'd polyurethane him with guilt, not that he shouldn't feel guilty, but I'm betting he feels that all on his own. "Forget about that. Our job is to figure out next steps."

"Should I call a lawyer, you know, to get ahead of the game, just in case?" Jake stammers. He is a man who likes to put things right, with a plumb line straight to the heart of those he loves.

"Please do." Legal theory is a discipline of which I have a flimsy grasp, no matter how many episodes of *Law & Order* have been shot in my neighborhood, nor are suspense novels my literary crack.

"Gary practices criminal law."

The word stings. "Micah is no criminal." I want to believe that. "But go ahead. Call."

Jake leaves a message for our friend Gary, then dials again. I assume it's to phone Micah, but he says, "Mother," and soon I hear, "Tomorrow? Six? No, I'll call the kids myself and tell them it's a command performance."

When he hangs up I peer at Jake as if I've just noticed he has a second nose. "Really? You had to involve your parents? You should have asked me first." New Orleans redux.

"Hell, Mel, if ever there was a situation that called for family support—"

"That's what we're calling intruding now?"

"Be glad you have a family that gives a fuck."

It is I who phones Micah to tell him about next Friday's mandatory showdown, disguised as a run-of-the-mill Shabbos dinner. It is Jake who sleeps on the couch while I check a clock every twenty minutes.

CHAPTER 12

Birdie

AFTER DINNER WITH HIS FAMILY, BIRDIE AND MICAH BOLT TO their sole means of personal transportation, one of his trucks. Its Mash logo and amateurishly painted mound of mashed potatoes dribbled with gravy sits on a spud-brown background. Birdie thinks whoever wrote that there is no such thing as an unattractive color has never seen this van. Micah climbs behind the wheel while Birdie buckles Alice into her car seat, adapted for the truck.

"About what just happened . . ." Birdie says as they rumble away from Riverside Drive.

"Later." Micah's jaw is slammed so tightly shut Birdie hears only a slur. His right leg shakes. "I can't get those shrews' voices out of my head."

Veronika and Mel hadn't shouted. They didn't have to. "Walk into any precinct and explain what you did," Micah's grandmother had said along with, "What could be so terrible that you two can't work it out?" Mel's comments were mostly echo.

As they'd yammered on, Birdie saw her husband shrink back to a boy. She felt mugged by each remark, and wanted to lunge and protect Micah from these female howitzers, more

alike than either of them would notice or admit. But throughout the evening Birdie sat still—an island surrounded by Midwestern reserve, good manners, and an urge to be liked—as she
told herself that she didn't need to justify a thing to any member
of her husband's family. Her life, her problems.

Birdie sees Veronika as an uncommon variant on the grandmother spectrum. Until they met, she thought a grandmother
was required to wear machine-washable clothes and wouldn't
dream of serving a dessert that wasn't homemade except for the
Cool Whip. A grandmother didn't have a waistline, and didn't
care. When she wanted fresh flowers, she cut her own. A grandmother couldn't imagine civilized life without jumper cables
in the trunk, and tended not to give advice unless it was about
stain removal or composting. If she found someone to be malig-
nantly incompetent, she kept her opinions to herself. She didn't
offer them up as if she were a judge at the Iowa State Fair.

And what of Mel, who seems to sail through life with an *ob-
la-di, ob-la-da* attitude? She may be the more complicated puzzle
simply because she presents herself as less complicated than Veronika. This should make her easier to like—which for Birdie is
not the case. Around her mother-in-law, Birdie sometimes wants
to arch her back like a cat and hiss. Is it because Micah's mom is
the emotional equivalent of a close talker, a woman who covets
connection like some men do a BarcaLounger? That she tries too
hard to be the quicker-picker-upper of problem-solving? That
she has almost a bloodlust for friendliness?

Now you're just being a dick, Birdie tells herself, because
these aren't vile traits or vile women. Maybe *she* is the problem,
blaming others for the miscalculations her marriage has deliv-
ered. Also, here is where it gets weird. There might be genius to
the older Tobias wives' tactics, because as she and Micah drove
in the stunned silence of his wobbly truck, united in boiling

anger, Birdie felt more connected to her husband than she had in months. She wanted nothing more than to put this recent incident behind them, and return to the denial and path of least resistance that was—until recently—her marriage.

It was late. She was sleepy. Birdie slipped into herself, focusing only on the lull of the truck's warmth, as comfortable as an armful of clothes fresh from a dryer. The muffled whoosh of light traffic. The breathing of sleeping Alice. They headed south, past a showy cluster of high-rises, and soon turn into the familiar cobweb of lower Manhattan. Birdie's eyes meet the Brooklyn Bridge with its tinsel of cables and cords, a structural poem honoring the city. She sighs.

She'd grown up hungry for history, for beauty. In her seven-stop-sign hometown, beyond its brick and fieldstone Carnegie library and a stalwart limestone post office, her world had been bland and sparsely landscaped, as if an artist had left his canvas unfinished before escaping. Yet despite Iowa's openness, Birdie couldn't find her place. This had drawn her all the more to New York, with its density, its layers, its promise. Grand monuments to forgotten heroes lit her imagination and sense of romance.

When she arrived, Birdie Peterson couldn't wait to meet her future. It did not take her long to discover that the Midwest was shadowing her as she tried to find her place. She saluted Mel who, though raised in the Twin Cities, seemed born for New York City, where Birdie couldn't keep pace. Every week, she felt as if she were falling further behind in a race she hadn't realized she'd entered. And the crowds! So many people, everywhere she looked. She became even more suffocated by the overkill of concerts, shows, movies, dance performances, exhibits, and restaurants a person felt compelled to sample.

The worst taunts came from free readings, when authors launched books. Too many of the writers were graduates of the very program she'd casually blown off, although it was the draw of being at the literary hub of the universe that had lured Birdie to New York City as much as Micah had. But Birdie could not walk back her past. Her decisions had created Alice.

After Birdie became a mother, she canceled her subscription to *The New Yorker*. She had little time to read, she told herself, it wasn't cheap, and their money was limited. All true, but the more important reason was that the magazine became a weekly admonishment of her indolence, which for a Midwesterner was like admitting you cheated on your income tax or lied about your age. Birdie's artistic aspirations evaporated like a drop of water on a sizzling city sidewalk.

The last short story she'd written, for a workshop she'd taken the first winter she'd moved East, was about teenage lovers who hid beneath a bridge. In the early days, she'd felt close enough to Mel to show her rough drafts, and her mother-in-law was an encouraging reader who praised the story. But when Birdie submitted the piece, her instructor red-penned, *Been watching after-school specials, have we?* and, like starving dogs, the other students savaged her work. *Derivative! Reductive! YA?* Birdie was too hurt and timid to question the critiques. Her confidence caved, and her passivity scalded her as much as the rebukes. She quit the workshop, regretting the four hundred bucks for tuition, and never wrote another story.

For the next two years Birdie was rewarded by a molten gush of glee whenever she checked her teacher's website and saw that he had no new work to his credit. Let his writer's block be so complete he can't sign his signature! Then a collection of short stories by the instructor received high praise by the *New York Times Book Review*. The reviewer singled out a story that had been written in the alternating voices of a teenage boy and girl who lived beneath the Brooklyn Bridge. Inflamed by the plagiarism, at Mel and Veronika's advice she'd fired off a letter to the newspaper. It was never published, nor did her former teacher answer her email. Birdie felt herself turn into a cynic, hunchbacked with spite.

Now, as the truck chugged along, she stole a glimpse at Micah's profile, with his strong nose and hair grazing his collar. She reached across the seat, took his hand, and felt a caress in return, which continued until they parked in front of their building. Tenderly, her husband bundled Alice into his arms. They unlocked the front door and walked up the flight of stairs to their apartment, where he carried their drowsing girl to her tiny bed. She and Micah stood side-by-side, admiring Alice's innocence and beauty. Her face was a blend of Peterson and Tobias—her mother Luanne's straight and narrow nose; David's deeply blue eyes; Micah and Jake's rosy cheeks; Mel's ears, protruding like quotation marks, covered by a halo of curls.

Loopy from the lift in mood between them, in the felted shadows, Birdie and Micah stripped each other of their clothes and, for the moment, crimes and culpability. Scented by the truck's unmistakable odor of garlicky mashed potatoes, they stumbled into their bedroom with Mel and Jake's hand-me-down brass bed, its wintry floor covered by rag rugs connecting like a Mondrian. Birdie held to the yoke of her husband's shoulders, wishing she could make right that which was wrong. Along with raising Alice, lovemaking was the sole element of their togetherness that remained intact. She let her hands slip down the narrow V of Micah's torso's and then, below.

From Micah she heard "I'm sorry" and "I promise I'll get better" and "Do you know how much I love you?" He answered his last question with his hands and lips divining exactly what she needed. The only sounds were the slap of sweaty limbs and moans building toward a crescendo, followed by collapse and an immediate descent into sleep, with Micah gratefully spooned against Birdie's tall, slender frame under a tangle of sheets.

She wished their marriage were a technical gadget for which she could call a help-line and hear a mild South Asian Jim or Jane tell her to press Control-Alt-Delete and correct all that was wrong. But in the morning a stranger came to the door.

CHAPTER 13

Birdie

A{\small LMA} H{\small ERRERA}, {\small A DETECTIVE FOR THE} N{\small EW} Y{\small ORK} P{\small OLICE}
Department, does not bring to mind Sherlock Holmes, Hercule
Poirot, or Jessica Fletcher. The stranger who rings Micah and
Birdie's bell on Saturday is short, sturdy, and dressed in a brown
raincoat and ironed jeans. "Is Micah Tobias home, ma'am?" she
asks Birdie after flashing her badge.

Sweat trickles coldly from Birdie's armpits. If she hadn't been
terrified, Birdie would recognize that when Detective Herrera
adds, "Routine procedure," there is no menace in her tone. "Please
follow me," Birdie says. "My husband is upstairs." They climb to
the second floor, each footfall sounding to Birdie like a gong preceding an execution in a historical drama.

Birdie leads Detective Herrera past Alice, who is watching
cartoons in the living room, and into the kitchen. Micah is facing away from the door, pouring himself a second cup of coffee.
When Birdie says, "We have a guest—a detective," she can't see
her husband's face, for which she is grateful.

When he turns around, any fear he might have revealed has
been cast off.

"Is there a problem in the neighborhood, officer?"

Micah once admitted to Birdie that he has practiced the art of how to make a good impression, and his work usually pays off. His voice is cordial, educated. Birdie hears the proper diction on which Veronika insists. The woman is still not above stopping her grandson midsentence to pounce on a *yeah* or a *gonna*.

What is the protocol for welcoming a law enforcement official into your home? "Won't you sit down, Detective?" Birdie says before the woman has the chance to respond to Micah. "Would you like some coffee? I can make a fresh pot."

"No, thank you. I'm following up on an accident a week ago Tuesday—October sixteenth—around midnight in Sunnyside, Queens," Detective Herrera says. "Mr. Tobias, were you in Queens that evening?"

Birdie thinks Micah should have answered the question immediately, not wait a beat longer than necessary to ask, "What kind of accident?"

"A car accident at the intersection of Skillman and Forty-ninth?"

He rests his eye on their bulletin board, with its collage of photographs, dry cleaning receipts, luckless lottery tickets, outdated discount coupons, and invitations.

"Not ringing any bells, sir?"

"No." Micah scratches his chin. "Sorry."

"You weren't involved in an accident? Or observe one?"

"No, ma'am. I did not."

"Are you the owner of a brown van, sir"—the detective refers to her notes—"with the logo 'Mash'?"

"I own two food trucks like that."

"I see," Detective Herrera comments with no visible expression. "One was spotted in the area of the accident. If you'd let me know where you were that night, sir?"

Micah looks at Birdie. "Hon," he asks, innocent as Alice's

stuffed monkey. "Do you remember what we did on Tuesday night last week?"

"Nothing special. We were here." Birdie despises Micah for roping her into a false alibi.

"Could you tell me the name and phone number of the individual who drives your other van, sir?" the detective asks.

Micah does. Archie Simco works for him part time. He is harmless, one fry short of a Happy Meal, counting down until his girlfriend delivers their baby. He is only eighteen and doesn't deserve scapegoating, Birdie thinks.

"This accident?" Micah asks, as Detective Herrera takes down Archie's contact information. "Was it bad? Not a vehicular homicide, I hope."

Birdie forces a chuckle. "My husband watches too many police procedurals."

"I'm not at liberty to say," Alma Herrera responds. No laugh. She thanks them for their trouble and leaves.

Birdie counts to one hundred, to be sure the policewoman is out of earshot, before she lets it rip. "Asshole," she begins.

CHAPTER 14

Mel

Is TOMORROW ACTUALLY MONDAY?" JAKE HAS SPENT THE LAST three hours sprawled in the prone position. "Already?"

My husband's weekends, when his stores are busiest, end with fatigue and anxiety. My clients often complain of the same, as if they were all freshmen who forgot to study for a midterm. Not me. Mondays? Bring 'em on. Except this weekend, when I twitch with trepidation.

"Don't you think that symbolism was a little on the nose?" Jake asks as the television goes dark after we watched a beloved series.

What symbolism? Usually, as soon as a show ends, my husband and I parse the plot with such rigor I could publish a scholarly paper about the plight of the lady cop, the lady lawyer, the lady sex researcher or the Lady. Tonight, all I recall is a con woman and a crocodile.

"Mel?" Jake says, waving at me as if I'm lost.

"You're right. That symbolism was too heavy-handed to discuss." I bring our ice cream bowls to the sink—I wasn't too zoned out to mainline Trader Joe's Coffee Bean Blast—and try to robotically check my messages, only to discover that the battery in my phone has drained. As I get ready for bed, I eye Jake's Ambien stash.

Regarding meds, a bottle of ibuprofen hits its sell-by date before I finish it, and my Spartan streak extends to my nearest and dearest. At Micah's ninth-birthday party, he whimpered after he collided with a bigger kid on the ice-skating rink. "You better rush that boy to the emergency room," Veronika skated over to chide. (Yes, she skates like an Olympic medalist.) "He may have fractured his arm."

"I can't leave twenty-five hyenas unsupervised on an ice rink," I said, gnashing my teeth. "I'm in charge here."

Two days later, with Micah still whining and weeping, I took him to the ER. He'd broken his arm and wore a cast for weeks. Since I learned of that grown-up boy's most recent accident, I haven't slept through the night. If I don't get some rest, tomorrow I'll be snoring mid-session. Jake's Ambien is not much bigger than a kernel of couscous. I swallow it.

Thirteen hours later, a gravelly voice calls out, "Wakey, wakey. Are you alive?"

I don't want to open my eyes. Quentin Tarantino and I are editing our movie. We have to finish it for Cannes.

"You've been wailing like a sick oboe," a Jake-voice says from what sounds like the bottom of the Hudson. My film collaborator has turned into one of the talking heads on CNN. Nerdy, with glasses. My type.

"Mel, you're spooking me," the voice says.

In my dream it's time for an audition. I stand up straight, thrust out my chest, adjust my décolleté, and sing, "If I were a bell I'd be ringing." I sound sultry, like Diana Krall, not off-key, like Mel Glazer. I struggle to open my eyes. I am in the shirt and leggings I was wearing Sunday evening and have overslept by more than an hour. I wish I were back in my dream. Now I'll never know if I got the part. My throat feels coated with peanut butter.

I rush through a shower and replace my usual oatmeal and banana with a double espresso that does nothing to eliminate a walloping headache. Only when I am in an Uber do I turn on my barely charged phone. Norah, who had canceled her session because of a trip to the Galápagos, is coming to therapy after all.

"Weren't you supposed to be communing with blue-footed boobies?" I ask her a few hours later.

"The trip is postponed," she sighs. "We're mid-crisis. Delia is in a bad way."

Delia is a young woman from Utah who keeps the moving parts of Norah's fast-lane life greased and humming. Norah runs a restaurant, with weekend work, twelve-hour days, and employees who quit with regularity. She has three children, each with a schedule complicated by teams, tutors, lessons, and homework. That her mother-in-law—capable, unemployed, and conveniently around the corner—has yet to cover for her should there be a childcare lapse is a constant grievance.

"Is Delia ill?"

"Not exactly. But very banged up and traumatized."

"That's horrible. I'm so sorry. What happened?"

"She never showed up at her boyfriend's apartment in Queens last Tuesday night. The next morning, someone called him from a hospital—a passerby had found her bloody on a street." Norah plucks a tissue from the box by the chair and begins to dab her eyes.

"Good God. Was she mugged?"

"No."

"Please don't tell me she was raped?"

Norah shakes her head from side to side.

"Collision?"

"Delia doesn't own a car. She was walking from the subway when someone must have run a red light, hit her, and took off. Didn't even call for help."

Her hands clench, as do mine.

"She can barely remember the accident, so I don't have any

other details." Norah rocks back and forth in her chair. "I can't begin to tell you how upset I am by this. I want to believe most people are essentially good, but Delia, who's an angel and beautiful and smart—my girls worship her—was left like garbage on a filthy New York street. What kind of lowlife would do this? It's reprehensible."

"Nightmare," I mumble. A thought bubbles. "Maybe the person—the perpetrator—didn't realize he or she hit her?" I wish to instantly retract my remark, as much for lack of logic as insensitivity.

Norah makes the face of someone who has just learned that the IRS is planning to audit them. "Really? What kind of dirtbag just drives away?"

I am grateful that it's considered normal for a therapist to pause in radio silence. I let the question hover until Norah realizes I won't answer it and adds, "Since Delia lives with us, I feel it's my obligation to take care of her." Norah sits up straight. "But it's turned my world on its head. Not only is our vacation off, I've had to hire another au pair to handle my girls, who hate her because she's not as much fun as Delia. I'm getting flak from Brian, too, who thinks I have a martyr complex."

Norah looks for my reaction and perhaps, praise. When she receives neither, she continues. "Delia doesn't have anyone else here but us. Her boyfriend hasn't called in days. He's a kid himself, and this is probably all too much for him to handle, but not hearing from this boy makes her even more depressed. Brian doesn't feel Delia is our obligation, even though her father was his fraternity brother. The guy tracked down Brian and called him out of the blue. That's how Delia came to live with us. But the dad recently lost his job so neither he or his wife can afford to come here all the way from Utah. I want to send them plane tickets, but Brian flat-out refuses. I feel she's our ethical responsibility. Delia is only twenty."

I'm in free fall, trying to separate Norah's rambling story from what I know of Micah's, and want to end the nosedive and steer us to safer ground. "How do you feel about all the additional work you've taken on to care for Delia?"

Norah hesitates and almost smiles. "You know I'm not the nurturing type. We've talked about this. I'm embarrassed to admit it, but I'm proud for rising to the occasion. Kind of a breakthrough, yes?"

I nod.

"But no good deed goes unpunished. Brian and I are bickering because I think he should be more supportive, not chewing me out. It's lose-lose, everywhere I look."

After discussing Brian for a few minutes, prurient self-interest returns. "I want to make sure I understand your circumstances. Do you know any more about this hit-and-run?" I let the question sail lightly, glad no supervisor monitoring the session can send me to therapist detention hall.

"Only that Delia has broken ribs, a broken arm and leg, a concussion, and a spinal fracture that may require surgery. She's also terrified, afraid something like this could happen again, a truck coming at her like an enraged elephant."

A truck. "I thought you said it was a car."

"Really?" Norah raises her eyebrows in pure skepticism. "I don't think so. Delia remembers a truck with a weird logo on the side."

The tectonic plates beneath me shift.

"What's her prognosis?"

"Too soon to know. She may get out of the hospital soon, but then she'll be in rehab. And the bills! Christ, the bills! She has no health insurance. Do you have any idea what hospitals charge?"

I do. Micah should be footing those bills, which probably means Jake and I will have to cover them.

Norah is speaking at twice her regular pace. "Brian and I are paying, which is pissing him off, the cheap bastard." She sighs. "It's a real dumpster fire."

My voice cracks as I ask, "Do the police have any suspects?"

Norah shrugs. "Are you kidding? The cops aren't all that interested. And did I mention there may be legal fees?"

The words are a bone in my throat.

"We're looking for a lawyer, in case there's someone to sue."

I feel panicked and ashamed, not only on behalf of Micah—I'm miles beyond the point in my session when I should have said, "Stop here, please. I may have a personal connection to the person who caused this accident . . . highly unlikely, but you never know. Six degrees of separation. Who'd have thunk?" But the loving mother on a fact-finding mission overrides the honorable therapist. If I wait, I may hear something, even if I don't bait.

Norah begins to complain about her head chef. I end the session four minutes early. Only after I transgress every rule of client confidentiality by dialing Micah's number and reporting what Norah told me do I realize I forgot to give Norah a monthly bill.

CHAPTER 15

Veronika

AFTER LOVEMAKING, THE ONLY SHABBOS RITUAL THE OLDEST Tobiases scrupulously observe, David tried to convince Veronika that Micah would take to heart her good advice. He'd come around. She'll see. Forbearance. But it was Birdie who came around. She called Veronika first thing Monday morning, sniffles and hiccups disrupting her words like heckling.

"Shall I send a car so we can talk in person?" Veronika offers after a minute of halting sobs. Birdie does not protest.

"I've never been in your office," Birdie says two hours later, her eyes landing on a fawn suede chaise illuminated by late-morning sunlight. "Do your patients lie down here? I've only seen that in movies."

"Not all." Veronika watches Birdie survey the room, her eyes settling on a silkscreen of yellow day lilies on a chartreuse background, the room's sole hit of vivid color. "It's an Alex Katz. From David when I turned sixty-five." Nearly ten years ago, when life had been simpler.

"It's strange being here, almost as if you're my shrink." Birdie has never visited a psychiatrist or therapist of any stripe.

"But you're not my patient. Though as Micah's grandmother"—

and presumptive head of the family—"I'd like to help. Why
don't you sit here?" She points to an embracing loveseat whose
sandy color suggests a beach. The other chair is clearly hers,
high-backed, tobacco-brown leather. A throne. "Cup of tea? I
was just going to have one myself." She wasn't, but she's learned
that a hot drink softens people up.

Birdie thanks Veronika, who disappears for a few minutes
and returns with two steaming cups of Earl Grey in bone china
cups and saucers that she places on a low coffee table next to a
white orchid. "Now," she says with her practiced reassurance
and enigmatic smile, "how may I help?"

The morning's tears reboot and Birdie says, "Everything's
wrong."

"Can you narrow that down?" Veronika uses her psychiatrist
voice, soft but firm.

"Micah should go to the police, like you said the other
night. But he refuses. He's a child." She demonstrates this by
sticking fingers in her ears, looking like a child herself. "We
were struggling before, but this accident has made everything
worse. Micah has no focus."

Veronika leans back in her chair, folds her hands into the
here's-the-steeple position, props her chin on her pointed index
fingers, and asks, "Is this something you've discussed with Jake
and Melanie?"

"No, though I'm sure it's no secret. I don't know what to do.
Which is why I called you. You've always been so . . . supportive."

It doesn't surprise Veronika that a grandmother would receive confidences denied to a mother-in-law, though she thinks
there's more to it. Birdie is sufficiently perceptive to know Veronika's opinions reflect sounder judgment than Melanie's. She
suppresses the urge to smile.

"Every day, I wake up thinking I want to get away," Birdie

says, kickstarting a second round of tears. "Not permanently. But we—or at least I—need a break."

"Would you take Alice with you?"

"Of course," Birdie says. "I worry about her overhearing our fighting. She's been throwing things at day care, running out of the room at nap time. Having accidents. She needs peace and quiet."

Veronika isn't surprised by Alice's behavior. "I understand that you and Micah need détente, but where would you go?"

"Home, I imagine."

"But this is home." The look on Birdie's face tells her everything. "In that case, we're going to have to work out a plan."

Melanie isn't going to like it.

CHAPTER 16

Mel

ON MOST ALICE-AFTERNOONS, BIRDIE OR MICAH DELIVERS my granddaughter to the Upper West Side. This Tuesday, however, since we are going to a story hour at the Brooklyn Public Library, I am picking her up. I grab the overhead bar of the subway, and cast my eyes on the sandwich of humanity piled high and wide around me. Families in pickpocket-proof pants speak the rat-a-tat-tat of broken English, Spanish, Russian, German, and languages I can't identify as they look for the 9/11 Memorial Museum. A Sam Cooke impersonator deftly panhandles the car while crooning, "Don't know much about geography." I put a dollar in his cup, and he grins, perhaps in recognition. This is not the first time I've given a buck to the same inner-city popstar. He should write me a receipt for a tax deduction.

At the first stop in Brooklyn, a mother tries to Tetris a double stroller into the car. Another woman hisses, "Watch yourself!" when the baby vehicle bumps her leg.

"Hey, it was an accident," Stroller Mom protests.

"How about 'Excuse me'?"

"You coulda moved."

"Cunt."

I cannot resist jumping in with, "Miss, there's no need for profanity."

The aggrieved commuter swivels to waggle a finger in my face. "Bitch, you correcting me?"

Is she simply rude or one more deep-fried mental health disaster kicked to the curb by American medical care? I hear Jake's echo beseeching me to please mind my own business; there are safer soapboxes than the train. As a seat opens at the other end of the car, I walk toward it and dive in, burying my face in the first piece of reading material I yank from my bag, last month's *American Journal of Psychiatry*.

I scan the table of contents and find an entry from . . . Dr. T. The accompanying photograph shows an older version of my once-upon-a-time lover. He has hung on to his hair, which has greyed, but judging from his double chin, he looks rather rotund. I'm curious to prospect for nuggets of his wisdom, especially when I see the topic, "Childhood Separation Anxiety and the Treatment of Subsequent Adult Anxiety." "Pathological early childhood attachments have consequences for the later adult . . ." his treatise begins.

Despite his unrelentingly pedantic tone, usually when I study Dr. T's work, it's impossible not to think of how his hands held my face as if he wanted to memorize it. How the stroke of his finger set my body aquiver. I can hear his voice—low, with a slight Brooklyn inflection. But today I am thinking of Micah, which decimates any fantasy.

Is my son's current behavior connected to potholes in his personality? Boyhood separation problems? When nursery school began, I was the last mommy permitted to leave the classroom, where he clung to me like an opossum pup while the other mothers marched out for coffee, no doubt washed down by gossip and guffaws about therapists' wacko kids. What I want to say to the Dr. Ts and self-satisfied moms of the world is that people often find my son charming, and charmers aren't, in my clinical experience, anxious types. Narcissists, perhaps— especially if they're card-carrying psychopaths or sociopaths. But I'm not going *there*. What I will cop to is that Micah might be feeling trapped by responsibility, rendering him incapable of taking next steps regarding what I now call The Incident.

We haven't spoken since Friday night's drubbing at Veronika and David's because I have unofficially declared a ceasefire— award me the Nobel Peace Prize—nor has Micah called me or, to my knowledge, Jake. I've become one more mother in nature who can no longer identify the offspring she raised to adult- hood. The boy I remember is gone.

When I emerge in Brooklyn, I notice the comparative si- lence, as if the borough has extra sound-proofing. I walk five blocks to my kids' brownstone. In this urban Mayberry of deep front lawns known as Carroll Gardens, strangers offer friendly eye contact, sometimes even hellos. Here and there is a bakery or funeral home proving that before Millennials colonized, this neighborhood was heavily Italian. I expect to see *Moonstruck* Cher saunter down the street. I like this place.

I reach Micah and Birdie's building, ring the bell, and through the cloudy window watch Birdie race down the stairs to let me in through the locked front door. Her face is flushed, her hair gathered into a loose ponytail. In place of her customary black yoga pants and immaculate white T-shirt, my daughter- in-law is dressed in cutoffs and one of Micah's old shirts, as if she were ready to wash a car. She offers a cheek kiss and vaults up a flight of stairs, two steps at a time.

Luggage crowds the small foyer like stumps of felled trees. Alice runs toward me, holding a purple unicorn backpack, tags still attached.

"Gran," she shouts. "Look what Mommy bought me for our trip. We're going to the farm! On two planes! Then a car!"

Oxygen leaks out of me. I don't take my eyes off Alice, though it's Birdie who speaks. "Micah didn't tell you?"

I'm too stunned to respond.

"We need a break. To think things over."

I'd like a break, too; I'd be happy to start with a pedicure. "Now?" I snort. "This is when you've decided to take off?"

"What's a 'break'?" Alice asks.

"A vacation," I say to Alice. "A short vacation," I add, hopefully, and turn to Birdie. "You'll be back soon, yes?" I assess the volume of luggage, enough for relocation to New Zealand, and rephrase. "You'll be back for Thanksgiving, of course?" Veronika and I alternate, and it's my year to host. I've constructed a centerpiece of pheasant feathers and birch branches, spent hours poring over recipes, and have ordered a ninety-nine-dollar Heritage turkey, possibly raised in its own penthouse. "I bought tickets for *The Nutcracker*!" I screech.

Alice beelines to her mother, who kneads the child's elfin shoulders. "Mommy said we're having Thanksgiving with Grandpa Russ and Grandma Luanne."

"Alice, may I have a word alone with your mom?"

"Go ahead, honey," Birdie says and dutifully, Alice trots to her room.

Before I can add that I also ordered bespoke turkey cupcakes for place cards and a Williams-Sonoma tablecloth "with turkeys in full plumage amidst a lush landscape of fall foliage"—I don't celebrate Christmas; perhaps I overcorrect—Birdie says, "Please don't make things harder than they have to be."

"I could say the same." My body heats up in the way older friends profile a hot flash. "Can we discuss this like adults?"

"Mel, this isn't about you. If you take it that way, I'm sorry."

"Not about me? Alice is my granddaughter."

"Micah and I need some breathing room." Birdie turns her

back on me and summons Alice. "Gran is taking you to the library now, sweetheart. Go pee, then grab your jacket."

My granddaughter does just that, then hurdles into my arms. I want to crush her with love. I paste on a grin, lift Alice, and swing her around, though later, my back may pay for the gesture. I love Birdie, regardless of whether she returns the sentiment, and I'd ache for Micah's mangled marriage and shattered family if the two of them would split. But to have Alice ripped away is inconceivable. Alice is mine, too. My blood.

"Birdie, you can't go." My voice trembles. "Please stay."

"Mel—"

"You're making a mistake."

"Maybe, but it's my life."

No tremble in Birdie's voice. This is as feisty as I've ever seen her get. "You'll regret—"

"I repeat: my life," she says. "My decision."

CHAPTER 17

Birdie

When Birdie deplanes in Des Moines, she balances a bulging backpack and tote as she pushes Alice in her stroller across the sleety tarmac. Inside the terminal, she thinks she spots the Ericsmoens, a trim couple in khakis and sneakers who attend her parents' church. The woman is wearing a straw fedora and a grin that says, *Screw winter—I've packed my SPF 50 sunscreen and I'm joining my tribe in Scottsdale.*

This crowd avoids the Atlantic coast, overpopulated by fast-talking Easterners able to mute Midwesterners with a glance, causing the latter to fret about being judged for their DIY dye jobs and mall clothes. Now that Birdie has been an outlier in New York, she believes the paranoia is justified. Midwesterners and Southerners are the bacon and eggs in one Denny's Grand Slam breakfast of a Northeast Corridor joke.

Only when the couple walks past her without glancing her way does Birdie realize they are neither Janice nor Chipper Ericsmoen, who'd fought in Vietnam with her father, but another man with closely barbered hair hidden by an Elks Club cap. Birdie is disappointed again at baggage claim, where she thinks she identifies a teacher, a neighbor, and one of the other sax players from the marching band. Wrong, wrong, and wrong. Birdie had willingly jilted her home state, and it is throwing no welcome home party. She hadn't expected a flash mob to welcome her, but she wishes her Iowa homecoming merited at least a "Hey, Big Bird." Big Lindsey, Big Jen, Big Stacey, and Big Bird: a quartet of cheerleaders all in the honor society who once ruled their regional high school. She lived forty miles away from this airport for the better part of her life. Someone should know her.

What she gets is, "Mommy, I'm tired." Hunger and sugar have sharpened Alice's sniveling. They'd devoured PB&J's Birdie had packed, and in a reversal of personal nutritional laws, an economy-sized bag of M&M's. In her daughter's enthusiastic ripping, the candy had scattered by the lug-soled shoes of the woman chattering in the next seat. In the last four hours, Birdie has learned more than she wants to know about spa music, but she is grateful to this stranger for forcing her mind off Micah. Off the step she is taking. Off the reception that she can't predict from her parents and grandmother. Off Mel, who tries too hard as she constantly advises and admonishes.

Birdie reaches baggage claim, locates and hoists their luggage into a cart, and continues to push Alice in her stroller, regretting that she hadn't informed her parents that they were coming so someone would have met her at the airport and helped. Like a mirage, the rental car sign looms in the distance. They'd left New York at dawn and changed planes at O'Hare. It feels like midnight, though it's been only six hours.

"Do you think you could walk, Alice?" If her daughter gets out, Birdie could dump her back-breaking tote in the stroller.

"No, Mommy," her daughter informs her with a dowager's dignity. "I can't." Every other kid Alice's age whom Birdie knows gave up a stroller by three. Iowans might assume Alice is disabled, though they'll be too polite to mention it. When a stranger—a woman her own age—offers to push the luggage cart while Birdie mans the stroller, she thanks her generously. *Score one for Midwestern niceness*, she thinks.

They reach the rental car counter, where after completing a sheaf of inscrutable paperwork, Birdie is handed keys and, with the other woman's help, pushes Alice and their belongings to the parking lot.

"It's red!" Alice says when they find their car. "My other favorite color." But her smile fades as fast as it arrives. "Where's my car seat?"

"We left it in Brooklyn," mounted in Micah's truck. Birdie will be breaking the law by buckling in Alice with merely a seat belt. She'll take that risk and, tomorrow, drive to town and buy a new car seat. Birdie turns around to once again thank the woman who helped her, but her guardian angel has already disappeared.

Whenever Birdie looks at a map of the United States, her eyes nail Iowa first, with its thumb of land suggesting a hitchhiker hoping to travel east. With all due respect to Madison County and its notorious bridges in the southwest, residents of her neck of the woods—people who still use that expression— believe they live in the state's true scenic corner, with one arm waving over the Mississippi to Wisconsin and the other to Illinois. Here and there is a hill, a bluff, a cave, a trout stream.

If this were high summer, Birdie might have admired a field of corn, oats, or alfalfa, along with the efficiency of a shiny combine harvesting grain. Having left her cynicism in New York, she'd hum "America the Beautiful," meaning every word. But November is a better month in which to leave Iowa than to arrive.

As the sun sinks in the sky over tundra plowed under, ready to be frosted by snow, the air carries a bone-lancing nip. Wind whistles through bare trees. A skein of Canada geese flies south. Birdie drives for ten minutes without seeing another vehicle on a ruler-straight road that would never be cast in a Mercedes commercial. Despite the whopper dimensions of her SUV, the farther she travels, the smaller and lonelier she feels.

"Look, Alice," she says, halfway home, relieved to find a subject to narrate. "That's a silo." A silvery phallus stands erect near the barn on Big Jen's grandparents' property. "And there's my friend's rope swing."

Birdie is ready to explain what a silo and rope swing are, but when she looks in the rearview mirror she sees that her daughter, who'd been maddeningly animated throughout the trip, is slumped like a sack of potatoes, asleep. Birdie, too, is exhausted. She dreams of eating her mother's pot roast, then curling up against Alice under the canopy of her four-poster, once the envy of her friends. Her bed had functioned as the enchanted 54-by-75-inch kingdom where her imagination had filled notebooks with poetry and lists, doodles and half-finished short stories.

She'd never considered her childhood exceptional, but preserved in the amber of memory, even feeding the hogs (the *trayf*, in Micah's lingua franca) now strikes her as far superior to the life she and he are cobbling together twelve hundred miles away. Evidence to the contrary—as a teenager she resented her smelly chores and the limitations of her world—Birdie files under Revisionist History. She makes one more turn, and shouts, "There it is Alice, the farm."

CHAPTER 18

Birdie

Birdie had always wished their family's farm had a name. At nine, her inner Laura Ingalls Wilder lobbied for Rocky Ridge, to which her father pointed out that the land's lack of even one rocky ridge in three hundred thirty-three acres is its finest feature. When she discovered *The Secret Garden*, Birdie pushed for Misselthwaite Manor; as she advanced to *Pride and Prejudice*, Pemberley. Russ Peterson would have neither. "If the Peterson Place was good enough for your grandpop, it'll have to be good enough for you."

The house—foursquare and solid—hasn't changed since Birdie's visit a few months earlier. The sun's dying rays glint off solar panels. Overlooking a dormant vegetable garden, a trellis where clematis bloomed is empty. Logs are split and neatly piled nearby, ready for the fireplace. Russ's pickup sits in the driveway along with an old-model fuel-sucking RV, the transport for national park vacations distinguished by bad plumbing, sibling protests, and bears stealing her bloodied sanitary napkins. There is no sight of Luanne's car, and except for a low-watt lamp in the hallway, the house is dark, as if it's glowering at her.

Birdie gently wakes Alice and lifts her to the gravel driveway.

"Welcome to the farm, Alice Joy-Ellen Tobias," she says as they walk hand in hand to the front porch.

Alice's eyes sweep from left to right until she shrieks, "What's that?"

Birdie squints into the dusk at a spook wearing an Iowa Hawkeyes sweatshirt in bumblebee colors. "A scarecrow, sweet pea."

"He's creepy."

"Remember *The Wizard of Oz*?"

Alice does not. She death-grips Birdie's hand. There will be much to unpack, not all of it clothing. An American flag, attached to a pole jutting from the front porch, flaps in the wind. In compliance with local taste, potted chrysanthemums in shades from saffron to citron yellow frame the front door, where a wreath proclaims *Autumn Blessings*, testimony to Luanne Peterson's abiding faith and skill with a glue gun. When they reach the door, Alice stretches to touch one of the wreath's dangling green ribbons, saying, "It's pretty, Mommy."

"You're right—it is." Birdie is glad Micah or Veronika aren't functioning in the capacity of taste police, though Mel, a bornagain craftswoman, might admire her mother's efforts.

Out of courtesy, Birdie knocks on the door. When after six good whacks there is no answer, she steps inside—no need for her key—and takes in the familiar musk of lemon Pledge, cedar paneling, and Buckshot, her father's deaf and arthritic black lab, decommissioned from hunting duty, who limps in from the kitchen. Birdie passes the sniff test. He barks and leaps an inch.

"Buckshot, old boy. Glad to see me?" She is glad to see him, partly because his presence means her parents can't be far away. It hadn't occurred to Birdie that at five-thirty they'd be anywhere but home. Her mother would be stirring a pot, earbuds in to listen to Chopin concertos. Her father would be in front of a crackling fire, reading the *Des Moines Register* or *Successful Farming*, assessing cattle futures and the price of sorghum the way other dads track baseball or the stock market. She'd imagined the table vivid with Fiestaware, though when she glances to the right, the French doors to the dining room are closed, and the table is bare except for an apple-filled pottery bowl she doesn't recognize.

Birdie hangs their coats on hooks in the front hall, shivers and checks the thermostat. Sixty-four degrees. She cranks it up to seventy-two, hopes she won't catch hell from her parents, rips open her bags, and finds sweatshirts for Alice and herself.

"We'll leave these here," she says, pointing to the luggage, "and get something to eat. Remember the way?"

Alice grins and runs to the kitchen, the polar vortex of her Iowa grandmother's domain. Luanne Peterson may refer to herself as a farmer's wife, as ordinary as a chicken dinner, her head jammed with agricultural factoids she aligns on tidy computer files. But she is also a registered nurse who earned her diploma when Birdie and Clark went to high school. Currently, she heads an obstetric ward, yet Luanne still raises the art of homemaking to a level Birdie has no desire or ability to reach. Her mother comes from a line of women whose mastery of tasks could easily be seen as a moral rebuke to other people's efforts.

To Birdie, this kitchen is her family's beating heart. Oak cabinets that she and her mother had stripped and refinished glow with a subtle luster. Plaid café curtains sewn by Luanne frame large windows. Community notices, church schedules, and grandchild drawings and photos plaster the refrigerator door. Next to the breadbox an iron cools on the soapstone counter. Does Mel even know how to iron, Birdie wonders, meanly?

The iron is another smoke signal that her parents can't be long gone, but Birdie's glee crashes when she opens the refrigerator. No leftover pot roast or apple crisp. Carrot and celery sticks swim in ice water next to sesame oil, oat milk, and a heretical package of ready-made piecrust.

Dinner tonight will be scrambled eggs.

After a few bites Alice rests her head on the table, closes her eyes, and drops her spoon. "Bed, Mommy, I wanna go to bed," she mumbles. Birdie carries her daughter to the back staircase and climbs the steps to the wide hall with its many doors. Her bedroom's DO NOT DISTURB sign is intact, but her desk now features decoupage supplies—brushes, sealer, and half-filled bottles of Mod Podge. The bed is covered with quilt pieces that Birdie carefully moves to her chair—assuming she can still call it hers. She pulls back the flowery chenille bedspread, slips Alice under softly starched sheets and Hudson Bay blankets, and whispers good night to her small, sleeping daughter.

Only as she plugs in the nightlight does Birdie notice that the bed's canopy is gone.

CHAPTER 19

Mel

WHEN FOR THE THIRD TIME JORDAN MENTIONS KIT, LAST month's travel buddy to Tangier, I suggest she invite Kit to join us for a dinner we'd planned for that evening.

"I already did," Jordan replied.

"How long have you been together?"

"About three months."

"What kind of work does Kit do?" My favorite busybody question.

"She's a novelist."

I can't imagine writing a book. My deadline would chase me like a squad car. "Anything I might have read?"

"Nothing yet."

I worry about Jordan being pursued by a gold digger as much as I would if my daughter, with her hard-earned income and boundless generosity, were a son. Are you entitled to call yourself a novelist when your work is unpublished? I imagine a dog-eared manuscript with participles dangling like mismatched earrings, then regret my skepticism. Kit might be a wunderkind who camps out at the most selective literary retreats, on her way to snagging every plummy prize.

Hours later I collapse onto a leather banquette at a restaurant chosen by Jordan. For the last ten hours, I've been the lion-hearted therapist. I'm relieved to stand down.

"All they serve is roast chicken?" Jake asks, looking up from the menu. "At Costco you get six birds for the price of one here." He sounds crabby, petulant, accusatory, and bored, the four corners of an aggrieved husband.

I refuse to be infected by his mood. "Costco's are raised in poultry concentration camps and are certainly not draped with foie gras," I protest. Even a vegetarian would find herself ravenous in this restaurant, calculated to allow diners to pretend they are blissed out in the home of an ambassador. Plush rugs absorb the babble of a crowd with enough good juju to get a reservation. At a brass-trimmed rotisserie oven, showy as a vintage Cadillac, chickens surrender to a steady, slow twirling, skins crisping on the spit. The garlic perfume could cure a thousand sniffles. Like the chickens' fat, my cares begin to drip away, though when I catch my reflection, even the flattering candlelight fails to mask that I can no longer pass myself off as thirty-five.

"Have you heard from Micah?"

"No, and do you think he's the only thing on my mind?"

"What else is eating you? I'm not psychic."

Jake laughs. Not a friendly laugh. "Really?"

We can scrap with the best of them. Last year Jake slept on the couch for a week, though I don't recall what offense landed him there. Has the statute of limitation on civility once again expired? If we were clients, I might suggest a coolheaded, measured approach. Repeating an acronym, I'd spell out. Or similar bunk.

I notice a woman of the type who gets called statuesque striding in our direction. It takes a few seconds to compute that this is Jordan, dressed as I rarely see her, in a shapely green jacket and silky pants that billow over shoes pointy enough to slit an envelope. In lock-step is a tiny woman in a red dress with a disciplined bob, a sharp nose, and a lipsticked mouth to match her dress. Jordan bends low to whisper in her ear. I turn to see if Jake is taking this in. I hope his waterbug-ugly mood will skittle away.

Jordan steers her companion toward her father with the slight locomotion of a hand on the woman's lower back. "Dad, meet Kit," she says. Jake stands and plants cheek kisses first on his daughter, then Kit. His charm—passed down by his father like their broad shoulders and size-eleven feet—is a dependable lubricant. I watch Jordan show off her handsome daddy, who is ten or more years younger than most of her friends' papas, then turn to me.

"Mel, Kit."

Kit could be eighteen or twenty-eight; that I can't tell the difference is a measure of how old I've gotten myself. I try to slow down and take in this snapshot, should Kit be elevated into the pantheon of permanent influencer. Do they already have matching tattoos? Is Thumbelina a hiccup in Jordan's life or someone who'll alter it ad infinitum?

"Lovely to meet you," I say, stiffly extending my hand. "Do you live in New York?"

"I share a loft in Bushwick with my brother. Harry's a lighting engineer for Broadway shows." She mentions the Tony Award–winning musical where her brother works, for which I've refused to blow hundreds of dollars for tickets; I'd sooner spend the money on a flight to Dubrovnik. We discuss theatrical revivals produced at the expense of original, risk-taking material. Kit's voice is comically high. Has she gone through puberty?

We attack our dinners, and Jake calls for a second bottle of wine, then a third. Jordan tells story after story, while I track Kit tracking Jordan, her eyes on my daughter like a laser pen. As we finish dessert, Jordan winds up with one last tale of corporate skullduggery, leans forward, and asks, "Ready for our news?"

I've grown skeptical of dramatic developments unspooled by children, but I don't have a choice.

"Ta-da. Kit and I are moving in together."

They exchange a look of almost religious sincerity. It's been years since I've seen her love-struck. She had boyfriends in high school, and starting in college, girlfriends, followed by a brief return to men, then strictly females. All the while, she has defended her domestic parameters. No live-ins, as far as I know.

"That's great, Jordy." Jake invokes the nickname only he can get away with. I hope others miss the slur I hear, and have failed to notice him drinking two glasses for everyone else's one.

I know congratulations from me, too, are in order, despite the unreliable scent of love at first sight. After years in my ringside seat treating brokenhearted clients who were once as convinced of their mutual devotion as they were their beating hearts, this is a state about which I have become skeptical. "We need a toast," I say nonetheless, and raise a glass, which remains half-empty. "To Jordan and Kit."

"To my girls," Jake clicks with both of them, and turns toward me with heavy lids. "To Jordan and Kit. To us, Mel."

"To all of us," I say.

"To the future," Jordan says.

"To you two."

I jolt at the sound of Micah's low voice, my spine involuntarily straightening as I turn to face my son.

"My good man." Jake stands up, stepping toward him, slapping his back. "Glad you could make it."

"Brother." Jordan hugs her twin. "Meet Kit."

I watch Micah small-talk Kit—"I've heard such good things!"—whose returned smile suggests that Micah is still to first impressions what dessert is to dinner. "How's my gorgeous twin?" he asks Jordan.

Since Birdie's departure, I've heard nothing from Micah.

This doesn't surprise me. At fourteen, when I asked him Mom-questions, he informed me that he released information strictly on a need-to-know basis, and I had no need to know. Nor is an A-list restaurant where Micah belongs. As if I've tossed a match on dry leaves, my anger ignites. He owes the police a visit, after which he should sprint to Iowa to make right what is wrong.

"Mom," my son says as he reaches my side of the table.

"Sit down and have some coffee." Does my tone sting? Perhaps. The others dine out on the domestic trivia of Jordan and Kit's life, slipping past the topic of Birdie and Alice, while I wait for Jordan and her lover to leave. I'm leery about their forthcoming household arrangement, but it's not my way to interfere. Okay, I intrude plenty, but in my humble opinion, my opprobrium and suggestions are elevating, improving their lives in the way vanilla and confectioners' sugar upgrade plain whipped cream.

"You've heard half our news." Jordan and Kit share grins deserving of a dancing cheeseburger meme.

"There's more?" Is my daughter getting a promotion? Will the company go public, letting us buy friends-and-family stock? Maybe it's Kit's announcement. A college graduation? She looks young enough.

"We're going to have a baby!"

Micah whistles and Jake stands to bear-hug both women as I choke on this information. Call me crazy, but as the mother of a single lesbian, a surprise baby has never made it into the worry diary I occasionally suggest that my clients keep.

"A baby?" I bleat.

"Yeah, Mom," Jordan says. "With any luck, healthy, seven or eight pounds, twenty-some inches long, hair optional."

Let these women share a life for a few years, then consider motherhood, I think. It's not as if my daughter is rescuing another dog.

"This is"—dare I say harebrained?—"unexpected."

"Fair enough." With conviction, Jordan adds, "But we know we want a family together."

"Are you adopting?" I could get behind an act of social justice. Perhaps Jordan has discovered an orphaned asylum seeker to mother.

"That isn't the plan."

"Taking in a foster child?" My cousin Laurie in Chicago did just that.

"We want a baby who's connected to us, Mom, and don't want to wait years, then suffer through IVF hell."

"You could freeze your eggs. Lots of my clients—"

"Will you stop? Kit and I plan to find a summa cum laude sperm donor, ideally one with dance moves." Despite my daughter's many gifts, she brings two left feet to a dance floor.

"Jordy, we're thrilled, and we don't need to know everything," Jake says.

My husband is thoroughly accepting of our daughter's sexuality, but the fine print makes him squirm. I, on the other, am getting an unexpected contact high as I begin to imagine Jordan's show-off genes mingling with those of, say, a Nordic God who is also the country's most sought-out orthopedic resident and opera singer. I force myself to annul that image, however, because I have a more pressing family concern. He's sitting at this table, smiling and drinking, most likely relieved that his twin has provided parental distraction when his moral, legal, and marital failings would otherwise be front and center. After a second pear liqueur, clutching leftovers in foil swans, Jordan and Kit depart. If my daughter's going to get pregnant, she better quit the booze.

Micah faces Jake and me and says, "Big news, huh?"

"I'll believe it when it happens."

"Aren't you the fucking buzzkill?"

I wish Jake would take our son to task for speaking this way instead of asking, "Mel, why so cynical?" His voice is thick and syrupy. "Be happy for your daughter."

I ignore Jake and with an acid tongue say to Micah, "Forget about your sister. What's going on with you?"

He freezes.

"Well?"

"I don't know if I can do it," he says as seconds calcify into a minute.

"And what is *it*?"

"Meeting again with the police, marriage, fatherhood, the works."

Jake covers Micah's hand with his own. They are both broad with tapered fingers. The sight of them together, each with a simple gold band, usually softens me, but tonight I hear the drink that varnishes Jake's words with sentimental goo. When did he stop being helpful? He's going soft on our son, but I'm not ready to give Micah a pass.

"Show some moral stamina," I say. "Turn yourself in. It may not be as bad as you think. Your incident wasn't intentional, and at this point no one can prove you were drinking, though I assume you were. Think of this poor girl you hit. She has a name, you know. Delia." I tell him what I've learned.

He stares at me, stony.

"Stop with the pressure," Jake says. "This should be Micah's decision."

"When you make mistakes, you should learn from them," I insist, ignoring Jake. "That applies to your family as much as it does your accident. You have to clean up your mess with Birdie before it gets worse. If you're going through hell, keep going." Sorry, Winston Churchill, for my lack of attribution.

Micah's eyes ice me, but I preach away. "Being a husband and a parent requires accountability. That's the least you owe your family. On a good day the return on the investment is joy and on other days, angst, but you try. You always fucking try." I stop only to catch my breath, dimly aware that in my desperation, I am speaking loudly, attracting stares. "Have you even spoken to Birdie since she left?"

"Yesterday, but not today."

"Because?"

"Enough," Jake barks.

"I'll say what I want."

"Mom, we need time. Both of us. That's why she left."

My voice climbs. "Are you trying to nuke your marriage so irrevocably you'll lose both Birdie and Alice?"

"Mom, I love them, but—"

"You're missing the point. Once you're a father there's no 'but.' It's 'I love them *and*' so I'm going to do X, Y, and Z to make it better, even if it's hard. They deserve it."

"Stop," Jake growls. "Our son is not one of your clients, though God help you if this is how you address them."

"I'm speaking as someone who loves her son and daughter-in-law and granddaughter, as someone who would be broken if we lose Birdie and . . ."

I can't finish the sentence. Nor, as I walk through the restaurant on my way out, do I acknowledge a young woman who gapes at me, her mouth hanging open. Only in the taxi going home does it register that she was Bambi, my new client, rendezvousing with an older man.

CHAPTER 20

Birdie

Birdie tiptoes down the back stairs and stands outside the kitchen door. A clock is on the wall that wasn't there yesterday. A hammer sits on the counter.

"If you wait a minute a birdie will come out right here and say 'cuckoo' ten times," Joy-Ellen Lindstrom, Birdie's grandmother, explains to Alice.

"A birdie? Why?" Alice giggles and wonders. *Alice Wonders* is the name of a children's storybook Birdie keeps telling herself she should write.

"To tell the time."

Alice scrunches her face. Someone has French-braided her hair. "Mommy looks at her phone to see what o'clock it is. Isn't that rib-dick-a-lis?"

"*Ridiculous* is a long word for someone your age." Joy-Ellen smiles fleetingly at Birdie before returning her attention to Alice. "Your Grandma Luanne, your mother's mama, wanted a clock like this when she was almost four, same as you. I'm only fifty years late."

Birdie had forgotten how flat and unhurried her grandmother's vowels sound, as if every word skates on patience. Until she heard her hearty chuckle, Birdie had also forgotten how much she missed her.

"With a bird on top of a little house?" Alice asks.

"The house is called a chalet and the clock comes from a country called Switzerland. In the mountains, shepherds call their goats and cows like this. *Oh-di-lay-ee-ay, di-lay-dee-oh, de-lay-ee.*" She demonstrates. Loudly.

As a girl, Birdie found her grandmother's yodeling as mortifying as when she skinny-dipped in the creek or polkaed around the living room with a broom during Saturday night babysitting, accompanied by her wunnerful-wunnerful Lawrence Welk records.

When her giggling stops Alice asks, "Why don't the shepherds just text?"

"Sometimes the old ways are the best." Joy-Ellen peers at Alice through glasses that magnify her eyes, which are the blue of a sunny winter sky. "Say, can you yodel?"

Birdie watches her daughter hesitate before she explains that, "People don't do that in Brooklyn. They yell."

"In that case, miss, why don't you finish your cocoa and cinnamon toast so I can give your mother a proper greeting." Only then does Joy-Ellen turn to Birdie and open her arms, doughy but strong.

"Grandma, *so* good to see you." Birdie flicks away a tear. Joy-Ellen offers kindness, solidity, and a large bosom to snuggle against. Had the cuckoo bird not done its duty, which startles both of them, Birdie wouldn't have let go. "You're looking great."

Joy-Ellen's is one of Birdie's favorite faces. Unlike Veronika, she is not, and has never been, beautiful. Birdie can't remember when Joy-Ellen's hair wasn't salt-and-pepper—now, mostly salt—tautly permed, and her face crosshatched with wrinkles.

"Where are my parents?" Birdie sits at the kitchen table.

"Your mom should be finishing her shift and your dad's in

Minnesota with Russ Jr., at an equipment auction. I came by to
walk Buckshot. Imagine my surprise." She gestures beyond the
other kitchen door, toward Birdie's duffels and suitcases in the
hallway. Joy-Ellen steps to the stove. "Hope you still like oatmeal." Birdie watches her grandmother ladle thick, creamy ce-
real into crockery bowls and add milk, sugar, and a pat of butter
to each along with a hefty handful of raisins. "You're all bones.
You sure don't take after my side of the family."

A pity, Birdie thinks, because while Grandma Lindstrom
might be built like a Doric column, she is also a pillar of sound
judgment. Joy-Ellen tried to instill in Birdie and her brothers
that if they've been brought up properly, any decent human
instinctively knows the right thing to do in virtually every situation, and people fritter away far too much time justifying
answers they know are wrong.

Wasting time is on the list of what flips Joy-Ellen's wig, along
with lying, bamboozling, stealing, and a sweeping category reserved for—in no particular order—racists, right-wing shock
jocks, hypochondriacs, foreign cartels that poison Iowa with
drugs along with the meth-heads dimwitted enough to buy the
stuff, braggarts, homeowners too lazy to keep up their property,
corrupt politicians who throw hard-earned money at the Iowa
primary, NRA members who use guns for any purpose other
than hunting, and people unable to keep their nose on their own
face. She doesn't consider herself political, just sensible.

Joy-Ellen places the bowls and two spoons on the table across
from one another, sits down to face Birdie, and asks, "How's the
hubby?"

Birdie pictures Micah two days ago, when she told him
she was leaving. He protested, but not enough. She hoped to
sense outrage, regret as deep as a well and for Micah to be as
sure of his passion as she was once sure of hers for him. She pictured peaks of emotion, not a gentle rolling plain. She especially

wanted to know why he'd made her lie to the detective. That alone deserved an apology.

"Next question."

"I see," Joy-Ellen says.

She has never spoken ill of Micah—nor have Birdie's parents—but in the implicit Lindstrom-Peterson bylaws, adulthood begins a few months past college graduation. After that, you pull your own weight. Birdie's older brother, Russ, has been farming as an equal partner with their father for years, and Clark, at twenty-six, is an architect in Minneapolis. A commission for designing an art gallery has allowed him to repay his student loans and buy a condo overlooking the sculpture garden of the Walker Art Center. Since Micah's food truck business is deep in the red, Birdie knows this certifies him as an inexplicable slacker, though her family keeps that opinion to themselves.

"Micah's parents?"

"Mel and Jake are fine." If fine means overwrought. Birdie has been trying, unsuccessfully, not to think how her departure will affect them—Mel, in particular. She knows her mother-in-law will take this escape to Iowa personally, as if Birdie's sole intent is to hurt her by taking Alice a thousand miles away.

"That charmer, David?"

On the one occasion when David and Joy-Ellen, a widow since the age of forty-seven, met—during the Tobiases' trip to Iowa for a church hall wedding reception—David acted the chivalrous swain, refilling her grandmother's punch cup, bringing her deviled eggs and sugary white wedding cake, complimenting her on the high school's string quartet. All the while, Birdie suspected that he was speculating on where the Petersons were hiding the booze along with the dinner.

David Tobias had made an indelible impression, though not half as much as Veronika had. Joy-Ellen Lindstrom and Veronika Tobias are the same age, and when they met, Joy-Ellen was as intrigued by Veronika's story as Veronika was fond of repeating it. How she moved to America after her tragically widowed mother married Herman Berezovsky, one more shadow of a human being discharged from a Displaced Persons camp after World War II. How Veronika was forced to take Herman's last name, wiping out Ya'akov Marcuse, her phantom father, for a second time. How Herman had lost a daughter, Klara, at Dachau, along with his first wife.

As Veronika shared her story it was the only time Birdie saw her grandmother cry. The Lindstroms and Petersons had known stability since 1873 and 1875 respectively, when their forebears emigrated from Sweden and Norway. Their lives have been a slow but steady upward struggle from poverty to prosperity, from tenant farming to owning livestock and working their own land, which expanded over the years to large herds on many acres.

"And Dr. Tobias?" Her grandmother refuses to call her "Veronika," though Birdie guesses Joy-Ellen would sooner wear a thong than visit a shrink.

"Lately, Micah and I are falling short of her expectations, though she encouraged me when I said I wanted to come back here for a bit." That wasn't quite true. Veronika didn't discourage her. The two weren't the same. But neutrality was more than Mel, whom Birdie hadn't consulted, would have offered.

"She's a tough customer, that Dr. Tobias. But she earned it the hard way and the woman's no fool."

No fool: Joy-Ellen's highest accolade. Message received. Listen up, Birdie.

"Grandma Lindstrom," Alice says, "did you hear that?"

Birdie heard them, too—three short honks, her mother's signature. As a teenager she took the toots as a warning to hang up the phone, snap off the television, or stop making out in the living room. She peeks through the window to see Luanne's navy blue Subaru Forester pull into the driveway and park next to Joy-Ellen's shiny green pickup and her own red rental. As she hears her mother open the back door, Birdie involuntarily holds her breath.

"Hide, Alice," Joy-Ellen whispers. "You can be your Grandma Luanne's other surprise."

"Who's here, Ma?" Luanne shouts from the mudroom as she hangs her parka on a hook and pulls off her boots. She is wearing the watermelon-colored scrubs Birdie had sent for Christmas, the color chosen by Alice.

"See for yourself," Joy-Ellen shouts back.

"Good Lord!" Luanne says as her daughter gets up to meet her halfway across the kitchen. Luanne's expression rotates through astonishment, happiness, and confusion until she lands on concern. If she's lucky, in that face Birdie can imagine her own face, fast-forwarded twenty-three years. Sunbursts of crow's feet frame grey-blue eyes. Light wrinkles bracket her forehead. Delicate cords climb up her neck. Fair hair heavily macramé'd with silver hangs in a braid down her back. This is what female fortitude looks like, Peterson-style.

"Birdie!"

"Not just 'Birdie'!" Alice adds, popping out from under the table and running to Luanne.

"Look how tall you've gotten," Luanne says, lifting her for a hug. "You're your mother all over again."

"I'd say you're all John Lindstrom, the three of you," Joy-Ellen adds. "That man was half giraffe. Shoes like ski boots. The cat slept in them."

"When did you get in?" Luanne asks, circling her sinewy, competent arms around her daughter and granddaughter.

"Last night," Alice answers.

"I'm sorry we weren't here for you."

"Grandma Lindstrom told me Dad and Russ Jr. are at an auction," Birdie says.

"When it comes to the farm, your brother thinks big and your dad grouses, but he's more excited than he lets on. He'll probably come home all hopped up about a manure spreader." She pours herself a cup of coffee, which she drinks black. "You two had breakfast, Bird?" Luanne asks, her long fingers playing with her simple gold locket. Birdie hopes her photo, with her brothers, is still inside. Luanne is avoiding the obvious, asking why she is here.

"Grandma's taken good care of us," Birdie says.

"Alice and I are going to take her bag upstairs to get dressed," Joy-Ellen announces.

"You promised me a story!" Alice says.

"Have I told you about how we were so poor we could only afford three-legged dogs?"

Alice glances at her mother.

"That's a joke, Alice," Birdie explains to her grave and literal daughter.

"You'll have to show me which suitcase in that logjam is yours."

"'Logjam'?" Luanne says after the two leave the room, lifting an eyebrow.

For the last few days, Birdie has been so electric with indignation she'd stopped short of framing how she'd explain her visit to her parents. "We may be here for a while," is all she offers.

"I've been waiting for you," Luanne says, the words unadorned. She might have as easily said, "I like the color green."

Is there a secret language connecting mothers and daughters? As a girl, Birdie was convinced that Luanne possessed motherly telepathy. How else could she know which boy Birdie hoped would ask her to the homecoming dance or when she hadn't practiced the piano? In a daisy chain of love, Birdie feels bonded to Luanne as surely as she feels linked to Alice, and Luanne tethered to Joy-Ellen.

She'd remarked upon this once to Mel, who informed Birdie that she was among the fortunate; many women who sought her help had only chasms where they wished mother-daughter ties would be. Warm family connection was nothing to take for granted, Mel had said, as if her words were highlighted in neon yellow. Her subtext was a command: family comes first—which Birdie has interpreted to mean that Mel feels the Tobias family comes first. As for Mel and Jordan, whether they feel the emotional reward of a tight bond is anyone's guess, since her sister-in-law soars through life with what appears to be ferocious independence. Birdie guesses that Mel is deeply proud of her triple-crown daughter. But close to her? She wouldn't bet on it.

"You've been waiting for me?" Birdie repeats. "Why?"

"It isn't what you've said, it's what you've not said." Luanne's tone is neither tender nor frosty. "It's been clear for a while that you've been discouraged."

Discouraged was how Birdie felt before Micah's hit-and-run, when her biggest concern was his waste of time and money in bars. Discouraged was a froth of an emotion compared to the more recent karate chop.

"Not that your father and I endorse using Iowa as a hideout. If you have problems, you can't hide from them forever."

Her mother's thin lips purse so tightly Luanne looks as if she has no lips at all. The austerity of her indictment is like a burglar alarm going off. I should have seen that coming, Birdie thinks. She waits for more on the subject, but her mother yawns. "Now, if you'll excuse me, I'm going to collapse. Two C-sections last night, and one delivery of twins. No rest for the weary."

"Get to sleep, Mom," Birdie says, hugging her. "We'll be quiet."

Luanne brushes Birdie's bangs away from her face. "Please, don't take what I said the wrong way," she says, then turns to walk upstairs.

But is there any other way to take her mother's comments

than as a declaration that Birdie is at least partially to blame for her situation? She is no longer hungry and washes her bowl of half-finished oatmeal. From outside, crows caw. Through the kitchen window, she watches Alice follow Joy-Ellen into the barn. Birdie refills her mug and sips weak black coffee until it grows cold and the boneheaded bird in the clock says "cuckoo" eleven times. Birdie wants to break its neck.

CHAPTER 21

Veronika

Veronika waves to Jake, who waits at their standard corner table, as far away from other diners as possible at French Roast, a neighborhood restaurant more reliable than distinguished. For as long as Veronika can remember, she and her son have kept a Wednesday lunch date. Dinners with the entire family have their place, along with Sunday morning lox-eggs-and-onions brunches at Barney Greengrass or dumplings at Sum Dum Luk. But for a busy son to devote ninety minutes a week to his mother is a gift—Veronika believes any mother would understand—even if they jaw about nothing more personal than a Supreme Court ruling.

She is wearing head-to-toe camel, as colorful as Veronika gets. The jacket is from several years ago, because she is not the Queen of England, and everything in her wardrobe is purchased as a lasting investment. Veronika always dresses with care, but before lunches with Jake she gives her attire extra attention; she believes it would agitate her son to see his mother take a turn toward dumpy or disheveled, signaling that he needs to step up and take charge. That one day—two decades from now, God willing—Jake will be running her life is as unimaginable as appearing in public with an unplucked chin whisker.

Often when they chat over lunch, they tunnel down to the granular level of something personal, which gives Veronika an opportunity to unleash observations and wisdom, usually about Melanie, Jordan, or Micah. Today, she expects the topic to be the latter. Veronika is teed up and ready to go. That boy needs to do what's ethical and right.

It does not take long for Veronika to finish her onion soup and Lyonnaise salad or Jake, his tomato soup, grilled cheese, and *frites*. They order espressos and begin to discuss the next presidential race, though her opinions about Micah await, ready to jeté on stage. But before she can lead the discourse in that direction, Jake leans toward her and says, "There's something I need to ask you."

"Of course." Her son seeks her opinion on everything from cooking—which he does more skillfully than Melanie, who apparently never tastes a dish before she inflicts it on guests—to how she felt being one of only three women in her medical school class. (Petrified, which Veronika tried to hide under a blitz of bravado.)

"Just so you know," he says, "I haven't mentioned what I'm going to tell you to Mel."

Veronika is now interested, very interested.

Jake sits up straighter. "Have you noticed anything off about Dad?"

Veronika doesn't like where this is headed. Unsubscribe! She scowls. "*Off?* Whatever do you mean?"

"Forgetful?" Jake continues down the cognitive food chain. "Illogical? Scatterbrained?"

Veronika tosses off a laugh that doesn't match her resentful expression. "No more so than usual. You know your father could never remember a birthday or a name."

"Okay, but Dad used to do long calculations in his head, and the other day—"

Veronika interrupts. "Forgetting a bit is a normal part of aging." She wishes she was better at forgetting; she'd start with the first ten years of her life. "Someday it will happen to you. Show some compassion and common sense."

"Forgetting how to buckle a seat belt? What a Xerox machine does? Not knowing how to stamp a letter?"

Veronika feels her eyelid start to flutter. "Enough. Surely you are exaggerating. Your father is brilliant."

"Mom, I'm not saying he's not or trying to malign or insult Dad. You think it's easy for me to talk about this?" He hopes Veronika will help him out here, but she only fixes him with a cold stare. "I'm scared. Maybe he needs to see a neurologist to rule out—"

"Stop. You're deflecting. Worry about your son, not your father. What's going on with Micah? If he doesn't clear up the situation his accident is causing he may lose his wife."

"Mother, I'm worried about both." He and Veronika stop talking and sip their espressos, now lukewarm. He reaches for the check, but Veronika gets to it first and slaps down a credit card. Tenderness in her scalp is signaling an incipient migraine, and she knows that soon, pain will blossom in spots she forgot even existed. Inhaling deeply, she tells Jake to relax, though the person she's actually talking to is herself. "You're simply upset. You'll feel better when Birdie and Alice return." If they return. "And when Micah resolves his mess." She is no longer in the mood to discuss her grandson and looks at her watch. "It's getting late . . ."

Jake bends to kiss his mother goodbye and leaves the restaurant while she waits for her receipt. Veronika feels like a woman who has gotten off a plane, expecting summer in Algiers, but has landed in Antarctica without a shred of Polartec and no return ticket. She stares into her espresso as if she'll find an answer there. *Is* David losing it? She has noticed forgetfulness and eccentricity, attributed both to overwork, and has encouraged her husband to go to the stores later in the morning. He's refused.

David Tobias & Son's shops are where David is happiest, maybe even more so than at her side.

She flashes on the worst possible scenario: dementia. If David is truly sick, how rapidly will he deteriorate? Of the many ways for a life to ebb away, Veronika believes dementia is the cruelest, for its hostages as well as their caretakers. Veronika has treated people in both categories. She thinks of Alzheimer's and the like as psychological serial killers, and has never been convinced that the person who is afflicted isn't aware that they are losing their own intellect, bit by bit. Veronika can imagine the mean trick of having less and less of a warm, beloved mind and body present beside her, until one day only a fleshy ghost remains.

When she pictures life without David she envisions an empty box. He is her sole confidant, her lover, her playmate, and her favorite human being. Beyond Jake, Jordan, and a carefully curated short list of people—mostly analysts at her institute—whose relationships nourish her, Veronika is close to no one. She has never felt the need.

Veronika takes a long drink of cold water and a deep breath. Then she stands, straight and strong. This is *narishkeit*! Foolishness. Surely, she can help delay her husband's unraveling. Veronika will not give up. She is, after all, Dr. Tobias of Central Park West.

CHAPTER 22

Mel

WHEN YOU SAW ME IN THE RESTAURANT, HOW DID YOU FEEL?"
I ask Bambi at our next session.

"Honestly?"

"I hope everything you share here is honest."

She winds a shiny ringlet around her index finger. "It made
me feel better. Don't take this the wrong way, but I could tell
you were having some ugly words with your son and husband.
At least I assume that was your son and husband. Both lookers,
by the way."

"Why did that make you feel better?" Bambi's hair twirling
is starting to irk me. I'd like to slap her hand.

Her wry half smile becomes whole. "It's good to know I'm
not the only one who's a little psycho."

I laugh. Glad to be of service.

"Now it's my turn to ask," Bambi says. "What did you think
of Clyde?"

"Was that who you were with?"

"Pretty damn gorgeous, huh?"

"What do you wish I'd say?"

"That you get his appeal?" Bambi presents the statement as a question.

What I think of the man is irrelevant. I volunteer nothing.

"I've decided to come clean to Joe about Clyde."

"Why do you think that's a good idea?"

"I owe it to myself to clear my conscience before I sleep with Clyde. If I don't sleep with him, I'll always wonder if he was my true north."

Whoa, Nellie. I wait for more, but Bambi turns silent. "About your 'true north,' I feel it's my place to point out that your GPS might not be entirely reliable." It may not know true north from Tierra del Fuego.

Looking dubious, she continues to finger her curls. I wish it wasn't my job to get people to think. Why couldn't I be a Tarot reader who had only to say to clients, "Behold the King of Swords. He commands you. Dump Clyde." Done. Over. Out.

"Have you considered that honesty can be overrated?"

"I don't follow," Bambi admits.

How dense is she? Show me a therapist who hasn't thought this about a client and I'll show you a liar. "Truth-telling can have a seesaw effect. One person feels better for getting information off her chest but the disclosure may make the listener feel worse." I offer this tidbit along with a salvo of similar observations from my flea market of shopworn aphorisms. I hope they sound less hackneyed to Bambi than to me.

"But, Dr. Glazer, if I miss this chance with Clyde I could regret it for the rest of my life. What if Joe is the mistake and Clyde's my destiny?"

What if? The room feels noisy, though neither of us is speaking. I force myself to question why I have taken a deep dislike to Clyde. I've worked with adulterers whose pas de deux started in hot-sheet motels offering discounted matinee rates and seen their relationships blossom into marriages more fulfilling than what they left behind. Is it the age difference? When I glimpsed Clyde, my impression was of a Las Vegas high roller older than Bambi by, say, twenty years. Yet I know deeply committed couples with decades between them, so it can't be that.

"I'm awake all night," Bambi says. "Thinking about Clyde is better than my dreams."

Oh, do go on.

"What if I'm living the wrong life?"

Bambi has distilled therapy to a single question. *What if a client is leading the wrong life?* If so, I have made a commitment to help her find a better one. But wait. I'm conducting group therapy, though there are only two of us in the room. The honks and hoots in my head are so loud I'm surprised Bambi can't hear them. Are Micah and Birdie living the wrong life? No matter where I start, all roads lead to my son and daughter-in-law. May God and the licensing bureau for the New York chapter of the National Association of Social Workers please forgive me, but once again I've gone rogue, barreling down a mountain switchback.

I need to steer us to safety. "Please try to put your thoughts about Clyde aside and ask yourself, why did you marry Joe?"

Bambi rubbernecks the buttery yellow roses I bought this morning at Trader Joe's, and smooths the wrinkles in her pants. "Joe was a college buddy," she begins, "an adorable dork. One night we got hammered and slept together. I didn't know he was a virgin. After that he became a stray puppy following me, worshiping me, so persistent and cute I finally gave in and we became a couple." Bambi explains that it's she who decides where they live, what Joe wears, who their friends are, which movies they see or music they listen to, and on and on. She and Joe are romantic antonyms. The Veronika-David model. Veronika asks David his opinion about a play, movie, or candidate, and while he's mulling it over, she tells him what to think.

"For a while I got off on someone as sweet as Joe needing

me this much, but it didn't take long for it to become suffocating. Being with him can be like living in one of my parents'
Woody Guthrie albums."

The rest of our session flies while I strike a bargain: if I can
keep Joe and Bambi together, Birdie and Micah will stick it out.
When our hour ends, I tell myself we've done some real work.

"I'll cancel the appointment I have with Clyde to run lines,"
Bambi declares. "I'll also tell him I'm too busy to go to the reading he invited me to for tomorrow, and I'm going to plan a date
night with Joe."

"We'll have a lot to talk about next time," I say—if Bambi
follows through on any of the above. More if she doesn't. I try
not to think of myself as a fraud, leading a bull session that isn't
therapy.

An hour later I'm home, where I riffle through the mail as
I polish off a leftover empanada and look longingly at an announcement about a class two Saturdays from now on how to
make sock puppets. The card-carrying optimist in me hopes
Alice will be home by then, and sets aside the circular. I pour a
glass of red wine, from which I take a generous glug.

"I may have had a breakthrough with a client," I say to Jake
as I kick off my shoes. "Her name is Bambi."

"And I should care about that why?" My husband is into his
Scotch—Macallan, the good stuff—and his tone is uncharitable.
The haberdasher in him usually prompts Jake to hang up his
jacket as soon as he is home, but today he has committed the sin
of tossing it over a dining room chair. He has loosened his tie,
the same one as yesterday.

"Excuse me?"

"Your work, your work, your work." He does a fair imita-
tion of my voice, assuming I am an African grey parrot. "Who
gives a shit about Heidi?"

"Bambi. Her name is Bambi. And you're right. Mea culpa.

We should be discussing what's really important." I empty my glass of wine. "Did you speak to Micah today?"

Jake has accused me of smother-mothering. In return I've promised to call our son only every other day. But Micah may as well be standing between us in this room, a monument to parental failure. The burden of The Incident is crushing.

"We had lunch," Jake says. "Nothing's changed."

"Is he heading out to Iowa?"

"Birdie told him not to come. 'She needs her space.'"

"He should just show up. Ring her doorbell. He's her husband. He doesn't need an invitation." I have said as much to Micah. Jake raises his eyebrows. I can't tell if he agrees with me or not. "Any word back from that detective?"

"Nada."

I'd like a night free of motherly misery. Hence my eagerness to bend the rules and report on Bambi. But Jake is having none of it. Rather, he's saying, loudly, "What about my work? Do you ever think about the issues in my life?"

Since Jake isn't a quantum physicist, a video game developer, or a seismologist studying Japanese earthquakes, I should be able to track the minutiae that fills his professional psyche and produces sixty-percent of our income—okay, sixty-five or seventy—even if I find serious deliberation over ordering neoprene bomber jackets versus suit jackets with silk lapels mindnumbing. Since Micah's predicaments have piled on, I wish Jake would let some of my inattention slip by. I could mount a defense, but what's the point? I'm guilty.

"Your problems are my problems," I say.

"We're quoting my mother now?"

Your problems are my problems. Am I morphing into Veronika? Holy shit.

"Tough season?" I ask.

"We're up eight percent, which in this economy ain't bad."

"Congratulations." I weigh possibilities. "A personnel situation?"

"Getting warmer." Satisfaction colors Jake's face, unless it's the booze.

"Is Larry into drugs again?" Last month, Jake walked in on his first lieutenant snorting a line of coke on a Burberry coat.

He shakes his head.

"Is Sonia pregnant?" She looked plenty zaftig at her wedding last month.

Another athletic head shake.

"Is Nico retiring?" He and his wife have bought a house in Santorini. At least I recall the name of each store's manager. People, I remember. "Are we going to play this game all night?" The circles under Jake's eyes are sootier than usual and it looks like he's getting a cold sore. "I give up, babe." I walk carefully toward him, afraid he will rip my eyes out. I will take that risk. "I'm a terrible wife, ludicrously self-involved, an awful person. Can we agree on that?"

He lets me hold him. "Yes, Mel, all that, goddammit."

He pulls me close and I feel him swallow. I love the Jakeness of his smell, the heft of his shoulders, his day's end stubble. My husband could grow a prophet's beard in five days.

"Tell me, please." I turn my voice to tender.

"It's my dad."

"Let me guess. It's David who wants to retire?" Who could blame him? He opened his first store fifty-four years ago.

"If only."

"He's not sick, is he?" The night of our ill-fated Shabbos dinner my father-in-law reported that his cardiologist declared his heart to be as healthy as that of a man half his age. Veronika deserves partial credit, because she regulates his pill consumption like a pharmacist doling out narcotics.

"Physically, he's strong like a bull, but . . ." Jake looks away, as if he is watching David across the room. "I've been making up excuses for him for months, but there's no denying it. He's starting to lose it. Places orders twice. Forgets things. It's costing us, and I have to go over every damn form he touches. I'd be better off doing them all myself, but that would crush him." Jake turns away, but not before I catch the tears in his eyes.

"Oh, honey," I say. "I had no idea."

"You haven't exactly been bringing it to the marriage lately."

I dumbly consider myself, hiding in my snow globe of Micah-worry, Alice-missing, Veronika-resenting, Jordan-advising, and whatever the fuck I'm doing or not doing with clients.

"I can live with reviewing his paperwork," Jake continues, "but lately Dad's taken to yelling at the sales staff."

"What? The only time I've ever heard him shout is at the TV." Even when Veronika rips into his conversation, he yields to her with the deference of a head butler at a maidenly tea.

"We're at the point where my dad should stop waiting on customers. Yesterday he told a guy a blazer made him look like a tub of lard."

Jake is laughing, sadly. David is as mensch-y as men come, a fine papa, grandfather, and great-grandfather and—I think, selfishly—my loving champ, deftly deflecting Veronika when she claws in my direction. With my own dad on indefinite emotional sabbatical, I consider David another father. Why haven't I noticed a change? Maybe "rat's pajamas" was no joke. We're together all the time, but like an Impressionist painting, perhaps the closer I've been, the less I grasp the big picture.

Then again, Jake might be overblowing the situation, which a doctor can reverse. "Is there anything practical we can do?" I think aloud, remembering a case study about a man whose apparent dementia receded when his clashing pharmaceuticals were sorted out. "Your dad definitely needs to see a neurologist and I know just the one." He's the brother of a member of my book club. Though as highly regarded as my friend's brother is—she reminds us regularly that he's the head of a department at one of the city's major hospitals—Veronika no doubt knows a far superior neurologist.

I have never met a more adoring husband than David or a closer couple than Veronika and David. They've nursed each other through breast cancer (hers), a knee replacement (his), and pneumonia and shingles (both of them); they schedule colonoscopies for the same morning, and over the years have rarely slept apart. David allows Veronika to be Veronika.

On top of Jake's hand, I trace circles in sync with my heartbeat, attempting to calm both of us, and ask, "What does your mother think?"

"There's the rub. I brought it up, and she cut me off." Jake pulls away and examines his hands as if they are new. "I've tried and failed. I can't do it, Mel, but you know what? You can. You're tougher, way tougher. You have to talk to my mother. You've got to do this for me."

I can't even. Hearing about this from me, Veronika, blaming the messenger, might put me through waterboarding or at the least, force me to listen to a twenty-four/seven loop of Céline Dion singing "My Heart Will Go On."

Jake reads my face and says, "C'mon, I don't ask much of you."

I would sooner go on a hunger strike or repeat statistics. Yet I hear myself say, "Of course I'll do it, sweetheart."

CHAPTER 23

Birdie

JOY-ELLEN NIBBLES A CINNAMON BUN WHILE SHE DEFTLY KNITS mittens that look remarkably like Elsa, the barn kitten, if Elsa were powder blue. Alice named the kitten, who she insists is her pet. Luanne is reviewing her menu. As tradition demands, the family is planning a big Thanksgiving. A hefty gobbler, earmarked for the Petersons, struts in their neighbor's flock, unaware of the price on his head. Next week, swaggering Tom will be stuffed with cornbread and sausage, roasted glossy brown, and picked to the bone. There will be soup made from Joy-Ellen's butternut squash, a shimmery-quivery cranberry mold in the shape of a star, homemade Parker House rolls, Brussels sprouts, garlicky mashed potatoes, yams crowned by billows of marshmallows, corn pudding, a 1950s green bean casserole, carrot tart with ricotta and feta—because every year Luanne tries something new—and three kinds of pie: apple, pumpkin, and pecan.

"Your basic five-thousand-calorie bomb," Joy-Ellen says, patting her comfortable middle, and turns to Birdie. "Will we have the pleasure of your company?"

Yesterday, Mel asked Birdie the same question, as Micah has been doing via phone, text, email, and one beseeching note

attached to a 1-800-Flowers lavender rose bouquet. He has been
deeply apologetic, and last night Birdie had decided to return to
New York. When she powered up her computer this morning,
however, to book plane reservations, she asked herself, what's
the point if Micah won't come clean to the police?

"I've decided we'll stay," she announces to her mother and
grandmother.

"Does that mean Micah will be with us, too?" Luanne starts
to roll out pastry for pie shells. Her strokes are long and smooth,
stretching the dough thin. Birdie wishes her mother would give
her a lesson, but she knows if she asks, Luanne will say, "Not
now—I have to get to the hospital." She is in constant motion.

Birdie realizes that if she fails to invite Micah, her mother
and grandmother will most likely disapprove. Their tolerance
for her ambiguity, self-pity, and a struggling marriage is no
greater than it would be had she lied, cheated, or Botoxed all
expression from her face, though since she's been in Iowa, they
haven't pumped for information. No drama queens, they. Their
power comes from calmer waters.

"Micah won't be joining us." She hasn't invited him.

Joy-Ellen raises her eyebrows. This passes for a scathing look
she directs toward Luanne, who asks, "Does this mean you'll be
here for a while, Bird?"

Birdie's breath quickens. "I may." Until asked, she hadn't
admitted it to herself. Certainly not to Micah or Alice. Definitely not to Mel.

Luanne wipes her hands on a dish towel celebrating the great
state of Iowa and puts her arms around her daughter. "I don't need
to know the down-and-dirty, but your grandmother, your father,
and I are here if you want to talk. We'll leave that up to you."

Birdie isn't ready. She may never be ready.

"If you're here for a long stay, though, we suggest you look for
a job. Should you be lucky enough to find one, you'll need child-

care. I've asked around and heard your friend Jen from cheer-leading has opened a home day care. You may want to check it out." With merciful regularity, Luanne is thinking sensibly, emotions at bay.

"I'll do all that, Mom."

"May I jump in?" Joy-Ellen puts down her needles. "If you stick around, you're going to need your own wheels, not a rental. If you talk pretty to Russ Jr., he may be willing to lend you the truck he's trying to sell."

Would she never get beyond a truck?

"My neighbor is unloading a Honda Civic in pretty good shape," Joy-Ellen adds, "but for that you'd need real money."

Birdie sees this as her grandmother's way of asking how she's fixed financially. The truth is that when impulse and anger blew her to Iowa, she hadn't thought beyond her last paycheck and nearly maxed-out credit cards. She and Micah have a savings account fattened with wedding present cash, which—when they were feeling bullish about the future—they'd hoped would grow into a down payment for an apartment or house. A new place to live may have become a back-burner dream, but Birdie would never dip into this stash before discussing a withdrawal with Micah. She owes him that.

"I'll ask Russ about the truck," Birdie says as Alice walks into the kitchen and heads straight to Joy-Ellen, who presents her with a mitten. She slips it on her hand and dances around the table, meowing. "I love it. Thank you, Grandma Lindstrom." She stops before her great-grandmother to hug her, then turns toward Birdie. "Can I show it to Daddy on your phone?"

"Later. Daddy will be at work now," Birdie says, hoping that it's true.

AFTER SPENDING THE rest of the morning trolling through job listings within a forty-minute radius of the farm, Birdie comes up with exactly no possibilities. While she may wolf down their banana pudding pancakes, she can't see herself as an IHOP wait-ress. Nor does she want to be a laundromat lady, a Walmart greeter, or an exotic dancer at Dangerous Curves, a bikini bar. Birdie decides to go into town, wow the manager of the gym with her big-city résumé, and talk herself into a job.

She drives and thinks. Four years ago, she stood beside Micah Henry Tobias, strategically covering her convex belly with the anemone bouquet her future mother-in-law handed her before the courthouse ceremony she witnessed along with Micah's dad and paternal grandparents. It was a mixed mar-riage. Midwestern and Eastern. Dairy Princess and Tobias roy-alty. Pragmatist and *luftmensch*, an ID for a head-in-the-clouds person with an iffy income. Veronika taught her the term along with an appreciation for pickled herring and blintzes. Birdie has found these to be upgrades from the Petersons' *lutefisk* and *lefse*, foods that Mel, despite her Minnesota roots, has never sampled. Her mother-in-law comes from the Marais of Minneapolis, where if you tripped, you hit a pastrami sandwich or a poster for a Coen Brothers movie.

When Birdie met Micah, she'd been impressed. None of her previous boyfriends had attended a vaulted speck of a liberal arts college where they'd majored in Gender and Sexuality Stud-ies and performed West African dance, without shirts or irony. None of her exes were even from Texas. They all came from solid Iowa stock that led them to premed, to pharmacy, to ac-tuarial science, engineering, and agricultural economics with a minor in poultry nutrition, and ended with a degree from a state school. She'd married Micah before she'd hung out with peo-ple who served amuse-bouches at Sunday night suppers; before premed, pharmacy, engineering, agricultural economics, and actuarial science had belatedly sounded like choices a verifiable adult would make. Now that she is one child and a thousand miles in the rearview mirror away from her decision to marry, she doubts it more by the day.

In town she easily parks on the main street—called, literally, Main Street. During high school, postgame (football, basketball, or baseball, as the seasons turned) she and Lindsey, Jen, and Stacey drove up and back Main, waving and honking at cars full of boys, who waved and honked in return. Birdie tried to explain to Micah the kick-ass fun of this pastime. He remained skeptical; at the same age, he and his friends zigzagged the city by taxi, visiting bars whose managers looked the other way when they exercised phony IDs.

Where are her friends now? Only Jen is accounted for, thanks to her mother. For the last two years, Birdie hasn't exchanged as much as a Christmas card with her or the others. She doesn't want to think what it reveals that she has let these friendships go belly-up.

When she enters the gym, the receptionist says, "Hi, may I help you?" in that cheerful Iowa way, almost as if she means it. Sizing up the girl's toned arms, flat core, and tight buns, Birdie feels draggy and out of shape; during the last month, her yoga practice has also gone belly-up. Who is she to pitch for a job? But that's what she does, spitting out the speech she rehearsed in the car.

"Hi, I'm Birdie Peterson. I grew up near here and have been living in New York City for the last few years, where I've taught yoga at a popular studio." Does "popular" make her sound stuck-up, a major Iowa faux pas? "I also taught yoga for four years when I was at the U in Ames. I was hoping you might have an opening for a teacher." Birdie clears her throat. "Or a sub."

"Not as far as I know," the girl answers, too hastily for Birdie's liking. "We don't have many yoga classes and we already have a teacher. But why don't you reach out to Paula, the owner? Here's her card. She lives in Des Moines. This gym is its satellite."

Birdie takes the card, thanks her, and on the way out, turns to ask the girl if she has any ideas of where else she might look for a job.

"You could try the new place around the corner. I saw a help wanted sign in the window. I think it's a coffeeshop."

Birdie pictures a Lake Wobegon watering hole, where sunburnt farmers in caps and overalls spout off to reporters before the presidential primary or inhale donuts while shooting the shit about the price of soybeans. A sassy waitress, name of Mabel, would be asking if she can fill 'er up or top her off. But when Birdie enters Field of Dreams it isn't that at all.

For a moment—in the best possible way—she's back in Brooklyn. Floor-to-ceiling bookshelves dominate the soothing blue space along with overstuffed, thrift shop armchairs where customers are curled up, reading, some snuggled under granny afghans. One guy is snoring. At a long oak bar, patrons are nibbling pastry and drinking out of shiny orange mugs. Bach plays in the background as people tap on laptops at tables scattered around the room, which has stained-glass windows. In front of a fireplace—a fireplace!—preschoolers sit in a circle on a shaggy rug where a woman of about fifty in jeans and a denim shirt is reading a storybook. Vintage photos cover the walls. Birdie looks closely. They feature the Des Moines Demons and other minor league Midwestern baseball teams.

Is this heaven? No, it's Iowa.

Until this minute, Birdie never realized she wanted to work in a bookstore, which this is, along with a coffeeshop. She can picture herself introducing customers to her favorite Edith Whartons and inhaling the smell of new books. Alice is there, too, spellbound when Birdie reads *Madeline* aloud. "'In an old house in Paris that was covered in vines . . .'"

Forty-five minutes later, Birdie has talked herself into a job.

Gwen Nordbeck, the woman reading to the children, is the owner and until recently a professor in the Writers' Workshop at the University of Iowa. Birdie mentions that she had been accepted by the program but couldn't attend for "personal" reasons, and Gwen doesn't push her to explain. The salary for the barista/salesperson job Gwen offers is so dainty Birdie imagines it will scarcely cover day care, car expenses, and toothpaste. To buy the Honda Joy-Ellen mentioned, she'll need to take out a loan that she'll be repaying for years. But the job will give her what is most important now: time to think, time to breathe, time to decide. Maybe even time to write.

WHEN BIRDIE ARRIVES at her parents' house, Joy-Ellen is teaching Alice how to play checkers on the same set she'd used to teach Birdie the game.

"Look, Mommy—I have a king!" Alice beams like a hundred-watt bulb.

"Good for you, sweetheart. Can we play a game later?"

"At your own risk," Joy-Ellen warns. "This one's a quick learner and quite the competitor."

Like her Aunt Jordan, Birdie thinks. Like Veronika.

"How goes the job-hunting?"

"You can congratulate me. I'll be working four days a week in town at Field of Dreams."

Joy-Ellen high-fives Birdie. "Holy moly. That was a snap. Is it a gardening center?"

"It's a bookstore that doubles as a coffeeshop. It's owned by a professor from Iowa City. Gwen Nordbeck."

"Gwen Nordbeck, Gwen Nordbeck. Of course. She grew up here. You went to school—and maybe the prom, if memory serves—with her nephew, that kid whose little brother drowned." She does not add, "It was the older brother's fault."

"You mean the guy who tried to revive his brother with mouth-to-mouth resuscitation? The boy who took full responsibility for his little brother's death? That Nordbeck? Leif?"

These distinctions matter to Birdie, who has never mentioned—and does not intend to mention—Micah's accident to her family. If Leif could try to bring his seven-year-old brother back to life, her husband could determine the consequences of his own actions. Leif was what Micah isn't. Perhaps there is no moral equivalency in her reasoning, but in Birdie's mind the events are linked. Micah is as spineless as Leif was stalwart.

CHAPTER 24

Mel

"OUR REFRIGERATOR LOOKS LIKE A FORENSIC LIBRARY OF EVERY meal we've eaten this entire month," Jake says. In addition to remnants of takeout, it's crammed with Thanksgiving leftovers. No one will describe me as a minimalist—or much of a cook— but yesterday's turkey was juicy, the sides weren't incinerated, and Veronika complimented my stuffing.

Even better, everyone behaved. Jordan demanded that the Tobias cavalry not stage a public bloodbath, on account of her girlfriend, Kit, and Kit's brother joining us for dinner. This kept our deportment civil and forced banter about The Incident and Micah's marriage into the no-fly zone. Furthermore, unlike holidays of yore, Veronika did not require each of us to answer the fraught question, *Who do you feel most grateful to have in your life?* Our guests cleared out in record time, which left plenty of headspace for me to focus on David's mental state.

I'm desperate for a reason to be positive. As we drink our coffee, I point out to Jake that, "Your dad was the first person to shout 'pancreas' when someone asked, 'What's that internal organ shaped like a pear? You know, not the appendix, not the gallbladder, not the liver or the bladder?'"

"He knew all three verses to 'We Gather Together,'" Jake muses. His family insists this isn't a churchy hymn, as my father might have were he not celebrating Thanksgiving with my stepmother's relatives in San Diego.

"But he kept forgetting where Birdie and Alice were."

"And asking who'd be reciting the Four Questions."

"Or where the latkes were."

"My mom had to tell him to put his napkin in his lap." It was that breach of etiquette that clinched it: something is off with his dad. Hence, while other Americans flex their consumer muscles, loading up on flat screens and wine refrigerators, today is when I promised Jake I'd have a heart-to-heart with his mother. Black Friday indeed.

Veronika and I see each other often, but we never meet for breakfast, lunch, or coffee dates, nor do we rendezvous for walks, barre class, shopping, mani-pedis, lectures, or book club, like I do with friends or Jordan. The subject at hand is too momentous and sensitive to discuss by phone, in addition to which it would be far too easy for her to click off, claiming, say, a tornado warning exclusively for her block.

I plan to ambush Veronika when I stop by this morning to deliver the clean serving pieces that contained the sweet potato gratin and cranberry-pear pie she brought to yesterday's meal. Jake will have already picked up David to spend the day at their Long Island store. If Veronika has stepped out, I will invent Plan B—and on and on through the alphabet, as need be.

It's a short walk to her apartment. Too short. With every step, my grit chips away. By the time I arrive I am praying Veronika will be gone or suggest that I simply leave my delivery with the doorman. Yet after he announces me, I'm directed to go upstairs. I march to the guillotine. Who wouldn't want to kill the messenger who delivers this news?

Veronika greets me in her Saturday clothes—a starched

white shirt tucked into gabardine pants cinched with a Hermès belt that shows off her still-svelte waistline. The ensemble is crisp, matching her demeanor. "To what do I owe the honor of this visit?" she asks.

I hand off what I'm carrying. "Thanks again. Everything was delicious." Since waiting won't make the water warmer, I force myself to dive right in. "If you have a minute, could we talk?" I hope Veronika can't hear me gulp. I check to see if her eyelid has started to tremble. Not yet.

"Cup of tea?"

"No, thanks." I love an English accent, the word *whilst*, thatched roofs, Colin Firth, and Wellies as much as anybody, but I've never gotten the appeal of tea. The smell alone makes me gag.

"Coffee, then? I just brewed a pot."

I'm already hyper-caffeinated, but drinking coffee will give me something to do with my hands, which are itching to twirl my hair like Bambi. I accept a cup, take my time adding milk, and stir for twice as long as necessary. We sit on Veronika's uncomfortable iron chairs at a small marble table in the corner of the spotless kitchen. I admire her botanical prints, over which I linger, though they've been there as long as I remember. Never has a cabbage rose been more intriguing.

"I thought I might hear from you." Veronika smiles.

That my mother-in-law expected me to seek her out is puzzling. I'm stumped, but not for long.

"I expect you want to talk about your son and his issues. Which first, the accident or the situation with Birdie?"

I muster the chutzpah to look Veronika in the eye. "Neither, actually."

"Oh?" Frustration, surprise, and hostility crowd into that short word. A gulley I'd never noticed divides Veronika's forehead as she says, "Please do not tell me you accept the manner in which your son has behaved."

"You must realize I'm horrified. Micah——"

"Or the childish way in which his wife abandoned her husband?" As if she's been working with a dialect coach, the more Veronika speaks, the more mid-Atlantic her speech becomes. She is beginning to sound like Katharine Hepburn.

"Totally unacceptable."

"What, then?"

"I'm here on behalf of Jake. In his place." I garble my words. "What I mean is, there's something on our minds and it's difficult to discuss and I'm sort of a spokesperson, as it were."

"Can you please get on with it?" As Veronika frowns, parallel lines deepen between her eyes.

"Jake and I are both worried about Dad. About David." Veronika may have requested "Mother" when I became engaged, but Jake's father has been "David" since day one.

"I see." She shifts back in her chair and sits taller. Mistrust wafts from her like smoke announcing a new Pope. "Why is that?"

"I know the other day Jake tried to bring this up, about David's forgetfulness and confusion." I avoid *dementia* as if it were a land mine.

"When did my son get to be such a worrier?" Veronika lifts her shoulders in a shrug. I begin to speak but am interrupted by "Don't look at me that way, Melanie. It's a rhetorical question. Obviously, to avoid dealing with Micah's behavior, Jake is deflecting by picking on his father."

I try to speak but can't make a sound.

"Since as a physician I am versed in the mechanics of the human brain, let me help put yours to rest."

"Okay, but——"

"David's behavior is within the norms for a person of his age."

Is she claiming it is neurotypical for a man of seventy-nine to forget how to make change while plenty of his peers are winning duplicate bridge tournaments, composing chamber music, and gobbling up—and in some cases, writing—the latest twelve-hundred-word presidential biography? But I don't challenge Veronika. I say something worse. In an effort to streamline this ordeal, I skip to the end of the remarks I've rehearsed for the last few days. Bombs away. I blurt out that "we think David needs to step away from the business."

Color drains from Veronika's face and it takes her a minute—which feels like five—to speak. "Good God. My son is the one who has lost his mind. With all due respect to Jake, his father is the most valuable asset the stores have." Her voice climbs with each statement.

It feels spiteful to repeat what Jake has told me about his father mucking up orders, when he is isn't offending customers and suppliers. "Maybe it's best if you ask Jake." That sounds worse than spiteful. It sounds as if we are keeping secrets from his mother. We are, trying to protect her by an emotional firewall.

"What a bizarre and unfortunate turn of events." Veronika clenches her hands. Her face purples and I feel I can hear her silently count to ten before she responds with, "Melanie Glazer, have you finished patronizing me?" She hits hard on *Glazer*, to remind me I'm not a loyal *Tobias*.

I realize I have bungled the delivery of my message. I may as well have bludgeoned my poor mother-in-law with a dull knife. I wish I'd hugged her, or at least held her hand while I spoke my piece slowly and softly. It's too late to try that now, with Veronika looking embedded in ice.

"I know this is hard to hear," I say meagerly, "and how you must feel."

"Oh, do you, now? I doubt that."

Veronika is right. No one can know how she feels, especially if you're a decades-younger wife married to a man whose mind isn't turning to mush.

"We're hoping David can be helped, Mother." When I say *mother*, I realize how infrequently I call Veronika this. *Muth-er.* It doesn't even sound like an English word. "Would you like me to make a doctor's appointment? I've gotten the names of some top neurologists, and I'd be happy to go with David."

Veronika stares into the middle distance. "Do whatever you think is best," she murmurs. "You and Jake seem to have everything worked out." She leaves the room, possibly to graffiti my wedding picture.

On my walk home, I think about how Jake trusted me in this maneuver, which I botched, and that this may be the first time when he didn't triangulate by lining up with his mom. It doesn't feel nearly as good as I thought it would. I certainly don't want David to suffer. I love this man and wish his faculties were as sharp as they were even a few months ago. Nor do I want to visit heartache on Veronika, or for her to face the loneliness wreaked by a partner's dementia.

To myself, I can say the word, if that's what it is. I hope I haven't been cruel, but I suspect I have been, and I won't get a do-over. If my relationship with Veronika was lacking before, now it's probably shattered. Come for the intervention, stay for the remorse.

When I get home, I pull down the shades in my bedroom, turn off my phone, and crawl under the duvet. I fitfully doze and dream, cartwheeling through dark halls of self-reproach.

When Jake comes home he asks, "Are you on life support?"

"Barely."

"How'd it go with my mother?"

I turn myself to the wall. "I may not have been as gentle or kind or articulate as I'd hoped."

"How bad was it?"

"You know how some people are such smooth talkers they

could get hired to run a Holocaust museum after belonging to the Gestapo? I wasn't that person."

Jake sits next to me on the bed and rubs my back. I return to sleep. When I wake three hours later with a crick in my neck, he announces, "My mother called. She's going to make an appointment for my dad to see some big-shot doctor and wonders if you'd do her the favor of accompanying him because she doesn't feel up to it."

I am not dreaming. This is a day when I believe in God.

CHAPTER 25

Veronika

I HAVE WORKED HARD TO EARN MY HAPPINESS. VERONIKA silently repeats this mantra as she performs her nightly ablutions. She tissues off her makeup with Pond's, as she's done all her adult life, continues with four minutes of dental hygiene before she paints on cuticle oil and a potion that claims to remove sunspots, and ends with massaging an overnight moisturizer on her face, another formula on her neck, and a third cream, lemony and light, on her legs and hands. Her sacraments complete, Veronika slips into a short silk chemise and climbs into the left side of the sleigh bed in which she and David have slept for decades, making love, a son, and plans. They have rarely slept apart.

David lets Veronika be what she sees as her best self. She cannot imagine functioning without him. In her transactional mentality, he is her priceless quid pro quo for the loss of a father she can't remember, a glum childhood in a dour apartment, and long slogs through med school and analytic training. Since Veronika turns to her husband for a sound opinion on most topics, tonight she looks into his eyes and says, "*Liebchen*, forgive me for being unkind. I'll be blunt. Lately, you're not functioning at a hundred percent. Are you feeling amiss?"

"Amiss, Miss?"

"Do you think you might be getting a little foggy?"

There. Veronika has said it. She thought she never could.

"Foggy, eh?" David toggles to a geezer's voice. "What's that you say?"

"Don't make me pontificate like a clinician. I am not joking." Not that anyone would accuse Veronika of spontaneous kidding, which is different than her ability to repeat the rare joke.

"We're being serious?" David asks.

"As a heart attack, if you'll forgive the trite simile."

"Alexa, do I have Alzheimer's?" he asks the device on the bureau that informs him of the temperature and when National Cat Day is.

"According to the Mayo Clinic, everyone has occasional forgetfulness . . ."

"Is Miss Genius over there the only person who is going to answer me?" Veronika snuggles nearer to David and rubs her face against his stubble, which turned silvery only a few years ago. She ruffles his hair, as thick and white as a caricature of a senator.

"I'm aware that I can be forgetful," he says, after a minute. "But I can remember a quote I read somewhere, that an aging mind has a bagful of nasty tricks, and one is to tuck away names and words and facts in crannies where they aren't immediately available."

"Who said that?"

"I don't recall." He winks. "But, darling, if I realize I'm sometimes confused, doesn't that mean my brain cells must still be in decent shape?"

"I think only a neurologist could make that call."

"I'll go to a doctor, then, if you're concerned."

Veronika sees that defensiveness has crept into the room like a noxious vapor. Does it qualify as lying that she has already made an appointment? This sin of omission makes her feel sneaky when she has tried to operate her marriage with honesty and integrity. "In that case, I'll see if a doctor can squeeze us in for next week."

Veronika silences David with a touch to his lips. In response, with his strong, talented hands he kneads that place in the back of his wife's neck where he knows she carries her tension like an ox does a brace. "I should be taking care of you, love, not the other way around. Going bonkers isn't how I want it to be."

"You're getting ahead of yourself, darling," Veronika says, though she's gutted. "A doctor's appointment may be a fool's errand, but we'll feel better when he declares you hale and hearty."

David doesn't answer. Soon, Veronika hears the breathing of his sleep, though it will be hours until she nods off. Melanie's performance from yesterday rumbles through her mind, which turbocharges her indignation. Had the situation been reversed, would she have been a more artful bearer of toxic news? Without a doubt. Which is the last thing Veronika recalls about her terrible, horrible, godawful, very bad day.

CHAPTER 26

Mel

"YOU WANT *ME* TO PERSUADE BIRDIE TO COME HOME?" JORDAN and I have just finished our second lap around the Central Park Reservoir. "Me?"

My opinion of Jordan is sufficiently high that I believe there's little she can't do. In my daughter I see the dragon-fierceness that has helped to start a company on track to go public, its future stock enhanced by the creation of a must-have app. As we wind down from our run, I pant like a husky who's dragged a sled from Nome to Anchorage. I've tried to match my daughter's strides, but though I'm a fairly fit forty-four, I have twenty-one years on her and she has six strong inches on me. Her schedule is so booked, however, that if we don't connect for the occasional morning run, I may never see her.

I begin to stretch. "Weren't you trained in conflict resolution?"

"Yes, for one whole week with an emphasis on corporate dogfights. You hatch a killer idea in a meeting, a colleague writes a memo where she scours away two Oxford commas, changes two words, and claims your idea as hers. You start a war. That's where I come in."

I'm not sure if there should be an Oxford comma in that speech or not. "Couldn't you just talk to Birdie, then, as a friend?"

"I assure you, Birdie would not appreciate me butting in, nor would I call us friends. We've been alone together what, nine times in four years? We're *cordial*." Jordan slings the word as if it's profanity. "Every once in a while, we visit the dinosaurs at the museum with Alice or I swoop down like the Good Fairy after a trip."

My daughter returns from her frequent travels laden with souvenirs. Last year, I received a battery-operated rat from Vietnam. When Alice wore a T-shirt pimping Icelandic beer, I knew without asking that it came from Aunt Jordan.

I'd fantasized about my daughter and daughter-in-law becoming pals. Then again, I'm reminded of Micah telling me soon after he and Birdie got serious that since she was from Iowa he thought we'd be soul mates. Two Midwesterners! What are the odds? You'll have so much in common!

"You're the marriage counselor. Why don't you talk to her?"

We park ourselves on our favorite bench. A plaque quotes Helen Gurley Brown, who famously said, "Never fail to know that if you are doing all the talking, you are boring somebody." I try to remember this when I conduct a session. "How goes it with Kit?"

Like a waving flag, a smile spreads over Jordan's face. "Aside from the fact that I turn in at ten and she stays up 'til two and sleeps 'til eleven—in a furnace—she's adorable."

I had to give Micah a curfew, but not Jordan. To my knowledge, even in college, she never got home so late that it was morning and she has always cracked a window at night.

"Is she as OCD as you?" Jordan takes after Veronika, who labels her canned goods by date of purchase in order to know which corn kernels or tomato soup to use first in order to ward off botulism.

"When I asked her if she thought I was too persnickety, she said I was—after I explained what the adjective meant."

I will try to remember not to salt my speech with *jejune*, *hagiology*, or *callipygian*, though I'm baffled. "But she's a writer."

"Her books aren't exactly wordy."

"Do tell." When I met Kit, I knew better than to pry about her work. I've had clients who were screenwriters and authors so paranoid about revealing an idea they asked me to sign a non-disclosure agreement before they begged for my help in overcoming writer's block.

"A graphic novel."

"Like *Maus*?"

"More *If You Give a Pig a Pancake*."

That storybook is an Alice favorite, which circles me back to how much I miss my faraway granddaughter.

"I've been meaning to pick your professional brain," Jordan says. "Can a child inherit a parent's personality?"

Good question. "There's no definitive data as far as I know — though your grandmother might." As would Dr. T, who's lectured on the subject. "I doubt scientists will ever stop exploring nature versus nurture, but I'm inclined to say yes. Look at your dad. He's a replica of his own father." Except, thank God, for whatever is percolating in David's brain. "Why do you ask?"

"Kit is relentlessly upbeat, which grump here never thought she'd like. But now, I'd love our child to have that trait."

"Isn't this a moot point," I ask without fully digesting the information, "since you'll be the biological parent?"

Jordan's look suggests that I recently lost forty IQ points. "Mel Tobias, why do you continue to make that assumption? Have you not listened to one word I've said? Unlike me, Kit has an entirely flexible schedule. When we're pregnant we'll use her uterus. Full stop."

"You say *we* as if pregnancy is a team sport."

"Why are you refusing to understand how hard a pregnancy would be for me with my hours?"

La, la, la. I can't hear you. I don't want to understand. I don't want to understand at all. What I know is that if the child we're discussing is the offspring of a sperm donor and a ditz like Kit, I risk having another grandchild vanish from our life as Alice seems to be. Is it possible to suffer from motion sickness while sitting on a park bench?

I do not excel at much. I can't identify eighty percent of the newer singers on Spotify, recite even a third of the periodic table, or tell a Manet from a Monet, but I took to being a grandmother with the same ease Martha Stewart brought to spatchcocking a chicken. My love of this role began the moment my baby Micah had his own baby, not much bigger than an oven mitt yet looking strikingly familiar. I dropped in on Alice every day, watching her kick her legs while fixating on a ceiling fan as if it were Saturn. I, in turn, fixated on her.

I was an outlier: the first of my high school and college friends to have children, and then, the first to have a grandchild. The mothers of Micah and Jordan's friends have always been women older than I am. Peers who are childless or have only recently become moms seem mystified by my joie de vivre. The ballsy ones ask, Doesn't being a granny make you feel as if you've fast-tracked to old age? What they don't understand is that becoming a grandmother has flung me into a time warp that through some enchanted alchemy makes me feel ageless. As Alice and I read *Pat the Bunny* I could press her penne-sized fingers onto the whiskers of the book's daddy and see the future along with the past; those fingers might just as easily have been on the tiny hands of Jordan or Micah, and, once again, I was twenty-two.

Grandmotherhood reminds me that love is engineered for tender expansion, an emotion as elastic as a mother's belly. Perhaps someday, as a standard bearer for aging gracefully, I will be called upon to lecture on this topic. Maybe there's even a book in me.

When Alice was two months old Micah told me that Birdie felt ambushed by my constant visits—as if I cared whether her hair was dirty or her T-shirt splattered by baby spit-up. That's when I cleared my Tuesday and Thursday afternoons for scheduled visits, telling Birdie this was to give her some downtime to nap or get out of the apartment. The truth was that I wanted Alice to myself.

At first, I was as out of practice at caring for a baby as I was driving a stick shift. This made me wonder if a mother is biologically designed with a delete button that erases memories from her hard drive—*hard* being the operative word here—so she will forget about the fussing, frustration, and fatigue of infancy, and at least consider having more kids. Or maybe I had only a shallow store of knowledge to drill into, since when our twins were babies, Jake and I had all the insights of two stalks of celery. But gradually, whatever mothering instincts I had returned.

By the time Alice was five months old, the two of us were a lock and a key. I equipped our apartment with the extensive paraphernalia a baby requires—portable crib, bottles, snuggly animals, brain-expanding toys and music, high-chair, blankets, bibs, diapers, wipes, ointments, a stroller that cost as much as my first car, swings and slings and on and on. I secretly wished my friends would have surprised me with a baby shower. When yet another package would arrive, Jake asked if I was planning to kidnap Alice and spirit her away to an undisclosed location. Now that doesn't seem like such a preposterous idea.

As Alice got older, nothing felt better than chatting with my granddaughter while we strolled through her neighborhood or mine. Often, we were mistaken for mother and child. But flattered as I was, I proudly corrected strangers. "No, thank you very much. I'm her grandmother."

With Alice exiled to Iowa, I'm afraid our bond is fraying by the day, and I feel shattered every time I think about it. A screen cannot compete with my granddaughter's new life: a kitten; the family dog; oink-y little piglets; young cousins; a great-grandmother who knits, yodels, swan dives, and possibly break dances; and The Other Grandmother, the effortlessly beautiful, formidably efficient Luanne. There is even a rumor about a pony. This is, indeed, the winter of my discontent.

When I see Birdie online, I want to shriek and ask why she and Micah can't, for God's sake, reconcile their differences? Won't Birdie and Alice *please* come home? But Jake has made me swear on a stack of Alice's family drawings not to interfere. My husband insists that anything I might say will inflame the situation. He is probably right.

CHAPTER 27

Mel

Norah arrives for our eleven o'clock appointment looking like a blurred selfie. She is wearing a shirt and jeans that might have taken a coast-to-coast bus ride. Her nails lack their customary polish, and her hunky canary yellow ring (Diamond, sapphire, or agate? Veronika would know but I don't.) that usually sticks out on her hand like a caution sign is nowhere to be seen.

"It's been a while." She has canceled three appointments.

"Sorry. My life is spinning out of control."

Whose isn't? "Because?"

"Delia is doing outpatient rehab. She's moved back in with us, but still can't work. I love her, but now it feels like I have four kids, not three. Her arm and leg fracture are healing, but her back injury turned out to be pretty serious—she's using a walker now—and I'm getting second and third opinions on whether she needs surgery. Given all of this, she's a head case. I'm hoping you could suggest someone she could talk to—in a pro bono capacity, preferably, because she has no money or insurance, and Brian is furious about all the bills."

Much as I'd like that therapist to be me, I know I can't color outside the lines to that extent and say, "Let me come up with a name or two."

"We're also dealing with the police." Norah rakes a hand through her hair, whose grey roots encroach on its butterscotch shade with low-lights and balayage created by someone who isn't Mother Nature. "Finally, there's a detective who's taken a real interest in the case, a Ms. Herrera."

My motion sickness returns.

"Really? I'm surprised," I admit, at risk of sounding callous. "Not that what happened to Delia isn't awful, but so many accidents—"

"Accident? I'd call it a crime."

"I'm no lawyer, but doesn't a crime require premeditation?"

I can't tell if the look Norah gives me displays antagonism or confusion.

"What I mean is, I imagine many situations like Delia's never get fully investigated . . ." My voice trails off. "You're lucky hers is. Okay, not exactly lucky. It's awful that she was hit in the first place."

"This detective knows Delia's aunt." Norah looks older without eye makeup, which she usually applies so expertly I've been tempted to ask for a tutorial. "Apparently, networking matters as much at the NYPD as anywhere. In that respect, yes, we're fortunate."

While we may not be. My heart starts to thump. "Does this mean they found the truck that hit Delia?"

She nods. "We thought as much 'til a few days ago, but the woman they were zeroing in on had a solid alibi, so, no. Besides, Delia is pretty sure whoever hit her is male and young. She woke up the other day convinced she'd seen him in a dream. What do you call that?"

"I'd call it 'dreaming.'"

"Not repressed memory? Suppressed memory? Recovered memory?"

"I'm not sure what Delia thinks she experienced, but memories like this aren't always reliable. Sometimes we choose what to remember just as we choose what to forget."

This remark gets no reaction from Norah, who says, "As of today, they think they may have an eyewitness. Detective Herrera called just as we were leaving the house. This is why I was late."

Between David's medical misfortune and Birdie's exodus, I'd taken my eye off the ball and allowed The Incident to shift to my back burner, though I'd planned to give Micah a kick in the butt when we grab coffee after this session. I feel I'm being punished for my inattention.

"You haven't mentioned your mother-in-law," I point out as our time nears its end. Invariably, Norah harps on the woman for at least ten minutes, ten minutes I inevitably enjoy.

"Suffice it to say she sides entirely with my husband— 'You're way over-involved, Norah.' Like that."

We wind up the session. I enter my notes and when I leave to meet Micah, I am surprised to find him in my waiting room when we'd agreed to meet at Starbucks. "I found a parking space right in front of your office," he explains. "Good karma, huh?"

He needs a lucky day. We both do.

"The weirdest thing, though. After I locked the truck I felt an odd vibe and turned around. A woman was taking pictures of the truck."

Thanks just the same, karma.

CHAPTER 28

Mel

I hope you don't feel railroaded into this," I say with belated guilt as David and I find seats in the teeming waiting room of the neurologist.

"Mel, doll, what kind of putz would refuse to see a doctor when his family tells him he's slip-sliding away?"

"You're being a good sport." I lean over to peck David on the cheek.

He cups my face and strokes my cheek. "I'm sure this isn't where you want to be, either."

From the get-go, my father-in-law and I have reveled in a breezy relationship that grew from my belief that he understands why Jake loves me. There's also the V factor. He's a loyal husband who would never knock his wife—certainly not in front of me—but I'm convinced he knows how thorny she can be. Over the years, as if I deserve combat pay, he has compensated with a thousand civilities. David is my living, breathing malware, protecting me from Veronika. How will I manage without him? But I'm going all doomsday. Stifle yourself, Mel.

"What do you hear from Birdie?" David asks.

"Not much. She's keeping her own counsel."

"Why doesn't Micah get his tuchus to Idaho or Indiana or whatever and beg her to come back?"

The best I can do is shrug. "I've stopped understanding my son."

David opens his *Wall Street Journal* and offers me the first section, while he takes Money & Investing, loaded with numbers that would fly right by me. Can he still analyze them?

One by one, other patients are called, until the only people left are a handsome, turbaned Sikh; a doe-eyed woman shyly peeping out from a hijab; and an elderly Chasid from either nineteenth-century Poland or a cool part of Brooklyn. He is accompanied by a woman in long sleeves, long skirt, thick flesh-toned stockings, and a conspicuous wig. "Tati this, Tati that," she whispers. I never fail to be fascinated by the colorful salad bar of New Yorkers who unite in any doctor's office. God bless health care.

"David Tobias?" a nurse asks, finally.

"Do you want me in the room?"

"Please. I need a witness."

David stands, tightens his tie, and marches toward his destiny. He could be a presidential candidate accepting his nomination. The neurologist welcomes us and introduces her subordinates. Their manner is respectful, affable, professional. This won't hurt a bit. We're just going to ask a few questions to see how unglued you are.

After preliminaries, the doctor begins with, "We'll recite three words we'll ask you to try and repeat later: velvet, daisy, table." He slowly annunciates each word.

Velvet, daisy, table, I repeat to myself.

Then they fire away. David obediently answers questions, as do I, mutely. I've got to assume that identifying a rhinoceros, a giraffe, and a whale is a warm-up. From here, David is asked to start at one hundred and subtract by sevens, which he does at twice the pace that I do. The questions zip by. "What is today's date?"

"December fourth."

"The year?"

Two thousand eighteen, I say to myself. You've got this. But he comes up blank, then stumbles when asked to draw a clock face indicating ten past eleven. He is back in the game, however, when he's given a minute to name all the words he can think of that start with the letter R, no proper nouns allowed.

"Razzmatazz, red, run, rat's nest—oh, maybe that doesn't count—ruler, rose, really, realistic, Rudolf—oops, sorry, that was a name—rest, restraint, respiratory, roadrunner, robber, roach, rival, rancid, rent, refrigerator, ramify, rampart, racketeer, roly-poly . . ." The buzzer sounds and only now do I notice my father-in-law's socks. One is brown and beige stripes, the other solid black. For the owner of David Tobias & Son this is not a fashion statement.

The doctor asks him to repeat the three words that kicked off the exam twenty minutes ago. "Daisy, daisy."

Table. Velvet. Table. Velvet. I try to deliver the answers by ESP. David begins to droop. Not gonna happen.

The neurologist concludes the session and explains that an evaluation will be explained by phone, in a week. I advise him to call Veronika. We snake through the hallway to the waiting room.

"How do you think I did?" David asks, as a boy might.

I remember when Micah—small for his age at seven and years away from the superb athlete he eventually became—wanted to join Little League. It was a foregone conclusion that every kid would be welcomed, though the children didn't know this, and since the teams needed to be balanced, each player was required to try out. When it was his turn, Micah fumbled trying to catch three pop flies. Grounders rolled between his legs. At bat, after two strikes, he foul-tipped. On the way home, he asked Jake how he thought he did. My husband gave the matter grave consideration. "You know, son," he said, "I think you made the team."

"That's what I thought." Micah beamed, and in that moment, I could not have loved either of them more.

"I give myself a C minus," David says.

"Oh, c'mon, you did just fine," I fib as David and I wind through the halls and reach the waiting room. Veronika, whom I did not expect, is here. She and David fall into each other's arms as if he's a soldier returned from Afghanistan. After I explain to her that she can expect a call from the doctor, I hurry away, eager to separate myself from today's despair.

"How did he do?" Jake asks at dinner.

"Getting a full ride to Harvard."

"Seriously?"

"Comme ci, comme ça," I answer with the coordinating hand flip.

"I'm glad you went with him. I never could. I'm sure my mother feels the same way."

"Any information from Micah?" I ask hopefully.

"Yes, ma'am," he says. "He's heading out to Iowa."

CHAPTER 29

Birdie

When Birdie turns off Old Route 8 onto the crunchy gravel road leading to Jen's, Alice starts bouncing in her car seat. She loves day care—Jen, especially. In high school, at a hair past six feet, Big Jen was the tallest of four willowy cheerleaders. She's hung up her pompoms and, three daughters and thirty pounds later, has fulfilled her nickname in every dimension, but Big Jen can still execute a perfect pike, ride herd on nine preschoolers for an eight-to-five day, and tease a smile out of the crabbiest kid.

She can even tease a smile out of Birdie. At Jen's the coffee is always hot and the sweet rolls warm and fresh. Each time Birdie drops off Alice, she is tempted to linger longer, catching up on people she hasn't thought about for years. But today after a quick schmooze —a word now in Jen's vocabulary—Birdie kisses Alice goodbye and drives to Field of Dreams, her radio blasting the Beatles. Here comes the sun, indeed.

"Morning," Gwen says as Birdie hangs her down jacket. "Am I glad to see you. Can you lend a hand here, please?" There are five boxes of books to shelve along with platters to fill with pastry and fruit, signs and flyers to create about readings, story hours and puppet shows—faithfully attended by Alice—and the biweekly blog to write: Birdie's suggestion and responsibility. The bookstore's mail orders are growing exponentially.

An hour later, when the door opens, customers start to float in. Some claim their regular spot at a table and begin to nurse coffees and manuscripts that aren't going to write themselves; others leave after a browse that can be hasty or an hour long. Gwen and Birdie never rush potential buyers.

There hasn't been a bookstore within a thirty-mile radius in years, and Field of Dreams is rarely empty. The day flies as Birdie and Gwen switch-hit as barista, consultant, saleswoman, and schlepper. Once in a while, Birdie recognizes a face, or vice versa, but virtually all the shoppers are strangers, for which she is grateful. They ask no questions about why she is back in the boonies after bolting to Gotham, that cesspool of damnation, rather than the tamer destinations of Chicago, Denver, St. Louis, or Minneapolis.

Today is different. Today Leif Nordbeck, Birdie's high school prom date, looks up from the thriller section, brushes away his hair to reveal his green eyes and chiseled features as he squares his broad shoulders, and walks in his cowboy boots straight to Birdie, wrapping her in his arms. Staring soulfully, while seventy-six trombones toot in the background, he says, "The stars have brought us together," or similar hogwash, before he deeply kisses her. The years melt away.

This is how it might have played out in Birdie's dreams had she given a chance encounter with Leif or another old boyfriend any thought, which she has not. They do not meet cute. No fireworks announce their reunion. In fact, they don't immediately recognize each other. Leif's blond crew cut has darkened to brown and is long and floppy. He has grown a beard and a few inches.

"Birdie Peterson, is that you?" He peers through rimless glasses.

"Leif Nordbeck? Holy shit. When did you get so tall?"

"Freak of nature." He puts down the mystery in his hand. "What are you doing here? Gosh."

He actually said *gosh*, she thinks. "I work here, part-time." Should she add *temporarily*? Birdie and Gwen have never discussed if and when she may return to New York, which is fortuitous, because Birdie wouldn't know what to say. Don't ask, don't tell is working fine. "And you?"

"I'm finishing a residency in Madison. Pediatrics."

"You're *Dr.* Nordbeck?"

He smiles, sheepishly, it seems to Birdie. "Don't be too impressed. I fainted when I was introduced to my cadaver."

Birdie can't help but draw a reproachful comparison to Micah, certain that Leif's career choice must be an atonement for his brother's drowning. "What brings you back home?"

"In town for my mom's birthday. I'm looking for a present and wanted to say hello to my aunt Gwen, too, but I guess she's not here."

"You missed her. Dental appointment."

"My timing has never been great."

Birdie wonders if Leif is referring to the evening of the prom, when he asked to date her exclusively. She turned him down, not wanting to start classes three months later at the University of Iowa shackled to a high school boyfriend at State two hours away.

"The last time I saw you we were mustered in a pasture for a reading of the Declaration of Independence," he says.

"With mosquitoes big as model airplanes. I'm still scratching." In Iowa bugs, DEET has worthy opponents.

"We used to catch fireflies."

"Are they the same as lightning bugs?"

"Maybe it was Christmas I saw you last."

On Christmas Eve, their families always gather for candlelit services in the plain oak pews of the church that Birdie's people,

Petersons and Lindstroms, founded as homesteaders more than a century ago along with the Nordbecks, Bergs, Johansons, and Bakkes. She loved the church, where she'd been a choir soloist. With Joy-Ellen pounding away on the organ, her "Angels We Have Heard on High" used to be an annual request.

"I'll be back for Christmas," he adds. "Will I see you there?"

"I'll probably be there with my family—and my daughter," she says, though in their tight-knit community, this wouldn't be a news flash. "Alice is three and a half. She's being brought up both Christian and Jewish, like her father." Birdie doesn't know why she feels the need to add this, or if it's fair to say she and Micah have been raising Alice with much religion at all.

"What's it like to belong to a multicultural family?"

This is exactly the kind of provocative question Leif always liked to ask, a trait she enjoyed as long as he wasn't grilling her.

By the time she'd met Micah, her attachment to the Lutheran faith had become more cultural than theological. It hadn't been a leap to marry a man who was Jewish, and privately, Birdie felt it was rather worldly. When Alice came along, it was easy to promise that her daughter would be brought up with two monotheistic religions. But Birdie has never tried to define her philosophy, if it deserves to be called that. Now, she spits out the first thought that comes to mind, that what bedevils her about being in a "multicultural family" are the paradoxes and clashes of her childhood mindset in contrast to those of the Tobias family.

"Let's just say there are subtleties I haven't yet decoded, not even after a few years." She considers how Micah, his parents, sister, and grandparents rarely set foot in a synagogue and appear to consider a belief in God optional, yet they identify as Jews with the vengeance of televangelists. "Everyone in the family spouts off about Israeli politicians' tone-deafness to the suffering of Palestinians, but should a non-Jewish columnist or even a

Facebook friend express a similar view, they go ballistic about how Israel is the only democracy in the Middle East and has every right to defend itself."

"It's complicated," Leif says. "Where do you stand on this?"

Birdie hasn't taken a stand, says as much, and shifts to, "The other thing that baffles me is how every family member is in each other's business. The Tobiases feel an urgency to gather at least twice a month for a meal, punctuated by more personal questions than my parents pose in two years. If my mother-in-law would ask what bra size I wore or if her son and I are trying to have a second child, I wouldn't be surprised."

Leif laughs and Birdie remembers when, before years of braces, he had buck teeth. "It sounds very friendly and caring, quite gemütlich."

"I suppose it does." She wishes she experienced it that way.

"Are you trying to have a second child?" Leif is poker-faced.

At least he didn't ask about her bra size, Birdie thinks.

"Sorry. That was me failing to be funny." Leif grins at his gotcha. "Seriously, do you think all Jewish families are the way you describe or maybe just your husband's?"

Is Leif Nordbeck suggesting that she's a bigot-spewing stereotype? Birdie tries to say, "I wouldn't know," without annoyance.

Leif looks as his watch. Micah stopped wearing a watch years ago. "I better get moving." He leans forward to give Birdie a brotherly kiss on the cheek. She recovers a smile. Five minutes later he's bought his mother the new Ottolenghi cookbook, and with a hug says, "I've got to go, but I'd love to continue this conversation at Christmas."

Birdie realizes she'd like that, too, and says as much. For the rest of the afternoon she ruminates on how, to combat the home field advantage when she married into the Tobias family, she wishes she'd had an *Underground Guide for Clueless Shiksas*. It would include a lexicon explaining that *Nova* is smoked salmon you buy in an *appetizing store* to pile on a *bialy*, and answers to questions like how guys with shaved heads keep their yarmulkes on. Forget short stories. This is what she should be writing.

Field of Dreams begins to empty. It's past sunset. The streets will be icy. Gwen returns. "Why don't you pack it in?" she says and, gratefully, Birdie does. Tonight, she and Alice will be celebrating Hanukkah.

The door chimes and opens. A man looks around, reaches Birdie in long strides, and pulls her toward him in a tight embrace legitimately worthy of a romance novel. The man is Micah.

CHAPTER 30

Birdie

Mɪᴄᴀʜ's ʜᴇᴀᴅʟɪɢʜᴛs ꜰᴏʟʟᴏᴡ Bɪʀᴅɪᴇ's ᴄᴀʀ ᴀs ᴛʜᴇʏ ʜᴇᴀᴅ ᴛᴏ Big Jen's. Despite Birdie's repeated insistence that he shouldn't travel to Iowa, for the past five weeks she's expected him to waltz through the door. In a game of marital Double Dog Dare, every time Birdie said, "No," she suspected her husband heard the opposite. She has been comfortable in limbo, freed from thinking about next steps, but now that Micah's here, he'll expect answers she does not have, though she knows the questions: Does she still love him? Is he reporting his accident to the police and suffering consequences that may bring?

They pull off the main road, park near Jen's trim, vinyl-sided farmhouse, and kick off their boots inside the mudroom. Alice is dutifully waiting in her red parka, striped pom-pom hat, kitty mittens, and Minnie Mouse boots. "Daddy," she screams. "Daddy!" She dashes to her father, catapults into his arms, and they dance into the kitchen and around its island. Birdie thinks she sees tears in Micah's eyes, though Alice is all giggles. "You came for Hanukkah!" she squeals. "Mommy told me I'd be getting a surprise."

A play kitchen waits for Alice in a big box wrapped in blue-and-silver paper festooned with dreidels, ordered online. Gifts from her parents, Joy-Ellen, Veronika and David, and Mel and Jake also stand by—a supermarket's stash of miniature plastic food and a monogrammed apron. Birdie reads Micah's face: he has no clue that the holiday begins tonight, though if he pulls a live puppy out of his ass later, she won't be surprised.

Jen walks into her kitchen and takes in the hoopla. "This is Micah," Birdie says. "Micah, Jen." Her friend was giving birth during Birdie's wedding reception; she has never met Micah. Her face reacts with *Birdie Peterson, why did you not tell me you're married to a movie star?*

Balancing Alice in one arm, he flips on his swagger and offers Jen his best *head cheerleader, huh?* banter, white teeth flashing. Birdie is not inured to her husband's appeal, but dashed hopes have tarnished its gleam. If only another woman's appreciation was all it took to put things right.

"Will I get to meet Darrell?" Micah asks Jen. Birdie might have mentioned Jen's husband once or twice, and Micah has the gift of name recall. Jake has often said he'd make a great salesman. Life would be easier if Micah accepted his father's standing offer to work at David Tobias & Son. But, of course, he'd be expected to put in ten-hour days, six days a week.

"Sorry, evening chores," Jen says. Darrell raises hogs, oats, and corn. This is not a hobby farm, and the man never rests. "He'll be sorry he missed you, but maybe the four of us can get together this weekend? I make a mean pizza."

Micah thanks Jen as if he's never eaten pizza. Birdie hustles her family out the door. Her mother will be serving dinner at six, sharp; her shift starts at eight.

As the three of them enter the Peterson kitchen, her parents' conversation with Joy-Ellen stops short as they take in their unexpected visitor. "Son, what a surprise," Russ Peterson says, clapping Micah on the back. Birdie wonders if her father knows

Micah from a bale of hay, and that this visitor, who has been to Iowa only twice, is her husband.

"What a wonderful surprise," Luanne says, giving Micah a hug and once-over. Birdie sees a flicker of wariness in her mother's eyes that fails to match her words. "You got here in time for supper." She says it almost as if he was expected. "Birdie, we'll need another place setting."

"I'll grab it," Joy-Ellen says, "after I give Mr. Tobias here a proper greeting." From her grandmother alone does Micah receive a solid, meaningful squeeze.

Tonight, because it's a holiday, they are eating in the dining room. "Daddy, look at my menorah!" Alice trills, pointing to the sideboard.

Please, please, give it its due, Birdie silently prays. The candelabra is made of nine chunky washers Gorilla Glue'd on an oblong block of wood painted blue and covered with sea glass. She and Alice worked on their project for days. It catches the topaz light cast by a Mission-style chandelier hanging over the table.

"Alice, no way you made this," Micah says.

"Really, Daddy. I did. With Mommy. Promise."

"Can I take a picture of you with it? Hold the menorah up high. I'll send it to Gran in New York."

Mel will appreciate their handiwork, Birdie thinks, then be pissed that she wasn't the one to make it with Alice, and more importantly, that the entire Tobias family isn't celebrating Hanukkah together.

"Hey, why don't I take a picture of all of you?" Joy-Ellen shoos Micah and Birdie toward their daughter. Later, when Birdie sees the picture, she and Micah will be pale as condensed milk, their astonishment plainly illustrating what love can turn into when it mutates.

"Do we light the candles before or after dinner?" Luanne

asks as she brings to the table a juicy brisket surrounded by carrots. Joy-Ellen carries in potato pancakes and homemade applesauce.

Birdie looks to Micah. "Before, right?" He nods, and with Alice between them, they stand together in front of the menorah. Micah, blushing, sings three short blessings that usher in the holiday. Birdie is relieved that he can remember them and wishes she could be inside Luanne's, Russ's, and Joy-Ellen's heads, taking notes.

During the meal, they keep the chat as light and neutral as air, inquiring about Micah's family, steering clear of his business. Mostly, they debrief Alice. What did you do in day care? Who are your friends? Can Daddy meet Elsa the kitty? And finally, the question that trumps all others, Do you want to open your presents?

"Can I get in on this?" Micah asks. He disappears to his rented car and returns with an unwrapped American Girl doll that looks shockingly like Alice, and a frilly, silly dress for her that matches the doll's outfit. His gifts preempt the play kitchen and its many accoutrements. Alice clutches her new doll and father's hand as he leads her upstairs for books and bed. Russ and Buckshot have retired to the living room. Luanne is off to the hospital. Birdie and her grandmother clean up after the meal.

"Handsome fellow, your man," she says.

"Not you, too? When Jen met Micah, she started to drool."

"Are you happy he's here, Bird?"

"Ask me again tomorrow," Birdie says as she loads the dishwasher. "We haven't talked much, not about anything important."

But an hour later, after she and Micah have gone to bed, talk slips their minds. As they undress each other in the chill of an Iowa evening, Birdie thinks that he *is* a fine male specimen, and that sex in her childhood bedroom never fails to disappoint.

Then again, scx with Micah has never been the problem. When they finish he says, "Birdie, I've missed you. Enough is enough. Come home."

"Have you gone to the police?" she asks.

"I called from one of those kiosks on the street. I got that far."

That is the problem.

CHAPTER 31

Mel

"HOW GOES IT IN IOWA? PLEASE REGALE ME WITH ANECDOTES from your day." Choke me with details.

It took arm-twisting and underwriting a plane ticket, but yesterday Micah flew to Iowa to surprise Birdie and Alice. After the third mournful message, he has returned my call, though all I get is, "Nothing much to say."

"How's your wife and daughter?"

"Alice seems a lot more excited to see me than Birdie does."

"Has Alice grown?" As we speak, I am looking at her picture, her eyes wide and wondering.

"Ah, no. Maybe her hair grew."

"Did she ask for me?" When Micah does not immediately answer, she says, "I'm demoted to Other Grandma, huh?"

"Stop it, Mom."

I feel pathetic, as unattractive as that may be. "What's it like now, Iowa?"

"Fucking cold."

I have visited the state only once, for Birdie and Micah's wedding party, after which Jake and I made a pilgrimage to the state fair. We spent two days gorging on foot-long corn dogs, cheese curds, and fried everything, including a whole stick of butter smothered in batter and cinnamon sugar, ending with chocolate fudge ice cream sandwiches, and I'm still lugging around the five pounds I gained that week. We marveled at the butter cow and the state's biggest boar (and no, I do not mean that windbag at the party), watched a sow give birth to ten little piggies, and tried to harmonize with my mother's favorites, the Beach Boys, whom I'd assumed were dead. It was a once-in-a-lifetime experience, accent on *once*.

"Do you think you can persuade Birdie to come home by Christmas?" I take off the last two weeks in December when many clients vacation, though not us. That's Jake busiest, holiest season.

"Not a chance. All the talk at breakfast was about going to a neighbor's farm to cut down the perfect Christmas tree. It sounds like a movie starring Bing Crosby. Alice is twitching, she's so excited. You really want your son to be the Grinch?"

Who can compete with Christmas—the glitter, the glitz, the gaiety? The color scheme alone tempts me to convert. "How's Birdie?"

"Quiet. Distant. Though she seems to love her job."

"She could get a job in a bookstore here."

"It's not just her work. She really likes being near her family. Her dad mostly grunts but her mom is a dynamo and you can't not like Joy-Ellen. But, Mom, there's Alice now. We're leaving on the tree hunt. Gotta go."

Micah clicks off and I allow myself a moment of melancholy. I know what it's like to miss family. Early in my marriage, I begged Jake to move to the Twin Cities, where I grew up. I would rattle off reasons. "Lakes right in town. Bike paths. Summer evenings with ten o'clock sunsets. Excellent public schools. The Saint Paul winter ice carnival. A house we could afford. My parents." I saved them for last.

"Hail storms that rain golf balls of ice and that's in the summer," Jake countered. "Velveeta. Lime Jell-O molds. People who say 'okeydokey' and 'jeez.' Those accents. 'Ruhtz' instead of 'r-o-o-o-t-s.' 'Ya' instead of 'yeah.' Miracle Whip instead of Hellmann's mayo. Blizzards. Bad blizzards."

At least my parents didn't merit his shit list. "Dairy Queen Blizzards," I lobbed back. "Sweet corn that's actually sweet. Lilacs. Craft beer. Fresh, clean air. The Guthrie Theater. The temple my grandparents helped found."

He listed, "Temple, any temple. Rhyming wrestle with hassle. Tornadoes. Windchill factor. Snow shoveling. Frostbite. Hypothermia. Ice-fishing, the most boneheaded sport ever invented. Cars that refuse to start in the winter, which doesn't end until May."

I knew Jake's real objection, a tale as old as time. He would never leave his mother, though he was down with me leaving mine. Veronika worships him like Sara Delano Roosevelt did her Franklin. When Jake told his mother a move to the land of ten thousand lakes was under consideration, she said, "How could you even think of abandoning your parents? Bringing you into his business has been your father's lifelong dream." After this she retired to her bedroom with a three-day migraine.

I hold a threadbare grudge about how Jake unilaterally blew off my fantasy of returning to the Twin Cities. I desperately missed my parents, who traveled to New York twice a year. My mother splurged on tickets to Broadway shows and sussed out obscure galleries and museum exhibits while my father saw the Yankees and Knicks with the kids and loaded up on pastrami and rye bread superior to that of their local deli. Chirpy as they were, on the last day of every visit they seemed relieved. My souped-up stress, which caused me to scurry from here to there as I barked at the children and Jake, most likely made them feel eager for retreat. This left me thick with remorse, more lonesome than ever.

Can I help it that my parents—compared to Veronika—led a fairly easy, All-American life? After I married—Jake and I were still in college, which was unremarkable anywhere but in a big city, where it was shockingly premature—Sam and Maxine Glazer considered their parenting job complete. My dad reverted to handball, vegetable gardening, and chess and spent even longer hours at his dental practice; my mother threw herself into first-grade teaching, Hadassah, mah-jongg, and aqua aerobics. When Veronika met them, I'm willing to bet she dismissed their prim politeness as the dullest denominator of Minnesota nice. My mother-in-law believes sophistication exists only on the Northeast Corridor and in New Orleans and San Francisco. Los Angeles, be damned.

I also suspect that because my parents didn't demand and butt in, Veronika assumed that meant they didn't care. I know that wasn't true, but they didn't want to intrude. If they would visit now, I'd cancel appointments and squire my folks to concerts, museums, plays, and restaurants. But my mother, one more non-smoker lost to lung cancer, will be making no trips east. Thirteen months after the Grim Reaper came for Maxine Glazer, my father replaced her with their neighbor, the Widow Dorfman, who vaporized every photograph not only of the first Mrs. Glazer, but of my brother Fred and me. The following year, the newlyweds moved to a gated community north of San Diego to be near her children and grandchildren. Now, when I call my father, we chat stiffly for a few minutes before—as if she's my mother—he puts my stepmother on the phone, though neither of us has anything we're willing to say.

I've become the one who makes twice-yearly visits I can't wait to end. During my most recent trip, when I worked up the nerve to ask my stepmother if I could have my mother's wedding china, she informed me that she'd donated it to Goodwill.

That evening, I wound up eating dinner alone in my hotel room while she and my dad blew me off for bridge.

Not that I'm bitter.

My phone pings.

Bambi: Can I c u?

Bambi who—with no explanation—stopped coming to therapy weeks ago. Hey, it happens.

Mel: Sorry no free hrs 4 2 days
Bambi: O shit. FT? Pls.😊?

I'm not a fan of FaceTime sessions. They not only make my face look as long as Seabiscuit's, I find the format flat and forced. Also, when verbal foreplay builds toward an orgasmic reveal, invariably, the screen freezes as my mouth hangs open so wide my gold fillings shine. On the other hand, this is tempest-tossed Bambi, whom I'd pledged to help. What would Veronika do? The answer is clear.

Mel: Can u b here in 1 hr?

No lunch for Mel.

Bambi: Yes yes yes ♥ ♥ ♥

An hour later, Bambi collapses in my office like a bag of rags. "Thank you for seeing me," she says, catching her breath. "I'm a wreck." She exhales and wails. "Joe left."

Jellyfish Joe, who Bambi was certain she could control? Ah, the arrogance of people underestimating one another. "Did he find out about"—I can't retrieve the name of Bambi's extramarital other.

"Clyde. You know how I vowed to stop seeing him?" She squeezes her eyes shut. "I lied—to myself and to you. Best intentions and all that."

I'm not surprised, because I've been there. "What made you start up with Clyde again?" Perhaps she never stopped seeing him, but I'll give her the benefit of the doubt.

Bambi sinks into her chair. "After a few weeks I couldn't stand how much I missed him. He's my OxyContin."

Dr. T in handy pill form. Keep away from small children and pets. Do not use when operating heavy equipment.

"Yesterday I didn't get home until after midnight and Joe was gone, leaving only this note." Bambi detonates into a fusillade of tears. Mascara dribbles down her cheeks. She sniffles, snorts, and reads from a sheet of yellow legal pad. "'I love you and I'm sad but I can't take this anymore.'"

I wait for her to get a grip, then ask, "What do you want to happen?" She heaves her shoulders. "Let me put it this way," I say when I get no response. "Do you see yourself with Clyde?"

Bambi gives me the side-eye. "I'm not a big enough fool to think that will ever happen, or even if it's who I want."

"Is Joe who you want?"

"Yes. Maybe, if I weren't addicted to Clyde."

I lean forward and speak slowly. "Bambi, an affair is a fairy tale."

"I'm not 'Bambi' anymore. Please call me Barbara."

"Okay. Barbara, an affair is not real life." Don't I know it. "Clyde may be a distraction from something you don't want to feel with Joe. Think of Clyde as a drug. If you take away the drug the feelings you can't face may move front and center. Eliminating Clyde is the equivalent of being in withdrawal—very, very hard—but it gives you the chance to try and understand your feelings for Joe in a clear, sober way."

When our time is up and we schedule another session, I let myself think I spoke with common sense. Another client is waiting. I am shoveling in spoonfuls of yogurt when the phone rings.

"Melanie, am I interrupting?"

Veronika's voice is shaky. I check the clock. "I have a few minutes."

"David's doctor called. It's . . . not good. Definite cognitive impairment, though he can't make a clearer diagnosis until he sees him again and tests further." Veronika chokes up and stops.

"Does David know?"

"Yes, we had the doctor on speaker. We'd discussed that before. David made it clear that he does not want to be treated like a child. He wants to know everything." Veronika may be hyperventilating.

"Take some deep breaths, please. I'm worried about you." I try to make my voice match hers.

Veronika's breathing calms. "I think David is taking this better than I am. Or else he's simply numb. Then again, I'm not sure how much he took in."

"I'm so sorry," I say, though the doctor's diagnosis is more or less what I expected. What I never expected is my mother-in-law revealing vulnerability. "What can I do for you? Should Jake and I come over tonight?" He works late every night during this season, but for his parents he'll make an exception.

"No, thank you," she says. "But if you could relay this to Jake . . ."

"He doesn't know what the doctor said?"

"I called you first."

I am dumbstruck. I do not look forward to sharing this with Jake, who I know has been hoping for a miracle. Just yesterday he found a post on a questionable internet site about a man whose slipshod memory was restored when a doctor removed embedded ear wax.

"Is there anything that can help David? Drugs or treatments?" Medical marijuana comes to mind.

"The neurologist said we'll sort that, but I'm not holding out hope. I've treated patients who are caretakers, and every one says the meds their loved ones take are no better than placebos. I'm . . ." I hear quiet weeping. "I'm scared."

I'm scared, too. The therapist in me asks a question, reflexively. "Veronika, what frightens you the most?"

After a long pause, she answers. "That David will forget he loves me."

I don't know what to say next. While I try to think of an appropriate response, Veronika preempts me.

"That is the wrong answer. I'm afraid David will forget who I am."

CHAPTER 32

Veronika

As David dozes in front of a Civil War documentary, he still looks like her husband—in his twenties, a dreamboat with the thick, dark curls Micah inherited; by his late thirties, becoming debonair; at fifty, still strong and virile; in his sixties, surprisingly rakish; in his seventies, distinguished. How much of David is left? How quickly will he vanish?

Veronika hurts in places that will never show. "Darling, are you there?" she asks. His answer is a guttural snore.

When Veronika met David at a college party she was out of step with her generation, a naïf impersonating a sophisticate. While other bookish women were going all in on *Ms.* magazine, flirting with feminism, Veronika Berezovsky was a drone, keeping her grades high to maintain a scholarship to Barnard and to prep for the MCAT. She attended one consciousness-raising group and fled, repelled, when called upon to vent about her personal oppression. Veronika didn't feel oppressed, personally or existentially, just short on cash and wiped out from a full load of classes and holding down a thirty-hour-a-week job in the library.

"What do you think of Joan Baez?" the only grad student

at the party in a navy blazer and rep tie asked the only woman wearing pearls and pastels.

"Is she a professor?"

He offered her a joint. She declined. "Bob Dylan?" David asked.

Had Veronika not been able to sing "Blowin' in the Wind" in a sultry alto the two might never have had their first date the following Saturday, when David introduced her to stuffed grape leaves at Symposium, a new Greek restaurant hidden away in a basement, and later in the evening, she introduced him to cherry cheese strudel at the Hungarian Pastry Shop. The following year, after David had acquainted Veronika with Woody Allen, Vietnam war protest, and sex, they were married in a rabbi's study. He'd gotten an MBA and was opening a small men's haberdashery. She was in med school and happy to replace Berezovsky with Tobias. Herman Berezovsky wasn't her biological father. Ya'akov Marcuse was, though she'd been stripped of his name as a child.

Veronika leans over David now and fingers his snowy hair. "I'm going to miss you," she says.

He opens his eyes and pulls her close. "Jumping Jehoshaphat, woman. I'm not gone yet. Come here."

She nestles her head on his shoulder and says, "I love you."

"And I love you." As they kiss Veronika feels tears coming but refuses to cry. "I hate this. It isn't fair."

"Whatever this is, stop it. Being a drama queen does not become you."

"Can I tell you something if you promise you will never repeat it to Jake?"

"Jake who?"

Veronika laughs, but not for long.

"What makes you think I'll even remember what you say?" he asks.

How long until David's sense of humor disappears?

"I promise," he says.

"I don't love being a mother even half as much as I love being your wife."

"Flatterer. Sycophant."

"Hand to God."

"In that case, will you promise me something in return?"

"What?"

"You have to swear."

"That's not fair."

"We're way beyond 'life's not fair.'"

"Is my promise legally binding?"

"By all means." David extends his hands, which Veronika admires—sturdy peasant hands, never without his wide gold band on his left hand and a black signet ring on the right. They lock pinkies and shake, laughing.

"Here goes." He kisses her again. "When I get truly cuckoo, you have to swear to find another man. And don't wait 'til I'm dead."

"Never."

He cackles. "Too late. You promised."

"I could never be with anyone else."

"Bullshit. Men love you."

Veronika doubts that's true. She suspects she intimidates most men.

"I'm thinking Art Greenberg," David says.

Veronika howls. "Not-Smart Art? Who mispronounces *heinous* and says *irregardless*? I think not."

"You do realize you're a snob?"

"You just noticed this?"

He twists his wedding ring. "Then Herb Martin, from your institute?"

"Née Metzenbaum? With that Liberace toupee? Next."

"Mike Bloomberg?"

Veronika recalls leaving a Park Avenue cocktail party years ago when David said, "Did you see that little short guy who got in the elevator after us? I know I know him, but damn, I can't place him."

Veronika only smiled.

"Does he sit next to us on Yom Kippur?"

"Guess again."

"My proctologist?" Veronika nods no. "The undertaker at Riverside who directs you to the right chapel?" They used to attend funerals there maybe once a year. Now they're up to two or three times.

"That was the new mayor," Veronika said. "And he's taken," she says now.

"Ok, then, Eddie Druckerman?"

"Who's Eddie Druckerman?"

"Loyal customer. Buys a top-of-the-line cashmere overcoat every other year, along with two suits for winter, one for summer, six ties, and eight shirts. Sits behind us at the opera. Widower. Lost his wife last year."

"The bald guy. I'm not ready for bald."

David says nothing. Veronika thinks he's drifted into one of his fogs. Then he rubs his hands together as if he's won on *Jeopardy!* "I've got it. Jordan's friend's dad, Jeff Ellington. Real estate developer. Hair to spare, runs marathons, house in Bridgehampton, owns a sailboat and a NetJet share. Calls himself a career philanthropist. Why shouldn't you be filthy rich?"

Veronika laughs, louder than usual. She wishes she could reveal that he's been her analysand for years.

"If Jeff Ellington is the best you can do, you are just going to have to hang on," she says.

CHAPTER 33

Birdie

ALICE AND BIRDIE FOLLOW HER FATHER AND MICAH AS THEY drive to their neighbors' farm. "Grab the chainsaw, will ya?" Russ says to Micah when they arrive.

There's a request I'll bet my husband has never gotten, Birdie thinks. She leaps to a dark place—Micah's accident and her anger about his unwillingness to take next steps—but wills herself to shut down the association for fear of ruining the morning's dreamscape. The temperature is a balmy twenty-nine, with a cloudless blue sky and almost no wind, a day that could illustrate the glossy calendar the heating company mails every year to her parents. Sun stipples snowdrifts that peak like meringue. Birdie is glad she remembered her sunglasses. After they walk for five minutes, she begins to sweat and loosens her scarf.

"Mommy, I didn't know snow could stay white," Alice remarks, considering its Brooklyn shelf life. Within a day or two, pristine powder turns to heaps that match a pewter sky and freeze into ice skids only the stroller-less can navigate. Where to Birdie snowfalls used to evoke images of sleigh rides and cocoa, in New York City what comes to mind is salt-stained UGGs and uncollected garbage bags piled as high as her head.

Russ leads the way, followed by Micah. Birdie and Alice trail behind in the men's Bigfoot-prints leading to a thicket of trees planted in neat rows.

"What'll it be this year?" her father shouts out. "Scotch Pine, White Pine, or Fraser Fir?"

While the Tobias family debates where to buy smoked fish, the Petersons spar over which evergreen species makes the best Christmas tree. Birdie's childhood favorite was White Pine, because of its long needles. Her mother prefers a Scotch Pine: its tougher needles can support more ornaments, of which she has hundreds—inherited, handmade by children and church ladies, and collected wherever the family has vacationed. Joy-Ellen and Russ, traditionalists, pledge their allegiance to Fraser Firs, which perfume the house with the greenest, longest-lasting scent.

"You pick, Dad."

"Alice should pick." Russ extends his arm as if he is asking his granddaughter to dance. Insulated by layers of clothing, she waddles toward her grandfather. The pair stomps through the groves, stopping at each tree as they assess pros and cons.

"My dad loathes a lopsided tree, so this could take a while," Birdie says to Micah. "He's big on symmetry."

"I don't think your dad's too big on me."

"He hasn't said as much." He doesn't have to. At least he's stayed sober when he hasn't said it.

Micah touches her wrist. In thick, borrowed work gloves his hands resemble giant paws. "Will you come back home, Bird? Please. I'm asking again, for me and for my family."

She has had weeks to consider her answer. "I'll think about coming home when you get the accident business straightened out. I don't want to open a closet one day and have a skeleton fall out that fucks up our life."

"Are you defining me by one mistake?"

"Don't we all get defined by our mistakes?"

"Hey, buddy," Russ shouts to Micah. "You, too, Birdie. The princess has chosen. Saw time. Chop-chop." He's the first to laugh at his yearly joke.

Birdie and Micah clamber through the snow. Micah slings the heavy saw over his shoulder like a dead animal in a display so on-the-nose machismo Birdie can't not chuckle. Alice stands proudly next to a fir tree that tops off several feet above Russ's ancient trapper hat, which he refuses to give up though it makes him look like Ted Kaczynski.

Birdie sizes up the stately tree. "Good choice, honey."

"The needles look almost blue. See." She lifts a branch to show its underside, and Russ beams. His horticulture tutorial has paid off.

"Want to do the honors?" Russ points to the chain saw.

Micah looks at the saw as if it's alive. "I've never actually used one of these fuckers."

Or many tools, Birdie thinks. His home repair skill set starts and ends with "Call the handyman."

"Nothing to it. Come here, Mike, and I'll show you how."

Her dad does know her husband's name, more or less.

"Here ya go." From a backpack, Russ pulls out noise-canceling earphones and plastic safety masks for both of them.

"Daddy, you look like an astronaut," Alice says when Micah puts on the equipment. She hops from foot to foot in her Minnie Mouse boots. Birdie hopes she doesn't have to pee.

"Get over there, ladies," Russ shouts to Birdie and Alice. He pronounces the word *git* and points to a hill about thirty feet away. "You throttle up this baby and place it on the wood." Russ's voice carries in the still field. "Then you press down as you slide the saw through here." He points toward the ground and demonstrates the movement. "Ready?"

From what Birdie can see of Micah's masked face, he is terrified.

"One, two, three."

The saw sounds like a symphony of dental drills. As Russ yells, "Timber!" Alice screams, but Birdie sees she's still smiling. Micah whoops. The tree falls. Not unlike like my marriage, Birdie thinks.

AT NINE O'CLOCK that evening, Birdie and Micah are sitting in front of the fireplace, admiring the tree, which they spent hours decorating with Alice, Joy-Ellen, and Luanne. Tiny white lights twinkle; Joy-Ellen forbids colored lights, which she deems appropriate only for a bordello. An angel Russ Jr. made in fourth grade looks down on the room. There are dozens of dangling ornaments, each with its own backstory: glass candy canes that belonged to Russ's parents; Smokey Bear, from a trip to Yellowstone; Judge Ruth Bader Ginsburg rendered in felt and lace, courtesy of Mel. Best tree we've ever had, they agree, as they do every year.

Luanne is at the hospital, working. Alice is asleep, as is Russ. Joy-Ellen left them a big bowl of popcorn before she went home. Only Buckshot keeps Birdie and Micah company.

Micah switches off "Feliz Navidad" and finds one of his playlists. He reaches for Birdie's hand. "How would you feel if I stayed here?"

"Stay? For how long?"

"Indefinitely. Your father asked if I'd like to help with the hogs."

"The *trayf*?" Birdie laughs.

"I could be like one of those guys who gives up Wall Street to move to the backcountry with his drop-dead photogenic wife who homeschools their kids and brags about their mail-order bacon crushing the competition and raises fancy Japanese pigs, and is verified by Instagram with a blue check mark because of all his followers." Birdie is one of them.

"When the wife's not shoveling shit?"

"Manure, if you please. We could be just like that couple."

"Except you skipped the part where they'd made so much money their ranch is half of Wyoming."

Birdie leans against Micah's shoulder while Buckshot's labored breathing and occasional dream-induced woof competes with Ella Fitzgerald. Where is it decreed that they must live out their life in Brooklyn? The fire turns to embers as Birdie muses on planting themselves as an authentic Iowa family, typical as one more field of corn. She takes the hand of her boy-husband and leads him upstairs.

Birdie has made up her mind.

CHAPTER 34

Mel

JAKE'S VOICE OVER THE PHONE IS LIKE A BUGLE PLAYING REVEILLE. "I hate to ask, but can you meet me at the Manhattan store?"

"Now?" My first session ended minutes ago, with back-to-back appointments filling the day.

"Now."

Powered by panic, I ask, "What's the emergency?"

"It's my dad. I'd like to kill him. We just lost a forty-five-hundred-dollar sale because he told a customer the Loro Piana coat he was ready to buy was a rip-off—the Ermenegildo Zegna is better at half the price."

"Was he right?"

"Of course. That's not the point." Jake is speaking in his eye-rolling voice. "His filter is shot to hell. Kaput."

My husband has ever so mildly suggested to his father that—given his recent visit with the neurologist—he might want to consider retirement, but has stopped short of saying he can no longer work in the stores. After all, David started all three.

"Retire—and do what?" was David's response the first time

Jake offered the proposition. "Play the ponies like your uncle Ezra, that bum?"

When I met Jake's uncle, I assumed his name was Ezra Thatbum, which was how the family referred to him. Only when Veronika called him "Ezra, that *mumzer*" did I get it. I may knock many Tobias traits but—with the exception of Micah—laziness is not one of them. The clan is hard-wired for the Protestant Work Ethic. That Ezra didn't do a day's work past the age of thirty-five was held in familial contempt until the man dropped dead right after his horse, Jock Itch, won big. From then on, he became Poor Ezra Thatbum.

When I heard Jake propose retirement to his dad a second time he pointed out that David complained about not visiting museums enough, and with more free time, he could make the rounds of MoMA, the Whitney, the Frick, the Met, and the American Museum of Natural History.

"But I only like going to those places with your mother," he replied, reasonably enough. Point, David.

This past weekend, Jake tried to sell his father on continuing education. "You're a Columbia grad," he reminded him, in case he forgot. "Maybe the tuition is discounted." A bargain might sway him.

This is when I broke in. Since his neurology exam, I have seen my father-in-law three times, and on each occasion, he has seemed increasingly befuddled. I worry that David is on the dementia fast track. I'm not sure he could keep up with a class. "We don't have to resolve this now," I said to terminate a conversation no one wanted to have in the first place.

"I wish I could zip over, but I can't, hon," I admit to Jake. "Full schedule. I'm so, so sorry. Crazed 'til four."

"I'll never last with him that long." Jake groans.

"Maybe I could cancel my last appointment," I think out

loud. It's Norah, who because of her issues concerning Delia comes in whenever she can rather than keep her eleven o'clock slot. I think she would understand about a family emergency, but she's also the client I most want to see, for glaring, unethical reasons.

"Riiiiight," Jake says.

His tone suggests that my work is on par with running a five-cent advice booth. Since involving Veronika is not an option, I suggest asking Jordan to stop by the store. "She and your dad could go out for lunch and afterward, a movie?"

"Okay." Jake sighs like an old man himself. "Let me know."

Jordan answers on the first ring, sounding spooked about getting a fully operational phone call from me instead of a text. "Everything okay?"

"Yes and no. I'll get right to it. Dad needs an intervention with your grandpa at the Manhattan store, and we were hoping you might be able to break free and help."

"What the hell? An 'intervention'? I've never seen him drink more than two Perfect Manhattans."

"Honey, I gather you haven't been with your grandfather lately."

"I'm sorry about that—I've been traveling, as you know."

"No need to get defensive. In any event, Grandpa is starting to . . ." How do I word this without sounding apocalyptic? "Get a little spacey—"

"Spacey how?"

"He's seen some excellent doctors, but they aren't giving his condition—"

"He has a condition?"

"—a formal name, though they agree something is definitely going on."

"This is a lot to take in. Why haven't you said anything?

You're a therapist, for fuck's sake." Jordan sounds outraged on top of upset.

"We can discuss this in as much detail as you want later, but right now there's an urgency. Could you possibly whip up to the Midtown store and spirit away your grandfather for lunch and maybe a movie? I'd go myself but I have a full schedule, and I'm late for my next session."

I hear breathing before she says, "Mel, I'm sorry, but I can't." She sounds genuine. "Kit and I have our final interview at the sperm bank. If we cancel, we're dead meat."

"Pardon me. I'm aware that donors are rigorously screened and interviewed, but why recipients?"

"I didn't ask. That's their policy."

"I see." Perhaps the sperm bank is trying to screen out potential parents they consider to be off-brand, wearing mullets, chewing gum, and in future reviews saying, "I graduated college" instead of "I graduated *from* college."

"It's the country's top-tier sperm bank," she adds. "Nana Veronika recommended it."

If it's top-tier, of course she did. Again, I hope Jordan has had a route recalculation about whether it's she or Kit who will carry their child, but this isn't the moment to renew that conversation.

"Why don't you ask Micah?"

"What good would that do? He's visiting Birdie." Groveling. Praying. Seducing. Perhaps not in that order.

"As of last night, he's not."

"Excuse me?"

"Birdie asked him to leave. Says their situation is hopeless until he comes clean with the detective."

I can be slow understanding what I don't want to understand. "Does that mean she and Alice aren't coming here over Christmas vacation?"

"It sounds to me like it's up to Micah whether they come back here at all. He's offered to move to Iowa."

"With the *trayf*?

"With the *trayf*."

I CLICK OFF and call Micah. He doesn't answer. I attempt to FaceTime, but get his unavailable message. I ping.

Mel: Important! Call pls.
Micah: Not ready to talk.

Is it possible to literally feel your blood pressure spike in your veins? My client's session should be starting. I pop out to tell a busy periodontist that I need to make a critical phone call that will take a few minutes. He grimaces. I call Micah again.

"What now?" he answers.

"It's not always all about you, Micah." I hope my wail isn't loud enough for the periodontist to hear through the wall. "And it isn't about Birdie and Alice and Iowa, not that I don't want to know what happened. It's about your grandfather." I deliver an abridged synopsis of what's going on with David and Jake and plead for Micah to drive to the store and take charge.

The sweet, kind Micah who I believe still lives inside my son—ready to spin a cocoon, molt, and emerge as a superhero—says, "I'll get right over." Fifty minutes later I take a call from a grateful Jake. David and Micah have left for lunch at Katz's Deli, where they will undoubtedly eat what the doctor never orders. All is well, for now, though Jake adds, "When I asked Micah if Birdie and Alice returned with him, all I got was the stink eye."

"Can we discuss this later?"

"More than fine with me."

The phone immediately rings. It must be Jake with one last thought.

The voice is deep, and as familiar as our song, "Moondance"—from his generation, not mine. His "Hello, Melanie"—like Veronika, to him I was never Mel—is a Brandy Alexander with plenty of liqueur to cut the sweetness.

It's Dr. T.

CHAPTER 35

Veronika

It is four in the afternoon. Veronika arrives home from her office a few blocks away, turns on public radio, and deftly sorts her mail, saving only an invitation to a couple's fiftieth-anniversary party and a solicitation from the New York Public Library. The doorbell buzzes, though no one has been announced. When she peers through the peephole, her first thought is how Micah is a dead ringer for David at the age when she met him. Only after she processes this nugget of nostalgia does she wonder why David is standing by his grandson's side.

"Sorry, love, but I can't find my keys," her husband says. This is the second set he has lost this month. "And if you'll excuse me, nature calls," he stammers when she opens the door. David drops his coat on the floor and makes a dash to the powder room. Veronika wishes his aging prostate was her husband's biggest problem.

"Nana." Micah leans down to kiss her cheek. His is cold and smells of cedar and lime. "What a surprise," she says, though Micah's face tells her it isn't a good surprise. "Are you coming in?"

"Only for a minute. I set the parking meter for a half hour."

"What's going on?" As if she has stumbled off a Ferris wheel,

Veronika senses a faint dizziness along with the scalp tingle that announces a migraine. She used to get brutal headaches a few times a year but now, they arrive almost weekly, her own *Masterpiece Theatre*. If she doesn't pop a pill in the next ten minutes she'll have to ride out the misery like a cowgirl on a mechanical bull, holding on for dear life.

"There was a scene at the store with a customer," Micah says, as if that explains anything.

"And?" The word may as well be a cattle prod.

"Grandpa ticked off Dad, who asked me to—" Micah stumbles for words.

"Babysit your grandfather?"

"That's harsh."

"Why not call it what it is?"

"We had a good time," Micah protests. "Went to Katz's, then saw a new animated movie."

Veronika scrunches her face, baffled. "You took your grandfather to a see a cartoon?" Her voice shrills. Protecting her husband's dignity, Veronika is realizing, may be the hardest part of what's ahead.

"It really didn't matter what movie Grandpa saw, 'cause he slept through most of it."

This does not make Veronika feel better. "I guess I should thank you."

"That's not necessary. Like I said, we had a good time."

How could he enjoy being with a grandfather who is . . . ? She isn't ready to say *losing his mind*. "Don't just stand there in your jacket. Can I offer you something to drink? To eat?"

Micah shakes his head. "Thanks, but I'm stuffed."

Veronika has never known her grandson to refuse food. He must want to get the hell out of here, and who could blame him?

David rejoins them and they head to the living room. "At

least sit down," Veronika insists. While most grandmothers might sweeten the command with a *honey* or a *darling*, the only person in her domain who merits such sweetness is David. She is fairly certain she must have terrified Micah—or Jake, for that matter—when he was a little boy.

In the living room, she and David assume their customary places in matching easy chairs placed across from one another so they share a large ottoman. Micah sinks into the couch. Only now, given her astonishment at seeing him escort David, does Veronika remember that he is supposed to be in Iowa.

"You're back early," she remarks.

"You were traveling?" David asks.

"To Iowa."

"David, you knew that," Veronika says.

"Why now, for God's sake? Isn't it colder than a witch's tit?"

"It was." Micah laughs. Veronika doesn't.

"Is someone sick, someone in your wife's family?"

Good, Veronika notes. David remembers Birdie is from Iowa.

"Damn, your wife's name is on the tip of my—"

"Birdie," Veronika and Micah say, more or less in unison.

"Birdie and Alice returned with you, I assume," Veronika says. Micah doesn't reply.

"Well?"

"They did not."

"Birdie," David says. "I remember now. Beautiful blonde. Twists that body of hers into a pretzel. I'm still waiting to hear why she's in Iowa."

"She wanted to see her parents, and we have some problems to straighten out."

"Going through a rough patch, huh?"

Veronika wishes David would stop nattering so she can unravel what's happening with Micah and Birdie. Perhaps protecting

David's dignity won't be the hardest part of what's to come. Getting him to hush up may be. "My turn to talk," she says like an egocentric teenager.

"By all means, take the floor, Your Excellency," the old David says.

"Can we expect Birdie and Alice to come home soon?"

"I'm not sure Birdie sees this as 'home' anymore," Micah admits, "or if she ever did."

"That's absurd." Veronika rolls her eyes to complete her scoff. Veronika and David's grandfather clock starts to chime. It's five o'clock. Her grandson looks as if he'd like to kick it. When the twins were in first grade, Jordan convinced her twin brother that the clock was a live villain that could chase him, giving Micah nightmares and causing him to wet the bed.

Micah stands. "Gotta run—the last thing I need is a ticket."

"Will you call me later?" Veronika asks. Micah answers, "Sure." But she knows she won't hear from him.

"Thanks for the lunch and movie," David says, though Micah let him pay for both. The elevator opens and as Micah steps in, David shouts, "Holly Hunter! Damn it. That's who voiced the movie. Holly fucking Hunter." Micah thumbs-up his grandfather as the door closes. "The mind is a terrible thing to waste," David sings out as he returns to the apartment and hears Veronika shout, "Back here."

"What's for dinner?" he asks, joining her in the kitchen.

"Halibut, broccoli, baked potato. It should be ready in forty-five minutes."

David pulls out the makings of a Perfect Manhattan—bourbon, sweet vermouth, orange, bitters, and a maraschino cherry—and begins to mix his nightly cocktail. "You know, darling. I'm thinking maybe I should pack it in at the store. I'm starting to feel . . . redundant."

"You could never be redundant, love." With David, terms of endearment come easily.

"I don't want to become a buffoon."

Veronika doesn't say, "That could never happen," because perhaps it has. Rather, "At some point, I imagine we all have to pull back."

"I don't see you doing that, Dr. Tobias."

As if it's a mantra, Veronika has often said that she hopes to follow the direction of her mentor, an ancient shrink—had the woman dated Sigmund Freud?—whose obit recently reported that in a concession to turning ninety-five, she had scaled down her practice to a mere thirty hours a week. Veronika pictures herself dying. It's years from now (twenty, if she's lucky), and after articulating an astute insight, she hopes to close her eyes mid-session, and never wake up.

CHAPTER 36

Mel

M ELANIE," DR. T SAYS. "I WAS AFRAID YOU MIGHT HAVE changed your office phone number."

Anxiety, curiosity, and apprehension somersault in my stomach. "Hello," I barely whisper, failing to match Dr. Theodore Trachtenberg's too-hearty-by-half tone.

"How have you been?" my long-ago lover asks, as if we are second cousins once removed at a family reunion, not a man and a woman who used to kiss for twenty minutes at a stretch in the back of a taxi.

"Fine, thank you." What is the point of this call?

"Still in practice?"

"I am." Should I toss a snippet of small talk his way? "You, too?" This is as small as talk gets.

"That's why I'm calling."

He's not getting in touch because for lo these many years he's been missing me and can't stand the heartbreak for one more minute? "What's up?" I manage to say.

He either clears his throat or mumbles something in Welsh, followed by, "I'm opening an office in New York, an extension of the treatment I'm doing with couples in Cleveland, which is going swimmingly, and I'll be hiring a therapist. Since I always had a high regard for the relationship work you did, I thought of you immediately, and hope you might want to meet and discuss this opportunity. I'll be in town later in the month."

Dr. T, the original TED Talk-er, aha moments and all, always did like the sound of his own voice.

"Melanie?" he asks, stunning me into a reply.

I know I should instantly decline. This is Dr. T, after all. T for transference, T for trouble, T-T-T-T for takes-two-to-tango.

In life, sedate years seem to follow one another like pearls on a string. Then, kapow, you hit a stretch with nothing but surprises and struggle, which is what now feels like. I have issues right, left, and center, not the least of which is that I got on a scale and have gained eight pounds. I owe my dry cleaner an apology; he did not shrink my skirt.

"I'm flattered you thought of me, Dr. Trachtenberg."

"Oh. C'mon, Melanie, it's Ted, for God's sake."

His voice has mutated to intimate. I could pretend I feel nothing for the man, were my body not betraying me. Sweat drips down my back and my shirt clings in clammy discomfort. I'm definitely feeling something. Can Dr. T tell? I used to believe he could read my thoughts as if they flashed like subtitles.

"Can we meet and talk about this opportunity?"

Instead of "No, stay away, get the fuck out of my life," I hear myself saying, "I'd be happy to talk." No harm, no foul. We set up an appointment that I tell myself I will cancel as soon as I click off the phone.

Although there's a mean rain outside, with wind thwacking nippy December droplets as if they were pinballs, I'd like to take myself on a long walk to digest what has just happened. But getting some air is out of the question. Norah is waiting. She is back to wearing nail polish and coloring her hair. Are Delia's medical troubles behind her? Is her mother-in-law mellowing? Has she experienced an epiphany that allows her to make peace with turning fifty?

"I fired my chef," she begins, and delivers an excruciatingly detailed recapitulation of recent confrontations.

I commend her on working up the grit to give this "arrogant scumbag" the axe. "And Delia?" I ask.

"She's a whole different story. Not so great. Out of rehab, but not ready to work. Still living with us, using a walker."

"What happened with the policewoman looking into her case?"

"Nothing. Delia took some pictures of what she thinks may be the truck that hit her—it was one of those food trucks—but she's dragging her ass on passing them on to the detective."

How very fortunate. "Why?"

"She may have a new boyfriend telling her what to do, but I don't know for sure. She's secretive and as far as the New York police go, intimidated—and frankly, skeptical. Delia thinks no one will take her seriously. I'm happy to help, but Brian and my mother-in-law insist it's time for me to stop interfering. They say I'm too controlling." Norah stares at the amaryllis plant I forgot to water. "What do you think?"

"Please try to answer that question yourself."

Norah avoids eye contact but eventually says, "Brian may be right. But I still wonder, should I call the detective?"

Please don't, Norah. I kick the ball right back. "What do you think?"

"I should call her. Brian can be a bully."

Norah spends the rest of the session amplifying this point. By the time the session ends, I am drained. The thought of listening

to Jake's play-by-play of what he experienced today at the store
with his father does not promise a relaxing evening, despite how
heroically my son came through as a Tobias family EMT. As I
lock up, the phone rings. Veronika. She's hatched a plan. It pivots
around me.

CHAPTER 37

Birdie

December twenty-fifth is the Petersons' day for wearing flannel pajamas 'til noon, exchanging gifts, gorging on mountains of waffles and sausage from their own pigs, singing carols accompanied on the piano by Clark, and starting thousand-piece jigsaw puzzles and new books. By midafternoon, they nod out, one by one.

Christmas Eve is the main event: holy and reflective. The treetops glisten and the children generally listen, with or without sleigh bells in the snow. Celebrating begins at six, at Grace Lutheran, followed by dinner served on Luanne's demure Lenox wedding china, thinly rimmed in gold, that she lovingly handwashes and dries with linen dishcloths. The meal pivots around either a hefty ham with homemade marmalade or a stately rib roast. This is a rib roast year. Birdie has volunteered to make dessert, although the most complicated confection she has baked since she left home is an apple pie with a crooked lattice crust.

It is three o'clock and her *bûche de Noël* hasn't begun to resemble a yule log, nor has Alice had her bath and changed into the red velvet dress Birdie wore twenty years ago. Luanne has packed it away with hand-sewn sachets she filled with her garden's lavender.

Joy-Ellen walks through the door, dressed for church, carrying a long Pyrex pan of macaroni and cheese. "Good Lord," she says, surveying the kitchen. "What's this?"

Birdie's hair is tied in what she now refers to as a *schmatte*, giving her all the flair of a shtetl milkmaid. "Chocolate cake, which I have to fill with this"—she points to a bowl of heavy cream whipped with Frangelico and ground hazelnuts—"and figure out how to roll up and decorate with these"—delicate mushrooms she's fashioned of sugared cranberries—"and confectioner's sugar to make it look like snow. I've been at it all day." It might be easier, she thinks, to assemble a modular home.

"What's wrong with a bundt? Dump a box of devil's food cake, chocolate pudding, and Cool Whip in a bowl and you're almost done."

"I was going for special."

"Show-off. You think these yokels you're related to can tell the difference?" Joy-Ellen slips off the jacket of her pantsuit, which is the blue of an IKEA bag. "Hand me an apron." She and Birdie begin to wrestle the dessert into shape, working without talking while tuned to Christmas carols on the radio. After twenty minutes she begs the question Birdie imagines her parents have made a pact not to ask. "What made Micah leave? He tried to convince me he could become a pig farmer."

Before she answers, Birdie places the last meringue mushroom on the *bûche de Noël*, now filled with whipped cream and rolled tight. "We don't see eye to eye on some important issues."

Joy-Ellen looks up from the cake. "Could you be any more evasive? These 'issues' suddenly appeared after you decided to marry him?"

Birdie wonders, When did her grandmother start following Mel and Veronika's pushy playbook? She turns her back on Joy-Ellen and stares through the ice-frosted window, as if a red-winged blackbird will reveal the answer so she won't have to.

"We have a tricky situation that's kind of festered and escalated. I'd rather not talk about it."

"Fair enough. But if you'll allow me to speak my mind . . ."

Do I have a choice? Birdie thinks.

"I have the sense you're letting life happen to you rather than figuring out what you want and helping to make it happen—if you can."

Birdie faces her grandmother. "Is this your philosophy?"

"Until I come up with a better one." Joy-Ellen stands back to assess their handiwork. "Not bad, huh?"

"It better taste as good as it looks," Birdie says.

"By the way, do you and Micah still love each other?" Joy-Ellen asks with all the innocence of the angel on top of the tree. Birdie is deciding how to answer the question when a leggy white puppy bounds into the kitchen, barking, followed by her brother Clark, here from Minneapolis. Bringing up the rear is Buckshot, incensed to see a visitor lap up his water, leaving puddles on the floor. Kids!

"Stop! Pringle!" Clark says sharply to his dog as he rubs Buckshot's back. "Sorry, old boy. I really must get this cur *Tiffany's Table Manners for Teenagers*."

"You really must give your little sister a kiss."

"And your old granny. I'm not in mothballs yet."

"And who is this vision in red?" Alice has entered the kitchen, transformed into Clara from *The Nutcracker Suite*. The room buzzes with greetings until Luanne's voice, like a whistle stopping a race, rises above the hubbub to remind her brood that church starts in one hour and fifteen minutes. They all better be showered, dressed, and ready.

Sixty-five minutes later, a blizzard of Petersons and one Lindstrom crowd into cars and pickups and reach Grace Lutheran as its bells stop pealing. Inside, candles glow, casting citrine light, lifting the room to meditative. Their family fills a whole pew and then some, middle right, as always. Russ Jr. and his wife and kids file in first, then Clark and Joy-Ellen, Russ and Luanne, and finally, Birdie and Alice toward the center aisle.

The church is packed, not unlike Micah's synagogue to hear Kol Nidre. As if a high school yearbook has come to life, Birdie waves to Big Jen, Darrell, and their children and other friendly faces. Pastor Paul, the minister she knows from her high school years—a man blessed with compassion, two chins, and eyebrows that call to mind grasshoppers—sits quietly on the pulpit. A pastor in her thirties greets the congregants. Her long, lank hair is tied back by a wide white ribbon that matches her vestments.

Birdie feels a tap on her shoulder. "Can I squeeze in?" It is Leif, whispering. "My family got here too late to sit together." Birdie wiggles toward Alice to make room for him.

When the choir to which she and Leif used to belong begins to sing, the honeyed four-part harmony rises to the rafters, and the room feels like a miniature Carnegie Hall. Birdie closes her eyes and absorbs the purity of the sound. Soon the music toggles to prayer, however, and the female pastor's words feel rote, more op-ed than spiritual. The room is stuffy. Birdie's wool skirt and sweater itch. Alice fidgets. Birdie fidgets. Her mother flashes a stern look.

The pastor preaches about beginnings and endings, and God's hope for His children to make peace with all of God's people. Birdie tries to take the message to heart. Can she and Micah begin again? It's been months—before she left for Iowa—since she has seen traces of the husband she misses and, in many ways, still loves. The man who has replaced Micah is distant, trapped in quicksand. She doesn't know when she'll see her body-snatched husband again, or if he has always been a mirage. She blinks back tears and tries to concentrate on the sermon, which is earnest and wordy. Her mind wanders until she hears her name.

Pastor Paul, the emeritus minister, is now at the lectern. "Tonight, it warms my heart to see our young friends Leif Nordbeck and Birdie Peterson. Welcome. For those who don't know Leif and Birdie, they grew up in our community. Before they left for their education and broader horizons they were each a vital part of this church, as choir members and leaders in our youth ministry. Will you come forward, Leif and Birdie?"

No! Birdie feels her face flush and shuts her eyes, as if that will make her disappear. She imagines this crowd of family, friends, and strangers rushing toward her like high tide. But Leif grabs her arm, drags her into the aisle, and grins, as if he is in on a joke.

They reach the pulpit, where the pastor with the preposterous eyebrows encircles them with his long arms—the men here are alarmingly tall—offers a short blessing, and asks, "Would you do us the kindness of singing tonight? Any carol or hymn of your choosing."

Birdie is sure her face is the color of Alice's dress. Her brain freezes. The last time she sang in public was at a karaoke bar with Micah, when after three margaritas she did a pretty fair rendition of "You're So Vain." She cannot remember one churchy tune. "I Had a Little Dreidel" worms through her brain. Birdie wants to bolt, grab Alice, and run. But med school has apparently turned Leif into a showboat. "'O Holy Night'?" he suggests, unruffled, and starts to sing softly, in the resonant baritone she remembers.

After a few bars, Birdie chimes in with a trembling alto, but Leif's voice is strong. A trapdoor in her soul opens and the words come back to her along with an energy charge. Soon, Leif's and Birdie's voices merge, a capella.

"The stars are brightly shining. It is the night of our dear Savior's birth." The choir and parishioners join in, rousing and heartfelt. Birdie can hear her father's voice booming above the others, and she finds her way to, *"O night, o holy night, o night divine."* She

can't help but smile and when Birdie turns to Leif, he is smiling, too, and they are eighteen. He's in a rented tux and she's wearing his gardenia corsage pinned on an aqua satin gown with eyelet trim sewn by her mother.

Birdie and Leif return to their pew, taking in the smiling *thank you*s. "Good job, Mommy," Alice says, and kisses her on the cheek. She feels a tap on her shoulder, turns, and Leif does the same, planting a kiss on her other cheek.

The minister offers a benediction. As her words float above them, Leif presses his thigh close to Birdie's leg and squeezes her hand. She presses his hand in return, which she hopes no one sees. Their contact hovers between platonic and erotic. Birdie does not want the benediction or the touch to end, but both do, and they tumble out of the church, wishing Christmas greetings to one and all in the starry, nineteen-degree evening.

Later, Alice is too excited to go to sleep. "No time for a story tonight," Birdie says. "Close your eyes, so you can wake up early and see what Santa left you."

"But what if Santa looks for me in Brooklyn?"

"Santa is smart. That's not going to happen." Birdie tucks Alice's quilt tightly around her and kisses her forehead.

"Mommy, do you miss anything from Brooklyn?"

Not at this very moment, Birdie thinks. "What do you miss?"

"Sidewalks," Alice says, after thoughtful deliberation. "We don't have them here. I can't scoot."

Alice had taken to her scooter immediately. A gift for her third birthday, it became her Jaguar, whizzing with shocking velocity along Brooklyn's tilting sidewalks, upended by tree roots. "You are a great scooter-rider. I'm sorry you don't have it here."

"That's okay, Mommy, but you didn't say what you miss."

Moving to New York City, she'd assumed she'd land in the Manhattan of her imagination. Micah, however, insisted on crossing the river to north Brooklyn, where she has lived in the parlor-floor apartment of a gently sagging brownstone that commands a heart-stopping rent. Birdie does not miss the apartment, which is small and dark, though some people might call it cozy, but she does miss her neighborhood. Kinetic energy seeps out of their hood colonized by people so diverse her farm-girl background fails to mark her as an oddity. This is—was—one of the best things about her city life. Should she explain to Alice that she misses hearing languages that aren't English, and seeing faces that aren't uniformly white?

"I miss pedicures," she admits instead. They were a monthly indulgence she justified because as a yoga instructor her feet were on display. She imagines she could find a salon here at one of the malls, but the closest one is almost an hour away and most likely the manicurists wouldn't be gossiping in Korean. It would feel all wrong, and anyway, no one sees her bare feet at the bookstore.

"I miss pigeons," Alice says. "Why aren't there pigeons in Iowa?"

"We have different birds—crows, grackles, sparrows, robins. And we saw a cardinal the other day."

"I also miss sushi. Especially tuna avocado rolls. Your turn, Mommy."

Now that Birdie thinks about it, she would kill for a tuna avocado roll. "I miss sushi, too, and pizza."

"Daddy told me Iowa pizza sucks."

"Alice Tobias, language," Birdie says, though Micah is right.

"Sorry, Mommy. One more?"

"Only one. You need to get up early. Santa, remember?"

"I miss Daddy."

She kisses her daughter and says, "I love you." Birdie feels no antagonism toward Micah. She isn't feeling much at all, which is worse.

Soon Birdie crawls into her own bed and thinks of sushi and pigeons, sidewalks and pedicures, and tries not to think of Micah, who makes her heart hurt. But mostly, like the teenager she was only five years ago, Birdie replays every minute with Leif until she begins to outline a story, her first in years. She decides it will have a happy ending.

O holy night, indeed.

CHAPTER 38

Mel

"HOW ARE YOU, ALICE HONEY?" TODAY HER GRANDDAUGHTER wears Pippi Longstocking braids.

Alice freezes and stares at Birdie, who says, "Please answer Gran."

"Did you have a good day?" I didn't, but this isn't about me. Alice says nothing. "What did you do at day care?"

"Tell Gran how you painted a picture of a Christmas tree," Birdie urges.

"Will you show me?" I say with sufficient gusto for a Louvre full of paintings.

Alice abandons the computer and that's the last I see of her. Given that at this hour she is hungry, tired, and cranky—as am I—on weekdays we have a short window to tryst. This is no way to be a grandmother and it doesn't get better when Jake joins our cyber-soirees on the weekends. But I hope this is a temporary problem, resolved by Birdie and Alice's return. I have not filled the Tuesday and Thursday afternoons reserved for Alice, which is why I couldn't say no when Veronika prevailed on me to stop by this Thursday to visit David. "I don't want him to be alone," she said and added, "please," which is as close to pleading as I suspect my mother-in-law will ever get. "He does best when he spends time with people he knows, and I can't cut back on my practice."

Can't or won't? I don't press. Being with a loved one whose mind is flickering requires inordinate patience. This is not among Veronika's many gifts.

As I walk to David and Veronika's apartment, Jordan calls. Not a text, a *call*, to which my knee-jerk response is a breathless "Is everything okay?"

"Better than okay," she trills. "We're in."

Getting accepted by a New York City co-op board is an ordeal requiring invasive paperwork and acid-tongued interviews, grueling and despised. "Great, but I didn't know you were moving," I admit. Or why. Jordan lives in a sunny downtown loft with a view of Lady Liberty. She has her own washer and dryer—a reality American suburbanites take for granted and two-thirds of New Yorkers covet—and enough room for a baby.

"Who said I was moving?" she asks, peeved. "Kit and I got approved by the bank." When in my confusion I don't respond she clarifies with, "The sperm bank. We're a go."

I let this sink in before I say, feebly, "I should congratulate you."

"You should, and ask about your future grandchild's daddy."

Do I have a choice? "Tell me everything."

"He's originally from the Netherlands, straight reddish-blond hair and tall like me, a history professor at Duke. Before grad school at the University of Chicago he went to Stanford, where he was a champion fencer."

Handy for family duels.

"No allergies, plays the banjo, used to edit a humor magazine . . ."

How about kindness? Sensitivity? Open-mindedness? Creativity?

"Light drinker, no drug use or smoking, two living parents

and three living grandparents . . ." Jordan continues with the exceptional résumé of her chosen sperm, which will arrive via very special delivery in a few days.

"He sounds like the right stuff, all right. When are you getting inseminated?"

"This is getting old." Her voice is a piercing keen. "*Kit's* carrying the baby. You're fucking relentless."

"I thought"—okay, hoped—"the matter might still be under discussion."

"It's not and never has been."

"Jordan, please hear me out," I say eventually. "My feelings have nothing to do with cockeyed prejudice about genetic superiority, if that's what's worrying you. If you adopt a child, that would be wonderful." And a better idea, not that I get a vote. "My goal is to protect you, sweetheart. If Kit is the biological mother and things get rocky between you, the child—who will have no biological connection to you—may disappear from your life. From our life. Like Alice seems to be. I don't want to see your heart broken, and frankly, I don't want to be hurt myself." I suck in a big breath before I let fly with, "Kit is very young. This decision to have a baby is rather . . . impulsive, and if she changes her mind about your relationship after she's had the child, I worry that she's likely to feel the custodial rights are more hers than yours."

"Did you read that from notes? You may be the most manipulative person I've ever met. I'm hanging up now," Jordan says, and does.

I guess I could have handled that better. As the day progresses, I consider calling to apologize, but for what—telling the truth? The more I obsess, the more convinced I am that neither Jordan nor Kit is ready to be anyone's mother.

CHAPTER 39

Mel

I ARRIVE AT DAVID AND VERONIKA'S APARTMENT, WHERE THE doorman hands me an envelope containing a key. *David is napping, so please let yourself in*, a note from Veronika says. Her cursive looks almost like calligraphy. *There's tuna salad in the refrigerator. Thank you.*

My in-laws' apartment is tranquil and orderly, with no overdue library books, unmailed packages and future dry cleaning piled by the front door, no plants starved for water, no pillows that need fluffing or baseboards that need painting. The only sound is a classical music station playing Brahms. I quietly call David's name. He doesn't answer and as I walk toward the closed master bedroom door, I hear him snoring.

I make myself a cup of decaf and a piece of toast, which I top with the tuna salad, to which I wish Veronika hadn't added grated carrots. When I finish I check David again. His snores, which drown out Brahms, are making me feel tired. I stretch out on the couch in the den under a mohair throw, and set the timer on my phone for a twenty-minute snooze.

My ear-piecing alarm wakes me from my power nap, refreshed. I visit the powder room, then knock on David and

Veronika's bedroom door. No answer. I knock again. "David," I call out. The snoring has ceased, so I add, "It's Mel. I thought we could take a walk after your lunch, but we better get going." No answer. "David," I say again, a little louder.

Now I'm worried. I open the door and step inside the bedroom. A pillow is out of its sham and a tousled afghan covers the bed, but David isn't here, nor is he in the master bathroom, whose door is open. I search the apartment. His phone is on the foyer table, but his shearling jacket is gone and so, apparently, is he.

I AM STANDING outside my in-laws' building, frantic. The doorman said Mr. Tobias left about twenty minutes ago. I don't know where to look first. In the park? There are two nearby, each stretching north and south for miles like giant cigars. Central Park is bigger and in the north end, near us, some of its winding, woody paths are, while enchanting, darkly clandestine. You could disappear for days. Riverside Park is smaller but, in places, dangerously close to the Hudson. David could have drowned—or be anywhere. He might have hopped on the bus or subway, since he loves to exercise his I-can-go-all-the-way-to-Coney-Island-for-half-price senior MetroCard. I shut my eyes at the image of my father-in-law surveying the city from the top of the Wonder Wheel, swinging his long legs while stuffing himself with a hot dog dripping mustard, onions, relish, and sauerkraut, which Veronika would forbid.

"You lost my father?" Jake says when I call, his voice sharp and needling.

"I didn't *lose* your father," I moan. "He was sleeping when I arrived so I conked out for my own catnap, just ten minutes"—I lie—"and I guess he woke up and forgot I was visiting—"

"Spare me. I hope that's not all he forgot and that he knows his address and the way home from wherever the fuck he is." I hear a heavy exhale. "Why don't you start looking on Broad-way? I'm on the way and I'll bring a few of the guys from the store to help search."

"Should I call the police?" The other day someone's beloved spaniel tied up outside a supermarket was liberated by a stranger. Within hours lampposts sprouted no-questions-asked flyers fea-turing a snatched dog with flowing blond ears along with threat-ening Grand Larceny notices from the police. But involving law enforcement and arranging for a Gold Alert—the one they issue for an impaired senior citizen—would be the equivalent of an-nouncing in the *New York Times* that David Tobias is non compos mentis. Veronika would murder me.

"Hold off with the police for now," Jake says, reading my mind.

I start to briskly walk down Broadway, casing every bar, pizza or ice cream parlor, open restaurant, bakery, and coffeeshop from Starbucks to old-time Greek. I hit Harry's, a venerable shoe bazaar David likes to frequent; bookstores, large and small; dry cleaners and barber shops; drug, hardware, liquor, office supply, cell phone, and dollar stores. I skip manicure, false eyelash and hair salons, women's boutiques, and banks. I have no idea which one David patronizes. Does he? I speed-walk through a shop selling rosaries, a Judaica emporium loaded with mezuzahs as big as challahs, and sprint through Zabar's, Fairway, Westside Market, and Citarella. I'll say this about my neighborhood: you won't starve.

Every few minutes I check in with Jake. "This is like look-ing for an ant at a picnic," I say after three hours. "Time to call the police?"

"Hold off."

"But it's going to get dark soon."

"We've got eight people looking. Let's give it another hour . . ."

I walk the aisles of more stores, and move on only when I'm convinced that David isn't lurking in a corner. As the sun fades, I imagine him dazed and disoriented. Then a man of my father-in-law's height wearing a similar jacket—and a buzz cut—walks in my direction, carrying a Dunkin' bag.

"Mel," he shouts, all chuckles and cheer. "What brings you here?"

This is my neighborhood. Why wouldn't I be here? "Looking for you. We had a date."

"We did?" he says, unimpressed, and from the greasy bag offers me a jelly donut, which I decline.

"Quite a haircut." Veronika will faint.

"Don't you think it makes me look younger?"

Or like a skinhead? "Shall we walk to your place together?"

"By all means." David offers me his arm, and sets off in the wrong direction.

I steer him right. "Damn it, sometimes I don't know which end is up," he says merrily, and polishes off one donut, then another. We walk for twenty blocks in silence punctuated only by a call to Jake.

When we reach the apartment, Veronika folds her arms around her husband as Jake and, to my surprise, Micah, stand by. "Darling," she says, "your beautiful hair is gone." But that is all.

As if it's a party, David goes to the kitchen to make cocktails. Standing next to Veronika, her eyes red-rimmed, this is when I offer to turn my Alice afternoons into David afternoons. Despite the demerits I may have earned for being a prison matron unable to prevent his madcap dash toward freedom, she accepts.

CHAPTER 40

Veronika

Y OUR GRANDFATHER APPRECIATES YOUR VISITS," VERONIKA tells Jordan. The last two Saturday mornings, after Nova and bagels, David and his granddaughter have raced through the crossword puzzle, still one of his daily rituals. Today he had no problem interpreting the clue, *Part of the brain that's always working*. He just can't make his own brain do the same. David's dementia is spotty, unpredictable, and aggressive. From moment to moment, Veronika doesn't know if the man by her side is her husband or a mystifying imposter.

"Does Grandpa like his aide?" Jordan asks.

"Kieran is a miracle," built like a mini-van and blessed with a brogue. He is trying to teach his charge the intricacies of Irish football and has introduced him to *The Simpsons* and fart jokes. How much of either David absorbs Veronika doesn't care to estimate.

"And my mom—I gather she's still coming over?"

"Two afternoons a week"—which Jordan would know if she and her mother were speaking. "Melanie actually appears to enjoy your grandfather's company," Veronika adds, though she can't understand how her daughter-in-law remains unflappable when David repeats the same weather forecast four times within the hour. Melanie is endlessly patient, with a temperament set at cheerful. Veronika cannot say the same for herself.

"All of us enjoy Grandpa," Jordan says. "He's still the same man we love." Veronika's face must convey her disbelief because Jordan asks, "Nana, is it hell?" and takes her hand, which tenses.

No one but Micah has asked Veronika how she's doing, not even Jake. This is what comes from a lifetime of stiff-upper-lipping enhanced by listening to patients drone on about loved ones who are miles away from interesting. Since Veronika is far more comfortable asking questions than answering them, she says, "Let's talk about you. Have you and your girlfriend—"

"Kit."

"—moved in together?"

"Last month."

"When am I going to meet her?"

"Soon," Jordan stammers. "Promise."

She's afraid I'll terrify this girl. "So, tell me. Is Kit the one? Are you compatible?" Such a sexless word. Veronika is glad it is fading from everyday vernacular.

"Like cookies and milk."

When Jordan smiles, for Veronika it's like looking in a mirror, circa 1970. "I hear you're exploring motherhood."

"We're trying to get pregnant, Mel's bent out of shape because Kit's going to carry the baby, not me."

"Because you're perpetually flying off to Silicon Valley or Dubai or Montenegro?"

"Precisely." Jordan sighs.

"I know your life is complicated, but I would not dismiss your mother's opinion." Veronika almost calls Jordan *honey,* but can't quite get there. "Your father has mentioned Melanie's concerns, that your girlfriend—"

"Kit."

"—that Kit might abscond with the baby like Birdie has our Alice."

"Pure batshittery, huh?"

Veronika sees no reason to sugarcoat. "Your mother has a point and you'd be a fool not to consider it."

Jordan looks older when she frowns, and Veronika can imagine her at thirty, with wrinkles etching her forehead. "The two of you," Jordan says, "you're both narcissists who want a little clone. I say this in the nicest possible way."

"Would a clone be so bad?" Veronika pictures a confident, capable, chess-playing child with a cascade of red curls. "And by the way, why are you making such a *tzimmes* about this when there's an obvious, easy alternative?" She snaps her fingers.

Jordan cocks her head and snaps her fingers in return. "I'm listening."

"Ask your brother to donate sperm." Veronika brushes her hands together as if she's wiping away a crumb or two.

Jordan suppresses a laugh and slowly shakes her head. "You can't be serious."

"When am I not serious?"

"Wasn't there one time when you put your underpants on your head? Or is that an urban legend?"

"Hear me out. Kit carries the baby, like you both want, but with your brother's seed instead of your Dutchman's. The baby will be half Tobias, your flesh and blood. Not only does this resolve the issue bothering your mother, that the baby will have no biological connection to you, you won't have to worry that your donor fathered hundreds of other children and in twenty years' time, your baby dates his or her own sibling. I'm sure you've read exposés on this." Veronika overlooks that it was she who suggested the sperm bank Jordan and her girlfriend use.

"Do you think Micah would ever say yes?"

That she's gotten Micah's consent already will be their little secret. "You'll have to ask him," she says.

CHAPTER 41

Mel

A RE YOU WORKING WITH MANY COUPLES NOW?"

"Not at the moment," I admit, "though relationships are often front and center in the issues my clients discuss."

"Do you enjoy your work?"

"Very much." It still amazes me that people pay good money for my observations and advice.

"Would you consider a change?"

I hadn't until he asked the question. "For the right situation, maybe."

I can almost pretend this isn't a job interview. Dr. T and I are at The Carlyle hotel on the Upper East Side of Manhattan sitting in a dimly lit room at a leather banquette the color of whiskey. The other customers are old and prosperous, some a full generation up from Veronika and David. I imagine them waiting for George Gershwin's ghost to play "Love Is Here to Stay."

This is a tourist trap Jake and I would never pick for a drink, with a ceiling too gold and red-jacketed waiters too fawning. If we were together we'd mock the snobbery—though as my eyes take in murals by Ludwig Bemelmans, who created the *Madeline* books, I wonder what it would be like to bring Alice here. I am eye to eye with a rabbit in a smoking jacket who may have just mooned me.

Dr. T has been the very definition of professional. We met at five in the lobby, where he was reading a journal he was published in this month. His peck on my cheek was gentlemanly, and his compliments, generous.

"Melanie, you haven't changed in twenty years," he cooed, overlooking that no one will ever again compare my waist to Scarlett O'Hara's.

"I could say the same of you, Ted," I respond, overlooking that his hair has thinned and his V-shaped torso has thickened to a meaty rectangle I'd describe as portly, were I to tell another living soul about this appointment, which I will not. Our conversation is entirely aboveboard, but I feel Dr. T undressing me. This feels disreputable. Flirtatious. Hot.

Since we're here to discuss troubled couples, I sip my champagne and tell him about the client formerly known as Bambi. "She was blindsided when her husband left, though she hasn't begged him to return. The other guy she's seeing is quite the player. I can't imagine this relationship lasting, but I hope my client comes to that conclusion herself. I like her."

Dr. T pushes his hair away from his eyes. He is wearing his wedding ring, as am I, a gold band embedded with a trio of modest diamonds. Jake designed it, inspired by a ring I admired from the third century at the Metropolitan Museum. I love it far more than any of the chunky diamonds and sapphires that weigh down the fingers of many of my friends.

"Do you feel you may have become overly attached to this Bambi?"

"Possibly," I add, though I am not going to share the irrational bargain I've struck with myself, that if I can help keep her marriage together, Birdie will stay with Micah and all will be rosy in Tobias-land.

We dissect Bambi's situation until Dr. T asks me to describe another couples' case on which I'm working. "There's Frank and Lizzy," I say, because why not? "They've been married for a few years and have a little boy. Recently, Frank got involved in a hit-and-run. He'd been drinking. He may have hurt someone, but was never apprehended, and no witnesses have come forward. Regardless, Lizzy feels strongly that Frank should turn himself in. It's ripping them apart—literally. She's left Frank and is living with her parents in Dallas."

Dr. T finishes his champagne, as do I. The sweet bubbles have put me at risk of getting giggly. He orders a second round for both of us. "That's it?" he asks.

"Frank has tried to get Lizzy to return from Texas, but she's dug in her heels and refuses. Lizzy thinks Frank drinks too much, and sees him as immature. He's heartbroken that she's left, and so is his mother, who misses their child terribly." I stare intently at an elephant in the mural. "The mother is my client."

Dr. T leans forward. I smell the same aftershave he wore way back when. "Is this another client you've gotten attached to, maybe overattached?"

His X-ray vision drills into my heart and mind. "Possibly."

"Would you call your client, Frank's mother, a meddler?"

"Never," I snap. "She wants what's best for everyone. She'd like to see the marriage repaired."

"Even if that's not optimal for the couple?" We lock eyes. His are familiar, the chocolate of a Milky Way. "I know you haven't asked for my opinion—"

"Go ahead. Please." Grudgingly.

"Your client sounds overinvested in her son's marriage. She should be encouraged to back off and live her own life, not his."

I hate Dr. T for being right. Fortunately, he doesn't ask, *How would you suggest she do that?*—because I have no idea—and shares a few cases of his own, discussing strategies that have and haven't worked, and particulars about the couples' counseling practice he hopes to create in New York, replicating his Cleveland model. "I'd like to start with hiring a female therapist. Sometimes we'll tag team and role play." He gets into jargon-y particulars. I try to nod attentively, but having been reminded of Micah and Birdie, seventy-five percent of my brain is now grieving for the Alice-shaped hole that will be the collateral damage if "Frank and Lizzy's" marriage dissolves.

I sit up straighter when Dr. T mentions a salary. It's large. I'd agreed to tonight's meeting strictly out of curiosity and nostalgia, not thinking about dollars and cents. But maybe a lucrative upgrade would take my mind off my mulish son and faraway granddaughter, not to mention my faultfinding mother-in-law, regressing father-in-law, stubborn daughter, and preoccupied husband.

Dr. T peers at me with a half-smile. "Might you be interested in the collaboration we're discussing, Melanie?"

For the first time, I wonder if I should actually accept the position, were he to offer it. Could we work side-by-side? I toy with a lock of my hair. "You've given me a lot to think about."

"In that case, shall we continue this conversation? I made a reservation at a little Italian place a few blocks from here, near my hotel."

I picture flattering candlelight, a table where we lean in to chat, a touch on the arm, sharing a dessert. I think not. I wouldn't trust myself, not after three champagne cocktails. I don't remember when the third arrived, but its empty glass is in my hand.

"Thanks, Ted, but I have to get to my book club." Though my book club doesn't meet until tomorrow. "It starts at eight."

When I stand I'm more than a little woozy. Dr. T flashes me an inscrutable look as he puts his hand an inch or two too close to my behind, which was once higher, rounder, and the focal point of his considerable attention. Comparisons to cantaloupes were made. I wobble slightly as he guides me toward the coat check while I try to demonstrate at least the dignity of a best-in-show Afghan Hound. I feel twice as blitzed as I did thirty minutes ago, and recognize Dr. T's leer. He helps me into my faux fur coat that no one will ever mistake for mink, since mink is rarely pink, and I drape an ivory scarf around my neck. I don't have enough active brain cells to tie it properly.

Madison Avenue is uncrowded and hushed. Locals who colonize the neighborhood have escaped to beachy places or are at home, reading in front of a fireplace, or so I imagine. I'm happy to be outdoors. It's one of those evenings that makes me want to do an I-Love-New-York happy dance. We start walking uptown, admiring window displays in stores that are almost like museums, so few people ever seem to shop in them. Dr. T offers to hail a taxi. In short order, one slows down in front of us, and he helps me in.

I turn to thank him for the cocktails and conversation, but before I know what's happening, he's sweeps me into his arms and pulls me close. "I don't think you and I are finished yet," he says and kisses me, long and deep. I taste champagne, chemistry, and a man who isn't my husband.

TRAVELING IN THE moving cab, I shudder. I didn't initiate Dr. T's kiss, but neither did I pull away. I close my eyes and try to pretend it didn't happen. I don't want to think about how I should be feeling. Guilty? Revolted? Both are on the menu.

Jake and Micah had scheduled a mano-a-mano dinner. Over ribs and beer, the plan was for my husband to jumpstart our son into action with a last-ditch pitch to call on Detective Herrera, because it's the right thing to do, and not incidentally, may help him win back his wife and child. I'm grateful Jake will be out so

I can put some distance between Dr. T and reality. When I open the door and hang my coat, however, I hear Jake's and Micah's voices, hooting and happy.

"Mel, hon?" Jake shouts. "We're back here." As I walk toward our family room, I hope Jake doesn't ask me where I've been, because I don't want to lie. I catch a break, because all he does is whistle and say, "Looking good. You should show your legs more often, babe." I'm wearing a sweater with a neckline halfway to skank, a pencil skirt, black stockings, and stilettoes. I had given some thought to my attire.

Empty bottles of beer litter the coffee table along with containers of Indian food. I kiss my husband and son, who offers me a Kingfisher on which I pass. The curry and cumin I smell are making me queasy.

"What happened to ribs?" I ask.

"We decided to celebrate at home instead," Jake says.

Celebrate? Micah called the detective! Birdie and Alice are returning! He sold his business for a wad of cash!

Jake claps Micah on the back. "Greet your daughter and her girlfriend's new sperm donor."

I'm drunk enough so that I have to ask Jake to repeat what he just said. "Whose idea was this?" I ask, incredulous.

"My mother's," Jake says, as if Veronika had negotiated peace between the Hutus and the Tutsis. "Brilliant, huh?"

"You don't think this will be . . . strange? And twisted? Being the father of your sister's child doesn't strike you as a little . . ." I say it. "Incestuous?"

"Why? I was already going to be an uncle," Micah says. "What's the big deal?"

"You're only questioning the idea because my mother thought of it—and that you're the last to know," Jake blurts out.

Suddenly, all I want to do is rip off my Spanx, chug a glass of cold water, and collapse under cool sheets. If I'm lucky I will pass out, and when I wake, lambast Jake on why he apparently never discussed The Incident and Micah coming clean with the detective, which was supposed to be the point of tonight, not anointing our son as his sister's sperm donor. "We're not done, but you'll have to excuse me, please," I say and slink off to our bedroom.

CHAPTER 42

Birdie

When Leif asks Birdie to go skating on New Year's Eve, her answer is no. Leif isn't the problem. Micah is. Skating will remind her far too much of him. They skated often, in Prospect Park, Bryant Park, and Central Park—before they discovered Donald Trump ran the rinks.

That a Manhattan guy knew his way around the ice surprised Birdie, which showed how little she understood a city childhood. Micah had played hockey in middle and high school, and Jake got up before dawn to drive him to Chelsea Piers for six thirty a.m. lessons. This led to watching the New York Rangers play at Madison Square Garden and Jake allowing Micah to toss F-bombs at the opposing team: variations on *cocksucker*, *motherfucker*, and *twat* limited only by his son's imagination. Micah excelled at this activity, and regretted that he couldn't list it on his college applications, since unlike Jordan, he hadn't served on Model UN, played varsity basketball or the flute, qualified for Math Honors Society, founded an anti-bullying organization, or run the manga club.

The second time Leif asks Birdie about skating, a month has passed. He is in town because his grandmother is visiting. This time, Birdie accepts the invitation. Tonight, at seven-thirty, after she's tucked in Alice with her emotional-support monkey, Leif rings the bell. Birdie has stopped replaying mental YouTubes of their moment at church, and has convinced herself that the warm touch she remembers was strictly chaste. She tells herself she isn't going on a date, though she's upgraded from ChapStick to lipstick and broken out her Jo Malone London Vanilla & Anise cologne.

Leif makes Birdie happy. It's unnerving how happy he makes her, in a completing-each-other's-sentences, life-doesn't-need-to-be-complicated kind of way. But Birdie realizes you can't compare a beginning to the thick of it that is marriage, especially one that includes a child.

Beneath his unzipped down jacket, Leif is wearing a red-and-white-striped sweater. Given his height, he calls to mind a peppermint stick performing in *The Nutcracker Suite*, an association Birdie regrets because it reminds her of Mel's disappointment in being unable to take Alice to see the production. Leif pulls open the jacket to give Birdie a full view of his sweater. "This is entirely my grandmother's fault and since she's visiting, wearing it is compulsory."

"Did I say one word?"

"Your face speaks for you."

"Are we going to the school?" Birdie asks when they're in the car. Every winter, the volunteer fire department floods the softball field, creating a glassy rink that freezes solidly through spring. A log hut functions as a warming house, heated by a pot-bellied stove. For Birdie, it invokes a Proustian memory of wet wool and the clean smell of melting snow mingling with the pipe smoke from the old coot who kept the fire stoked and tightened skate laces.

"You'll see. Patience."

Leif drives on back roads for miles in the opposite direction of the school, and parks near a pine grove. By flashlight, they hike to a clearing, where they are rewarded by the sight of a large frozen pond, partly cleared of snow and illuminated by a full moon hanging in a cloudless, starlit sky—a backwoods version of blazing LED streetlights. It is also magic.

"We can change here," he says. They each straddle a bench. He slips into timeworn hockey skates. Birdie laces Luanne's figure skates, their blue yarn pompoms bobbing, and heads toward the pond. This is her first time on the ice since last year, and she staggers like a drunken sorority girl stumbling out of a frat party, sure she will fall on her fanny. Within minutes muscle memory kicks in, however—as it will—and her gliding becomes almost like flying, making her feel as if she is living up to her name.

Whenever Birdie skates, she feels propelled by a purring motor and never wants to stop. With Leif's boom box blaring, they skate for nearly an hour, tracing figure eights and spins, practicing jumps and self-styled lutzes. They have the pond to themselves, observed only by a family of bored deer and, briefly, an owl who literally asks, "Who?"

"The judge gives you four points for skill and ten points for effort," Leif says in a hybrid accent of Russian and Italian.

Birdie futzes with Leif's boom box, and Patsy Cline begins to sing "Always." "The North Korean judge demands that you ask the lady to dance," she says. They attempt a waltz, for which they'd be lucky to get a middling score from even the most generous judge, but this does not dampen the mood. When the music stops, Leif doesn't let go. You're married, Birdie reminds herself as he holds her and she holds her breath, fearing yet hoping he will kiss her. To make sure he doesn't, she goes full-on Wikipedia and says, "You know Irving Berlin wrote this for his wife when they got married?"

"And gave her all the royalties. Some romantic, Irving."

Flakes as big as dimes begin to fall, and the wind kicks up, blowing powdery snow across their faces. Birdie shivers.

"How does a bowl of chili sound?" Leif asks. "I know this hole-in-the-wall that may still be open."

Birdie imagines tartan and taxidermy. She is right about the taxidermy. The head of a disgruntled elk hangs by the door of a dark, knotty-pine café. A few barflies nurse beers, along with various sad sacks you'd think twice about hiring to shovel your driveway. But the chili is hot and spicy, the beer is cold and earthy, the potato skins are piled with crisp bacon and gooey cheddar, and the cornbread is as tasty as anything Birdie has eaten in Brooklyn. Their conversation sticks to his residency, her bookstore job. She steers clear of Micah, and Leif asks no questions about him. If he has a woman in his life, Leif fails to mention her. Birdie gives the food a seven, the ambiance a two, and Leif, a nine.

It's almost ten o'clock when they pull into her driveway, her heart full of something agreeable and confusing. She wishes the evening didn't have to end. It is the best time she's had in . . . she doesn't want to think how long.

"May I kiss you?" he asks.

"Not yet," is her answer.

"May I see you in two weeks?"

To this she doesn't hesitate. "I'd like that."

Birdie lets herself into the house, which is still and toasty. Luanne has lit a caramel-scented candle in the living room and is curled beneath a quilt, absorbed in *The Liars' Club*. "Bird, don't you ever dare tell me our family or the one you married into is dysfunctional," she says, taking off her readers and looking up. Birdie perches on the edge of the couch beside her mother's feet in their bright red socks. Hank Williams is twanging away on the radio, so lonesome he could cry. Birdie has heard more country music tonight than she's listened to in a year.

"Have a good time?" Luanne asks.

"I did."

"The skates work out?"

"Perfectly. How was Alice?"

"Never made a peep. How's Leif?"

"He took me to a pond I didn't know existed."

"You know that's not what I'm asking."

Birdie meets her mother's gaze. Hank sings on about midnight trains and purple skies. "I forgot how much I like him, Mom. I might like him a lot. I don't know what to do."

Luanne's eyes narrow. "You know exactly what to do."

Her mother would know what to do. She always does. But that is not true for Birdie. She gets up, kisses Luanne's cheek, and starts to head upstairs, planning to add a page or two to the story she'd started.

"By the way, we're going to have a visitor tomorrow," her mother says, unsuccessfully trying to keep a straight face.

Birdie freezes on the second step. "Is Micah coming back?" They speak, text, or FaceTime every day. He's offered sketchy updates on his grandfather's mental state, but he hasn't mentioned returning to Iowa—or other bald-faced news that would make a difference in her life.

"Guess again."

Holy hell. "Mel?" No, no, no. Birdie is not ready to deal with her mother-in-law, though she'll say this for the woman, she's in touch with her feelings. If only Mel understood that her way of looking at life is not the only way.

"Wrong again."

"Clark?" She loves being around her brother.

"Nope. It's herself, Dr. Tobias."

CHAPTER 43

Veronika

I F YOU WANT A JOB DONE RIGHT, MORE OFTEN THAN NOT, YOU have to do it yourself. Veronika would have preferred not to fly to Iowa. She's busy—she's always busy—and had to prevail upon Jake and Melanie to stay with David so he has twenty-four-hour attention, not merely the afternoons with Melanie and the time with Kieran, their Irish Messiah. Nor is she looking forward to changing planes at O'Hare, with its tangle of concourses and pulsating chaos. But Veronika has appointed herself the emissary of sanity who will ensure that Birdie and little Alice hurry home. This stalemate has dragged on long enough. Micah's wife clearly needs to be talked down from whatever heartland ledge into which she's dug her heels.

How has the Midwest earned the honor of being called the heartland, Veronika grumbles as she wheels her bag to the gate. Veronika sees the region as a vast, under-landscaped wilderness clogged with cheese and bland white bread where people excessively apologize, judge one another by whether they've raked their lawns, and bake naïveté into Tater Tot hot dishes, which she's glad she's never tasted.

Veronika keeps these opinions to herself, of course, lest she be cast as that insufferable stereotype, the rude New Yorker who speaks like a Twitter feed. She boards the plane, finds her aisle seat, and immediately pops in earbuds to dissuade other flyers from launching a conversation. But before she has a chance to begin listening to an academic podcast, the woman in the next seat assaults her with friendliness. Veronika Mona Lisa–smiles and allows only that she's visiting her granddaughter and great-granddaughter. "Oh, for fun!" the chatterer chirps.

There's nothing fun about the assignment Veronika has given herself, she thinks, as she considers her seatmate's peculiar idiom. One of these days she must study the linguistic oddities of Middle-westerners. *Oh, for fun. Wanna come with*? Indeed.

When she deplanes in Iowa, Veronika is walking briskly toward the taxi stand when someone calls out, "Dr. Tobias!" She swivels, squints, and spots a woman waving at her while moving with greater agility than anyone of her age and sturdy proportions typically does. Veronika stops short and recognizes Birdie's grandmother. They met four years ago, at Micah and Birdie's Iowa wedding reception. The woman has one of those double-barreled names she associates less with the Midwest than with Southern family trees dripping Spanish moss and Confederate forefathers they shamelessly revere. Fannie-Mae? Norma-Jean? Jenny-Craig? Sara-Lee?

"Joy-Ellen Lindstrom!" the woman belts out as she reaches Veronika. "Hello there, Doctor. Thought I'd surprise you." Veronika is afraid the woman might hug her, but instead, she lunges toward Veronika's suitcase, saying, "Let me take that off your hands."

When she met Joy-Ellen several years ago, Veronika discovered they had three things in common. Both played excellent bridge and both knit, although Joy-Ellen chose yarn in cupcake colors, unlike the grey, taupe, or beige Veronika prefers, even for baby sweaters. The bigger point of commonality was that the woman didn't strike her as someone who lathered grand-children with praise. Rather, Veronika sensed that Joy-Ellen expected good behavior, which she didn't believe merited a re-ward every time it was demonstrated. She understood that su-perfluous clucking gave a child a swelled head—to exercise the local patois—and saved praise for occasions when children rose far beyond her expectations. In short, Veronika remembers that when she met Joy-Ellen Lindstrom, she had discovered a kin-dred spirit whom she liked. Not only was Birdie's grandmother the soul of her family, she was its compass. "How lovely to see you again," Veronika says, and means it.

"You, too, Doc."

"Do call me Veronika."

"Then you can call me Betty." The reference is lost on Ve-ronika and Joy-Ellen fails to get a laugh. "Have you eaten? We could stop for coffee."

Veronika also recalls local coffee, too watery to drink with half-and-half, the only way she likes it. "Thank you, but that won't be necessary." She checks her watch. "I should deposit my bag at my motel. Then I was planning to visit Birdie at the book-store for a chat before I see Alice. I'm only here until tomorrow."

"I'd be tickled if you'd stay at my place. I got the guest room ready. It has one of those heated mattress pads—heaven for old bones. Could I twist your arm?"

Veronika is always curious to see how people live behind closed doors. Can you sign your autograph in the dust? Do their medicine cabinets feature laxatives and Fleet enemas? Yet as tempting as Joy-Ellen's offer is for a student of human nature, Veronika also loathes being anyone's house guest, which too of-ten comes with a shifty, shedding cat who slinks along kitchen counters and the requirement to leave your shoes at the door, putting your bunions on display.

"You are truly kind, thank you very much. But I'm fine with my motel."

"Suit yourself. It's a real invitation, but I know better than to beg." Joy-Ellen belly laughs.

The women bushwhack through the airport, sidestepping slower travelers. Veronika tries to supplant her customary hubris with gratitude as she observes peers being escorted in wheelchairs or chauffeured in motorized carts. She'd like to pretend the age she will soon be turning—seventy-five—is the new forty-five, but what kind of drivel is that? How many more robust years remain before her body betrays her? Is she one broken hip or diagnosis away from a downward spiral? Like David.

How would it feel to travel with him now? More to the point, will they ever again take a trip? Veronika has quietly canceled the family celebration in New Orleans that they'd planned for her birthday. When she informed Jake, Melanie, Jordan, and Micah, she sensed palpable relief.

Leading them outside, the air hits Veronika like a blister pack of icicles. They reach a slippery parking lot and stop by a small green pickup truck where Joy-Ellen hoists herself into the driver's seat. Veronika follows suit. She can't remember being a passenger in a truck, ever. Joy-Ellen backs out deftly and as she begins to drive away on roads packed hard with snow says, "Birdie's looking forward to seeing you."

The chyron in Veronika's mind reads *I wouldn't put good money on that*, but she is glad to have her dreary sentiments interrupted.

"Birdie thinks very highly of you," Joy-Ellen adds.

"As she does you," Veronika responds. Birdie is not a big talker—at least not with the Tobias family—but within the parameters of her meager speech, she often invokes the woman. *Grandma Lindstrom says this. Grandma Lindstrom says that.* "And of course, your daughter," whose name she can't recall. "But that's irrelevant, isn't it? How Birdie feels about my grandson, Micah, is the issue on the table and all that counts."

"The only thing." Joy-Ellen gives Veronika the side-eye. "And not, in my opinion, for us to mess with."

Veronika draws in a long breath. "I respect you, Joy-Ellen. You are a woman of strength and principle. But this is where I hope we agree to respectfully disagree."

"I can't convince you not to interfere, if I can be so blunt?"

"Be as blunt as you want, but please understand I am here harboring only the best of intentions—and you will never change my mind." Ever. They drive in heavy silence. Veronika leaves her suitcase at the motel, Joy-Ellen drops her at Field of Dreams, and soon she finds herself face to face with Micah's wife, the second Mrs. Tobias clinging to her maiden name.

"Thank you for making the trip," Birdie says, one of several pleasantries she offers along with brownies and blondies, which Veronika declines. She walks Veronika through the shop, which would exceed Veronika's expectations if she had any. She does love a snug, independent bookstore, the only kind she patronizes. This one's a gem, with a good selection of mid-century British literature—Veronika's favored genre—here in the tundra. Yet certainly, Field of Dreams cannot be enough to keep Birdie from coming home.

Birdie settles them at a corner table. The double espresso she brings to Veronika isn't too bitter and only a lifetime of self-discipline prevents her from eating a second bacon-cheddar-chive scone.

"I imagine you know why I'm here," Veronika says, as if anyone in their right mind would casually jet into Iowa in the winter.

"I imagine I do."

Over the years, Veronika has noticed that Birdie never refers to her as Nana, as Micah does, nor does she invoke *Veronika*. Their relationship exists in a username Siberia. "Then let's get on with it. What's preventing you from returning to New York City?"

"I'm waiting for Micah to go to the police."

That again. "Let us assume he does." If need be, Veronika will haul him there by the ear.

"My family knows nothing about the hit-and-run, by the way, so I'm hoping you won't bring it up."

A miscalculation, Veronika thinks, to keep so significant a fact from your nearest and dearest, though in her practice, she observes this all the time. Joy-Ellen and Birdie's parents, Veronika is certain, would be appalled by Micah's behavior, and Birdie chooses not to risk their scorn. "In that case, why does your family think you and your husband are separated?"

"We're not 'separated.'"

"Nonsense. Perhaps not in the legal sense, but call this schism what it is."

Birdie zips her lips until they almost disappear.

"I would be grateful if you'd answer my question."

Birdie takes her time. "I'm not on trial." Metal glitters in her tone.

Veronika reboots. "We have never suffered a divorce in the Tobias family."

"Who said anything about a divorce?"

"In that case, may I assume you are reconciling?"

"Please don't make any assumptions at all." Birdie gets up. "And my break is over. May I get you another espresso? Something else to eat? Do you want to grab a book until we leave? I can't go for forty-five minutes."

"Thank you. I'll wait. I have plenty to read." Does she look like a woman who would travel halfway across the country without diverting reading material?

CHAPTER 44

Veronika

When Veronika sees Alice, she looks taller, though her face hasn't changed, with morning glory blue eyes like David's and cheeks as rosy as Jake and Micah's. Alice's first question is, "Where's Papa?"

"Home. He sends you his love. Do you miss him?"

Alice gives this some thought. "Yes, and sidewalks and pigeons." She reconsiders. "Black-and-white cookies, too."

"How about people?"

"Lots of people, like at the playground or on the bus?"

"Not crowds, Alice, or strangers. Special people."

"I miss Gran. She takes me to the library."

Birdie walks into the room. "The bookstore is almost like the library."

"And Daddy?" Veronika asks, ignoring Birdie. "Do you miss Daddy?"

With exasperation Alice says, "Obviously," a word newly added to her vocabulary.

Dinner is a family affair, with Birdie, Alice, Birdie's laconic father and conscientious mother, already in silly pink scrubs though she doesn't seem like a silly woman. Once again, Joy-Ellen arrives, carrying an immense, sausage-studded lasagna and a lemony dessert that she proudly tells the family was made from a recipe on the gingersnap box.

At Alice's bedtime, Veronika reads her great-granddaughter *The Snowy Day*, which she has bought her as a gift, then sits in the corner while Birdie does an encore with *The Wonky Donkey*. Then comes Alice's nightly name-checks, which she sing-songs. "Good night, Mommy. Good night, Daddy. Good night, Grandma Luanne and Grandpa Russ. Goodnight, Gran and Papa Jake. Good night, Nana Veronika."

"Enough, pumpkin. Lights out now." Birdie bends down for one last kiss. No matter what, Veronika decides, Micah's wife is a tender, loving mother but not offensively smothering, which she sees so much of now.

"I'm not done. Good night, Auntie Jordan. Good night, Papa David."

"Good night, Alice." Birdie is firm.

"Good night, Leif."

The color drains from Birdie's face. "I said, that's enough."

"When am I going to see Leif again?" Alice whines.

"Who's Leif?" Veronika asks.

"Mommy's boyfriend." Alice grins.

"Good night, Alice!" Birdie tucks her monkey under her daughter's arm, brushes away her platinum hair, turns on a night-light, and gives her one last kiss before she closes the door. She sits down on the top step of the stairs.

Veronika sits beside her. "Alice seems happy here."

"I think she is. She loves her day care, and my brother Russ's boys come over a lot."

"Are you going to tell me who 'Leif' is?"

"A friend from high school. No one important," she says,

although from the tension in Birdie's face, Veronika decides that is not the case. "Thanks again for the visit. I know the trip was hard, given what's happening with David. How is he?"

She wondered when Birdie would mention David. "It's partly because of David that you should return. A family needs to pull together in a crisis."

Birdie turns toward Veronika. "Trying to guilt me? Seriously?"

"Stating the obvious." Birdie doesn't make a sound. "And by the way," Veronika adds, because she is truly curious, "what do you make of Micah donating sperm for Jordan and Kit's theoretical baby?" Veronika expects some commendation for solving that particular family problem.

"Excuse me?" Birdie, scowls and swivels in Veronika's direction. "What in God's name are you talking about?"

"You don't know? Jordan has asked her brother to donate sperm for the child she and her partner are going to try and have." Veronika realizes she might be snickering but can't resist adding, "It was my idea."

"Could you back up, please? When did Jordan get a partner?"

"You really are out of the loop. Jordan and Kit have been together for months."

"Let me get my head around this. You're telling me my daughter is going to have a sister or brother whose mothers are Jordan and a woman she met fifteen minutes ago, and this baby, who Alice may never get to know, will be not just her sister or brother, but her cousin, fathered by her daddy?"

"*Half* sister or *half* brother. And it's *our* Alice, too. But yes, this is the plan."

After a minute, Veronika gets up and starts to walk downstairs.

"Did anyone think I should get some say in this?"

"Birdie, you have abdicated your vote in this matter. You

can't have it both ways. This is Jordan and Kit and your husband's decision."

"I think it's time for you to leave, Veronika," Birdie says, her voice rising.

Veronika agrees, but not before noticing that confidence becomes Birdie, who no longer has a problem using her proper name.

CHAPTER 45

Mel

Although it's been a while, the client formerly known as Bambi schedules a session, adding in her text that she wants to thank me. At the appointed time, a redhead with straight hair cropped short walks through the door in a flowery cotton blouse buttoned up to her neck, a long skirt, and lace-up boots that she may have last worn in a barnyard.

"In character for a new play?" *Little House on the Prairie*, perhaps?

"I'm done with acting," Barbara says. "I'm teaching drama now at a middle school." She smooths her hair. "And Joe hated my long curls."

"Joe . . ." I let her husband's name dangle until she grabs it like a gold ring and announces that she and Joe are once again living as husband and wife. "I followed your advice, which is why I want to thank you."

In the mist of memory, I recall suggesting that if she would delete Clyde from her life, Bambi-now-Barbara might be able to more clearly evaluate how she felt about her husband. I may have compared her affair to a picture postcard or a fairy tale—

both analogies are on my mental speed-dial—but I never assume, when I offer advice, that a client will follow it.

"Clyde turned out to be a liar," Barbara explains as she begins to pace. Perhaps she's trying to get in her 10,000 daily steps. "I wasn't the only woman he was seeing besides his wife, who found out about us and gave him an ultimatum. Clyde claimed he picked me, but my gut says I was just a hot little pepper to give his life a kick. I've decided I deserve more and that Joe is the better man. I'm lucky he'd even consider a reconciliation."

Barbara stops pacing and we spend the remainder of the session discussing how she can build her pubescent marriage into something mature and libidinous. Though I'm skeptical about her change of heart, I hope it's real and lasting. I haven't forgotten the magical bargain I'd struck, that if I could help Barbara and Joe get back together, Micah and Birdie will do the same.

"WHAT ABOUT THIS one?" Jake asks, later that night. On his laptop is an image of a porch big enough for a *minyan* of Adirondack chairs. I picture myself enjoying the blue-sky view of a sandy-bottomed lake on a cloudless July day. I am wearing a floppy hat and a swimsuit that fulfills its promise to make me look ten pounds thinner while also giving me *"Hola, mami"* boobs. In my hand is a fruity drink sporting an umbrella, in my date book are no client sessions, and in my head is not much at all. The breeze has blown away every worry.

I wish.

February is when Jake and I make summer plans. Over the years, many city friends have bought second homes in the Hudson Valley, the Berkshires, or near—not *on*—a Long Island beach. As modest as most of these residences are, some would be unaffordable at today's one-percenter prices, though we know people who brag as if they engineered their homes' appreciation through sheer cunning rather than luck. Smugness? Did I mention that is a trait I can't abide?

Jake and I don't own a vacation home, which means being enslaved to frozen pipes and leaking septic tanks while paying high taxes and in our case, assuming a second mortgage. Each year we rent, usually in a leafy region where the only competition is for who catches the heftiest bass in the fishing derby, and the only surprise is who still laughs at the joke Jake recycles about how I deserve first place in the large-mouth category. In winter we play hooky for a week or two somewhere with a palm tree.

Usually, before we commit to a rental, I fastidiously scrutinize dozens of listings to make sure we don't get suckered into a house plagued by balky Wi-Fi or tenured vermin. This year, I have neither the time nor patience to handle the search. "Book whatever you want," I instruct Jake.

"Done," he announces twenty minutes later. "The house is on the northern end of Lake George and there are five bedrooms—so we can invite the others."

The others? "Promise you won't," I plead.

"Does that include my dad?"

My afternoons with David are getting harder, because he has become quite the visionary. Twice, he has hallucinated in my presence. Once, he was convinced that a shaggy, four-legged Muppet—he called it a dog-sheep, not to be confused with a sheepdog—leaped from their Chagall print, a Metropolitan Opera poster for *Die Zauberflöte*, and was tear-assing around the apartment, defecating everywhere while singing "Mary Had a Little Lamb" in a falsetto. "I really stepped in it this time," he said and laughed, certain his foot had sunk into a pile of dog-sheep dung. He ran to the kitchen to clean his shoe.

The other time, he was incensed because after the mailman jerked off on the couch he proceeded to bed his next-door neighbor, a physics professor with a glowering New England-y face. I was able to stop David before he rang 11B to give Dr. Monica Kelly a piece of his mind, what little of it is left. His doctors are now fairly sure David's dementia is Lewy body, where hallucinations are part of the all-inclusive plan and deterioration can be swift. We're talking years, not decades.

Given David's condition, I am not sufficiently diabolical to say that he and Veronika can't visit us. "I'm sorry—I hope you'll invite whomever you want."

I doubt that will include Jordan. We haven't spoken for more than a month, though Jake—who continues to talk to our daughter—assures me she is not yet pregnant.

"Maybe we can entice Micah, Birdie, and Alice to join us," I say, fantasizing aloud. Last year, in northern Minnesota, we taught Alice to swim. Jakes gives me his *dream on* expression and I smell a lecture on the horizon about how I must learn to accept that Alice may stay half a country away. "Or at least Micah and Alice," I say. "Speaking of which, are we set for Passover?"

"I haven't heard otherwise." Jake wanders out of the room.

The holiday is approaching. As tradition dictates, Veronika and David will host the first Seder and Jake and I, the second. I am tired just thinking of the work, even if I am determined to keep our Seder small. These are the hardest meals of the year to prepare, requiring homemade matzoh balls in chicken soup, gefilte fish, shank bones, bitter herbs, multiple courses, and as many dishes to wash as Pharaoh had slaves.

Jake returns with a goofy grin and a large, red-ribboned box that he parks in front of me. "Happy Valentine's Day, kiddo," he sings out.

"Valentine's Day?" I say weakly.

"Uh-huh. Same as every year."

When the kids were little, I made Valentine's Day cupcakes for breakfast. Last week I sent Alice a plush puppy embellished with hearts, but Jake I have forgotten, though every other year

I've baked him a red velvet cake in my mother's heart-shaped pans. I am not a pretty crier. Soon, my eyelids will be as puffy as hotdog buns.

"Oh, boo-hoo," Jake says. "Open the box."

I rip off the paper to find a cherry-red suitcase. Like a shopping channel huckster, Jake proudly points out its four spinning wheels and other fine features. "Unzip it," he commands. Will I find a wisp of lingerie that will barely cover one butt cheek? An envelope falls out of the suitcase. In Jake's handwriting is scrawled, *Mel Glazer, you're going to Disney World!*

Jake loves Disney World. I fail to share his enthusiasm. The lines. The mind-numbing music. The industrial-strength chemicals "freshening" the air. Mostly, the disgust I experience watching people squander money they've saved for years on fifteen-dollar balloons and Swarovski-encrusted mouse ears.

"Open the envelope!" Jake orders.

I plaster a smile on my face and rip. A card reads, *Just kidding. Mel Glazer, you're going to . . . Paris.*

CHAPTER 46

Birdie

Whenever she finds a few free minutes behind the Field of Dreams coffee bar, Birdie chews through *Publishers Weekly* or another of Gwen's industry publications to try to get a bead on how words become books. Her reading is on the spectrum of useless to useful, bullshit to brilliance, occasionally inspirational: "Mood Boards and Creativity," "Christian Booksellers See Hope Ahead," "A Guide to Craft Software." Every night after her dad and Alice are asleep and her mother is at the hospital, Birdie writes. She has completed five short stories.

Today, it's snowing lightly but steadily, with several more inches expected. This means few customers in the store. The fireplace crackles and glows while Leonard Cohen growls melodically. Birdie wonders if Leif likes Leonard Cohen as much as Micah does. She hears from Leif every few days—almost as often as from Micah. Why doesn't she visit him in Madison with Alice? Leif has been trying to sell its wintry delights: sledding, snow tubing, skating on the lakes.

As she rearranges a table piled with memoirs, Birdie smiles at the thought of Leif's invitation, which she won't accept but is flattered to receive. She lets herself believe he is strictly a buddy, and that she isn't playing on a half-frozen pond through which she could easily plunge and drown. Leif and I are not reckless people, she reminds herself.

Gwen pumps the bellows, and the fire thanks her by blazing. She claps in appreciation and asks, "What's funny?" Birdie hadn't realized she'd been laughing.

"Thinking about something Alice said." Which is a lie.

"Beautiful kid, your daughter."

"Thank you." Birdie wishes she could engage her boss in a bigger conversation. She likes Gwen, who displays the occasional wry streak, but finds her indisposed to chumminess. This could describe half of the state's population, herself included. If anyone would ask who is friendlier, Iowans or New Yorkers, after having been back for a while she'd vote New York. Gwen never invites intimacy, asking Birdie few personal questions, and Birdie has asked even fewer of her. She has no idea why Gwen retired from the university at fifty years old (an age Birdie knows only because one day Gwen left out her driver's license), what gender identify term she might choose for herself, or if she is a writer.

She does know Gwen owns the brick building that houses the bookstore, and that she lives in a two-hundred-year-old farmhouse, which—in their most sociable interchange, a few weeks ago—she'd shown off in photographs. A green Aga stove, as big as an elephant and imported from England, is the centerpiece of the kitchen. The countertops are black soapstone and two stainless-steel refrigerators stand side by side like bank vaults. The room looks larger than Birdie's entire Brooklyn apartment. When she described the kitchen to her mother, Luanne was appalled at the enormity of its carbon footprint, but Birdie wouldn't mind owning a kitchen even half its size.

"When am I going to see what you're writing?" Gwen asks.

A startled Birdie had been reading aloud a paragraph that

she'd written, listening for its rhythm—or lack of—unaware of being observed. "I'm sorry. I only work when I'm on my lunch break, I promise. But if you want me to stop, I will. I didn't mean to overstep."

"Whoa. I'd be the last person on earth to tell a writer not to write."

"Spit-balling is more like it," she says, though one or two of her stories might be half-decent. Birdie is far too intimidated to ask Gwen for a critique. Professor Gwendolyn Nordbeck is the real deal, having taught for years at the Writers' Workshop in Iowa City. Several of Birdie's favorite novelists might have been her students, not that Gwen drops the names of luminous grads.

"Oh, no. I can see you're a writer," Gwen says. "You have the look. Beleaguered, eager, insecure. I could go on."

Birdie knows she is blushing.

"Takes one to know one," Gwen says.

This is when I should compliment her work, Birdie thinks, but there are no books on the shelf by Gwendolyn Nordbeck, nor has Birdie found such an author listed online. "What are you writing now?" she asks, to wiggle away from the discomfort.

"Another in my series."

This is not helpful. Perhaps Gwen writes sci-fi, young adult, or fantasy, genres Birdie never reads. "How many books have you written?"

"Some aren't published yet, but about sixty."

"Sixty?"

Gwen marches Birdie over to the romance section. "I picked the pen name Anastasia Aaron so it would be at the beginning of alphabetized lists and shelves." She hands one of the novels to Birdie. The cover features a sky like a Tequila Sunrise, his-and-her windblown tresses, biceps, and a kilt. "For erotic romance, I'm Brie McMarch. For paranormal, Lucinda Frost." This is the most talkative Gwen has been. "Did you think I could afford to buy and renovate a crumbling old house and this store by writing poetry or teaching?"

Gwen has suddenly become twice as interesting. Birdie would like to spend the rest of the day shaking her down for information. Are the other professors aware of her side hustle? Do they all teach their aspiring MFA students how to craft literary fiction while they personally write books of an altogether different genus and species? How long does it take to finish each manuscript? How much can you earn writing them?

None of the questions get asked because the bell at the door rings, announcing customers. A crew of women in their twenties step out of their boots, peel off hats and gloves, take seats at the bar, and cheerfully order lattes and pastries before they each buy several paperbacks as well as matching T-shirts that proclaim, IT'S NOT HOARDING IF IT'S BOOKS.

Only that evening does Birdie start spelunking in the netherworld of romance novels, whose pages are ruled by alpha males who practice seduction along with martial arts and can just as easily be Bollywood superstars as best friends' brothers. Whole categories of books are dedicated to secrets—secret babies, secret royalty, secret billions, secret identities, secret crushes, secret marriages, secret pasts, and secret supernatural talents.

Birdie can't imagine trying to write a romance novel, though she wouldn't mind living one. She becomes eager to polish the pages she wrote over the weekend. Only at eleven-thirty does she force herself to power down her laptop and turn off the light.

Usually, Birdie is asleep within minutes, but tonight she can't stop thinking about the love triangle category, one of romance novels' most compelling tropes. She imagines telling her own story, and wonders how it would end. This is when Micah pings. Hope I haven't woken u call if u can—which she does, although he'd FaceTimed with Alice at dinner time.

"I forgot to ask," he says, without apologizing for texting at almost midnight. "For Passover, are you coming to New York, too, or should I fly out to get Alice? My mother wants to know."

Of course she does. "What do you want me to do?" Birdie asks.

Micah takes too long to answer. "I want you to be there."

"Can I tell you tomorrow?" Birdie knows it's the wrong answer.

"Fair enough," he says. "Also, I hate being the intermediary, but I promised my mom I'd tell you to call her."

"Why?" Birdie asks, itchy with suspicion.

"Haven't a clue."

Birdie sleeps fitfully, wakes feeling exhausted, and on her lunch break at work, calls Mel, who answers on the first ring.

"Birdie!" she says as if they were long-lost roommates. "How are you?"

"You wanted to talk?"

She braces herself for a ten-minute dissertation on why the earth will stop spinning if she doesn't come in for Passover.

"Let me get right to it," Mel says. "How do you feel about Micah donating his sperm so Jordan and Kit can make a baby?"

Birdie gets right to it, too. "I hate it."

"Glad to hear it," she answers, buoyant. "That's all I needed to know. I'm sure you're busy. Kisses to Alice. Have a nice day."

CHAPTER 47

Veronika

Veronika cares not to advertise it, but she can be as sentimental as the next woman. Every card David has sent her is stowed on a high shelf in boxes labeled by the year. The keepsakes tend to be more saccharine than eloquent, but while Veronika knows she can be a harsh critic, she allows her husband's choices to fall beyond her purview. Where David is concerned, it really is his thought that counts, which is why it pains her that Valentine's Day has come and gone without his acknowledgment.

Last year's card dripped ribbons and pearls framing a shower of hearts. Veronika dismisses the question—why would anyone spend ten dollars on *this*?—and considers the Valentine's message. *Our love is a balancing act. We give and we take. We fall and we catch one another. We may not always know the answers. We may not always make perfect decisions. But we will always have each other.*

The words are more meaningful this year than twelve months ago. Veronika wishes they were true.

David enters the bedroom as she runs her index finger across the card's velvety texture. "Pardon me, madam," he says. "I must have walked into the wrong hotel room. I'm looking for my wife."

"You've found her." Veronika throws her arms around his neck.

He stiffens and backs away. "You hussy. I'm a married man, and you're not my wife. My wife is younger with long curly hair." He points to a family picture on the desk. "There she is." *Melanie.* "I would never cheat on her," he huffs. "We have a long, solid marriage."

Laughing. Crying. Cursing. Jousting with a man whose impairment has crashed their lifetime party. All come to mind, but instead, Veronika says, "Excuse me, sir. You look a great deal like my husband, and I get confused."

"No biggie."

Veronika never recalls David stooping to use that vapid expression.

"Give my regards to the raffish devil to whom you're married," he says as he doffs an imaginary hat and leaves the bedroom.

As she does nearly every day, Veronika reconsiders the hardest part of her new reality: perhaps it's learning that what David is thinking, feeling, and saying is nothing she should take personally. If that's the case, how will she manage not to be stung by his cruel remarks? How will she ever cope with the pain?

Twenty minutes later David is watching television. "This old movie has some terrific actors," he says, making room for her on the couch. "Kevin Spacey. Gabriel Byrne. Sit down and join me, Toots." Veronika does, though while David seems to be having a spasm of ordinary sanity, she's not sure who he thinks she is, and she doesn't care to ask.

When the film ends, she finds the *Times* and begins the crossword puzzle. Island off the coast of Tuscany? Oscar winner who appears in a candy bar ad? Qatar capital? Opera set in Egypt? Lag B'___? David fills in the answers as if dictated by God, and for several more hours, his wires connect and he is the David she knows. Later, they make love, which to Veronika feels more comforting than erotic. As she drifts to sleeps, she wonders, Is this the last time?

CHAPTER 48

Mel

O H, HAPPY DAY. UPGRADE: OH, HAPPY, FIVE-STAR DAY. I shout, "*Bonjour,* Paris!" while I'm still in bed, in the shower, in the kitchen. Like a birthday girl in her party dress waiting for guests, my new suitcase is packed and ready for our four o'clock pickup. Our hotel will be walking distance from everything I hope to squeeze into our abbreviated hop to my favorite city. I'm not even going to pretend that my new comfort shoes are remotely stylish and I don't care, because in Paris I will be uncomplaining about racking up 18,000 steps a day, even in the rain.

But first, work—Norah, Barbara, a new client—and already it's lunch. Dr. T is seated at a table set for three, his eyebrows knit together as he texts with one finger. His half-glasses are slipping down his nose. I remember when Ted got his first glasses, because he'd asked me to accompany him to the optician. I was so aflutter you'd have thought he'd invited me to the Academy Awards. The intimacy of sharing a wifely chore triggered my most tenderhearted emotions, and I felt linked to this man. But now all I see is Dr. Theodore Trachtenberg, long-ago colleague and poster boy for pleated khakis, who might offer a Gen X grandmother a job.

When Dr. T spots me, he switches on like stadium lights. Big grin, big hello, as if we haven't seen one another since a world war ended. He stands and kisses me once on each cheek. I guess he's been to Paris, too.

I consider that the table is set for three. Who's missing? Could Dr. T be staging a bake-off between me and another contender? Do I sit by his side or across from him? He must sense my hesitation and says, "I wanted you to be able to choose the seat where you'd be most comfortable." Is this a test? I pick across.

"The food here is outstanding," he says, as if he is complimenting himself for selecting this splashy restaurant, which is not exactly a hidden gem; I, too, read its recent review in the *Times*. He studies the menu as if he were required to memorize it for . . . what? A neurology test? A waiter—excuse me, Giovanni—appears to recite the specials, which he does, deftly. No cognitive decline there.

The carbonara sounds luscious, though I've never mastered the art of feeding myself fettucine, which has a habit of slithering off my fork like rambunctious baby eel. But since I'll be eating nothing but French food for almost a week, I decide to go for it, preceded by a Caesar salad. Will I reek of garlic? Too late. I have placed my order.

Dr. T mirrors my choices. Is this another hidden message I am supposed to unscramble? He gossips about colleagues I barely remember and attempts to discuss politics, since presidential primaries are saturating the airways and column inches, then asks, "What did you think of Penelope Chow's essay on how therapists' behavior can cause couples to abandon treatment?" I must look blank because he adds, "The *American Journal of Marital Therapy*, January issue."

"Sorry. Missed that one." I have let many of my subscriptions lapse. If there's buzz about a particular piece of scholarship, I assume I'll hear about it soon enough, which is how I also

approach politics. How could the article's point be other than
that inept therapists do more harm than good? Not only have
I not read that peer-reviewed article, I haven't submitted anything for publication in more than a decade. Let my colleagues
disembowel one another. Enjoy!

I feel a bump under the table. Dr. T's knee. I move my leg. A
few minutes later, there it is again. This man and I must be maxed
out on chutzpah to imagine we have either the right or the cre-
dentials to advise any couple tethered to hopes of togetherness.
Once again, I consider how lucky I am that Jake never found
out about us, and while I don't know Mrs. T, I have no interest
in ruining her life. Google has coughed up her name and photo:
Renee Trachtenberg, a pretty, plump woman about Dr. T's age
who runs a cat rescue organization.

The Caesar salad arrives without anchovies, a mortal sin.
The carbonara is on par with Olive Garden, our go-to restaurant en route to the Adirondacks. A noodle goes rogue and
dives out of my mouth back into its bowl, Giovanni talks up
the tiramisu, which Dr. T suggests splitting for dessert, but I've
decided that no matter how buttery the homemade ladyfingers
are or how high the salary of the job under consideration, I do
not care to share anything with this man. I'd like this lunch to
end, though for vanity's sake, I long to hear the honeyed sound
of a job offer, should one be forthcoming.

It is. After a round of "What would you do in group therapy
if client A said X, Y, or Z to client B?" and praise for my answers
("Uncanny intuition!") Dr. T pops the question: "Will you join
me in my practice, Melanie?"

I thank him profusely. I may come from Minnesota, but as
folks there say—though rarely by those from my former neighborhood, which was more or less a ghetto—I wasn't born in a
barn. I recite the boilerplate about being honored and humbled,
and stress that I will give his generous offer the serious thought

it deserves because it's a huge decision—*huge*. I promise an answer in a day or two.

Dr. T looks disappointed. I imagine he expected me to faint in gratitude and accept the offer when I came to. "Could you let me know by tomorrow, please?" he asks.

"I will. Promise."

My dexterity doesn't allow me to dodge a departing double cheek-kiss, but I am able to extricate myself from the restaurant in time to buy the deodorant I forgot, and get home forty minutes before the car arrives that delivers Jake and me to the airport.

Hours later, Jake and I are buckled up in facing aisle seats, relieved that there are empty rows in our section of the plane. This bodes well for sleep, helped by the Xanax we each pop as soon as we're heavenward. I contort into an ungainly fetal position and though I could swear I don't nod off, in what feels like minutes, Jake informs me that I have been snoring loudly enough to warrant scathing looks from the mommies nearby who couldn't get their babies to sleep. That, and we have landed at Charles de Gaulle Airport.

As we walk to baggage claim, the mere fact that everyone speaks French triples people's attractiveness, and I deeply regret—not for the first time—that I never learned the language. When we get into our Uber and reach the city, I see *beaucoup* confidence-oozing women with good haircuts walking at a quick clip in pointy boots, narrow jeans, and smart leather jackets. The men have pleasingly shaggy hair and three-day-old stubble. Everyone sports a cunningly tied scarf. I am proud to be with an American whose well-cut David Tobias & Son coat and jeans don't scream factory outlet year-end sale.

We reach our hotel, on a side street in the Marais. It's a jewel box that looks plucked from a vintage postcard. The lobby is a room in which I could happily live, dominated by dove-grey swivel chairs, a table strewn with glossy magazines in various languages, soft lighting, branches of white blossoms, and a life-size painting of a soulful, dark-eyed woman wearing a long scarlet cloak. She must be the French cousin of Bess, the landlord's daughter, who plaited a dark red love-knot into her long black hair. I take a spin in one of the chairs.

To avoid jet lag, Jake and I are committed to powering through the day. We head up to our room, which is crisp, simple, and serenely white. A tuberose-scented candle waits to be lit. The view looks onto the quiet, cobblestone street and I think, as unoriginally as every other visitor to Paris must, that this is a city designed for trysts.

For the next few days, I am determined to see Jake as my lover, and when we aren't exalting the architecture, food and *vin*, I hope we will talk about us, and only about us. I promise myself that I will not whine about problems on the other side of the Atlantic: David's decline, missing Alice, Micah's denial of The Incident and reluctance to fight for his marriage, Jordan's refusal to agree with my totally reasonable logic about baby-making, and my clients' jumble of complaints. Couldn't Barbara just grab a paper towel and clean up the damn hair she leaves in the shower so Joe doesn't bitch about it every day? Is that not a reasonable request? I doubt Veronika's patients waste her exorbitant therapeutic minutes with such beefs.

"Ready, Melanie?" Jake says after our showers and ten-minute naps.

Whenever we travel, we re-christen one another appropriately. Jake is pronouncing my name as if he is Napoleon and I have decided to call him Jacques. Two years ago, in Barcelona, we were Jesús and Maria; in Venice, Jacopo and Manuela.

"*Enchanté*, Jacques," I say, and we head out. Around the corner on Rue des Rosiers, a long line of customers leads us to the best falafel joint in Paris. We snack, stop at the Picasso museum, look for a *toilette*, spend an hour transfixed by Notre-Dame, browse the *bouquinistes* by the Seine, look for a *toilette*, cross one of the bridges to the Left Bank, feel sleepy and drink an espresso, buy a T-shirt that says TOUT VA BIEN!, take a wine and cheese break, and once again look for a *toilette*.

The weather is cool, though the sun, strong. We are as clichéd as tourists come, and I'm glad for it. This is Paris and I'm here with Jacques Tobias, the man I love. I notice that the streets and sidewalks are cleaner than in New York City though the trash bins are half the size and twice as elegant. I feel very, very lucky to be in this city so filled with charm, history, and one-Euro baguettes that I can think of no other place that compares.

We Metro back to our hotel, give ourselves thirty minutes to gussy up for dinner, and head to Montmartre. From Sacré Coeur we see the whole city spread beneath us like twinkling Lego blocks. But we don't stay long, because hunger has kicked in. We find our restaurant, clinging to the side of a hill, and manage to inhale a *poulet de Bresse* that could easily serve four, washed down with a bottle of Beaujolais.

"Shall I order a second bottle?" Jacques asks.

A wave of fatigue wallops me. "Not unless you want me to do a face plant in the *meringue glacé*."

"One last toast." My husband softly touches my hand and with his other hand, raises a glass. "To Melanie, my wonderful wife, with special thanks for looking after my father."

"To Jacques, for planning this trip."

We pay the bill and find the Metro, the hotel, and the chocolate on the turned-down bed, whose silky sheets beckon. I unpack the new snippet of black froth I am calling a nightgown, take my turn in the *salle de bain*, give myself a spritz of scent I splurged on this afternoon at *Fragonard Parfumeur*, decide my lacy lingerie is as alluring as the woman at Saks assured me it would be, and fluff my hair and attitude. I emerge, gift-wrapped and ready for love.

Jacques is nowhere to be found. Jake, however, is asleep. In less than three minutes, so am I.

CHAPTER 49

Mel

I SLEEP FOR ELEVEN HOURS, A PERSONAL BEST. WHEN I WAKE, Jacques is ready to roll. I notice that he hasn't shaved, which I interpret as a step toward trying to blend. He ate breakfast downstairs, which I missed, but he has thoughtfully brought me *café au lait*, two butter-bomb croissants, apricot preserves, and fresh strawberries. I am wolfing down the second croissant when his phone rings.

"Yes, Mom."

I'd hoped Veronika would resist calling us, since in New York all the better angels are on high alert looking out for David. Kieran is working twelve-hour shifts, Micah will stay over twice, and Jordan and Kit plan to bunk there on the other two nights.

"Everything's fine. We're going to head out in a few minutes," Jake says to his mother. "We'll start at the Musée d'Orsay and after that I'm not sure—we have a long list, plus Melanie—" He announces my name *en francais*. "Mel. Who else would I be talking about? . . . Yes, we'll definitely get to Angelina, but not 'til tomorrow, after the Louvre."

Veronika has fond memories of being taken on her tenth

birthday to Rumpelmayer's ice cream parlor in Manhattan. Angelina is a tea room run by the same family and, minus a few hundred plush animals, looks much the same. Its hot chocolate is like drinking a melted candy bar. I've worked a visit there into our schedule. If only my kitchen drawers were this orderly.

I point to my watch when Jake (alas, not Jacques) says, "What's Dad shouting about?" Alarm has crept into his voice.

"He said what?" Jake chokes out a sound between a grumble and a wince. "When did that start?"

"Can't Kieran calm him down?"

"He's calling for who? *Mel?*"

"Really?"

"What? That's nuts.

"Shall I put her on the line?"

Jake covers the phone. "Hon, my Dad's gone apeshit. He's convinced you're his wife. Could you talk to him, please? He insists you've abandoned him."

I grab the phone. "David, it's Melanie." I try to keep my tone airy. "Your daughter-in-law. Jake's wife. What's the problem?"

"Where are you, you bitch?" my father-in-law shouts.

"In Paris, with Jake, like I said." More candy-apple sweetness.

'Who's Jake?" David asks.

"Your son. My husband."

"Why are you cheating on me?" His voice is harsh and menacing.

"I am *not* cheating on you. You're married to Veronika, not me."

"I most certainly am not married to that rhymes-with-witch," he replies. "She's gaslighting me, insisting she's my wife, but you can't kid a kidder."

"Veronika loves you. You love Veronika. She is your wife of forty-six years. I'm Melanie, your daughter-in-law. I'm not your wife."

"Why did you leave me?" His voice has weakened and now he is crying.

"I took a little trip, with Jake. We'll be home in four days."

"Four days?" He sounds five years old. "Can't you get here sooner?"

"Can I bring you something from Paris? A box of macarons?"

"Don't treat me like a goddamn child."

I'm breathing hard. Jake and Veronika are each barking orders at top volume, but I'm trying to tune them out and concentrate on David. "Sorry. I wasn't implying you were—"

"Mel Glazer, enough with the bullshit. Get your bony ass back here immediately."

I toss the phone to Jake and bolt straight to the gilded birdcage elevator to escape to the lobby. My hair is a mess. I am wearing no makeup. No mistaking me for a local. I collapse into one of the grey chairs and weep, for David and for myself.

A few minutes later, Jake appears, his hands jammed into his pockets, his face tight. He sits in the other grey chair and starts to apologize.

"Not your fault," I say, cutting him off. "I feel sorry for your dad—and your mother. No one should have to deal with this."

He looks at his watch. "It's already eleven. Let's get going."

I see we're not going to talk about what happened. "Give me a minute."

When I return, I'm finished with trying to impersonate Melanie of Par-ee. We leave our hotel and walk, silently. Twenty minutes later, the sky cracks open like a Midwestern cloudburst. No beguiling mist painted by Gustave Caillebotte, this. I regret wearing my leather jacket. The umbrella we score from an outdoor vendor is just as crappy as those sold on the streets of Manhattan. My feet slosh and squeak in my new shoes, which are soaked to the soles. So much for Paris being romantic in the rain.

On the way to the D'Orsay, Veronika calls again with the same schtick. Twenty minutes later, I find it impossible to concentrate on the finest collection of Impressionist paintings under one roof. Veronika phones once more; despite a sedative she's given David, his harangues continue.

We abandon the museum after the first gallery, walk into the thicket of streets behind it, and fall into the first restaurant we see. My onion soup is excellent but Jacques has ordered today's *plat, lapin braisé au vin blanc*. The thought of Peter Rabbit giving his life so Jake Tobias can have lunch makes me even more depressed. I leave my soup unfinished.

"Maybe this trip wasn't such a great idea," Jake says. "Maybe we should head out to the airport and stand by for a flight." These questions are not rhetorical and I know better than to engage in debate. We return to the hotel—stat! I throw clothes into my suitcase, and my naughty little nightie taunts me as our shortest European vacation, ever, ends.

Jake summons his last reserve of charm, claiming a family emergency, and Air France lets us board a plane immediately. This time I don't need a Xanax to sleep because my battery has drained to zero.

CHAPTER 50

Mel

W E GO STRAIGHT FROM THE AIRPORT TO JAKE'S PARENTS'
apartment. Micah answers the door. In unison, we throw our
arms around our son and ask, "How's your grandfather?"

"You've got to give the guy credit. He has a lot of stamina."

"Your grandmother?"

"I'm here." Veronika steps into the foyer. "David is walking
with Kieran."

Another woman might be bedraggled, but the only sign of
Veronika's distress is the twitch above her eye. When she'll ignore
a spot on her blouse or let a hem sag, I'll know she's down for
the count. I've heard her quote Jane Fonda saying she considers it a public service to look pulled together, though I've never
been able to fact-check the statement. I believe Veronika's effort
is more for herself than whomever she imagines are her adoring
fans. There can be worse role models.

I embrace Veronika and she returns the hug, if briefly. Jake
and I do not say no when she suggests bagels and coffee. I am
hungrier than I realize, since I haven't eaten since France and
with all due respect to baguettes, nothing beats a fresh, lightly

toasted New York bagel, crunchy on the outside but soft inside, which I'd like to think also describes me.

"When did Dad start carrying on about Mel?" Jake asks.

"The medical term is not 'carrying on.'"

"Okay. When did he start vociferating like this?" Spoken like a man whose thoughtfully orchestrated, romantic, and not-inexpensive vacation got bayoneted by family obligation and all-inclusive worry.

"About a week ago, though most of the time he seems like himself. His doctor says delusions are not uncommon and can go on for a long time or stop as abruptly as they began. It's an erratic disease."

I believe Veronika's subtext makes the point that David isn't in love with me. I can handle that.

We have second cups of coffee and as Jake asks his mother if he should text Kieran to make sure his father is okay, we hear rowdy voices in the foyer. *"We'll sing a song, a soldier's song with cheering, rousing chorus."* I had no idea David knew the lyrics to the Irish national anthem.

David and Kieran march into the kitchen. My father-in-law takes one look at me, leaps in my direction, and plants a big wet one on my lips. Two days later, I can't un-feel his tongue in my mouth. I doubt I ever will.

THE FOLLOWING MORNING, I am leaving for work when the phone rings. I check caller ID. Dr. T.

This is when I remember that I've forgotten to respond to Ted's job offer. My lack of response is its own response, but I still must do the deed. I take the call and babble—"family emergency," "deeply sorry," and "thanks again—the offer means a great deal to me."

Dr. T lets me drone on with my repentance rhetoric, but eventually, I must gasp for breath, and he breaks in with, "Let's cut to the chase. Obviously, you're not interested in the job," because I haven't said as much, not in so many words.

"No, I'm not, but—"

Dr. T interrupts my second round of apology: "I see—no need to elaborate, Melanie."

"B-but—" I begin again.

"If you're not interested, that's all I need to know, though I think you're making a major mistake."

"I can explain."

He stops me. "Is the obstacle our romantic history?"

"Yes." Something else I can't un-feel. There are other reasons, but that one counts the most.

"Do you want to talk about it, because—"

"No." My turn to interrupt.

"In that case . . ."

"Good-bye, Ted." It's a door slamming.

CHAPTER 51

Birdie

"Y OU FLY SAFE, NOW," JOY-ELLEN SAYS TO BIRDIE AND ALICE with send-off hugs at the Des Moines airport. "Don't forget the care package for Mr. Charm." She thrusts a small parcel into Birdie's hands. "Homemade peach preserves may not cure dementia, but they won't hurt."

Jewish holidays never fall on time. Micah has explained the lunar calendar that marks the cycle of celebrations. Sometimes Passover arrives as late as May, heralding spring, but this year the first Seder will be in two days. It's April but still cold in Des Moines. Birdie and Alice clomp onto the plane in boots and layers of fleece and wool.

A flight attendant asks Alice how old she is. "Four, Thursday," she answers, puffed with pride. Mel has planned a unicorn-themed party, since Alice is a true believer. A four-foot-tall inflatable unicorn, a unicorn piñata, and other unicorn frippery will trick up Birdie's in-laws' living room. Mel and Alice diligently debated the merits of a cake versus cupcakes until Mel ordered both of them. She's tracked down and invited every playmate of Alice's she could find: Mabel, Quentin, Madeline, Fin, William, Hazel, Emil, and Tilda have all said yes. Mel hopes Alice will remember

who these kids are. She hopes her granddaughter won't miss celebrating her birthday without the Iowa brigade, but their visit to
New York is overdue—and there are developments.

"Daddy!" Alice screams when Micah meets them in the
terminal. He scoops up his daughter and they whirl around the
baggage collection area as if it's their personal soundstage. Alice
howls with a fizzy delight that reminds Birdie of a movie played
so relentlessly during the holidays she believes she could lip sync
the script. Her parents would find the scene mortifyingly theatrical, but Birdie is certain most tourists must wish someone they
loved had gone to the trouble of an airport reunion.

While Micah may not be the most dependable husband, he
knows how to put on a show. It takes only a glimpse of father
and daughter together for Birdie to be reminded that her husband didn't steal her heart—she happily gave it away. She'd like
to be that girl again, pink with hope, and the impulse lingers
past their group hug. Then, she remembers.

They pile into the truck, where Alice greets her car seat
like a friend and updates her father on how she no longer sleeps
with a nighttime pull-up, can write her name, and how Elsa the
kitty has become a fat, lazy cat. Alice has so much to say Birdie
barely needs to speak, for which she is grateful, and a half hour
later, Micah drops his wife and daughter at his grandparents'
apartment for a late lunch.

"Birdie!" David says at the door. "And Alice! You've shot
up like a tree."

Has Veronika, standing behind her husband, coached him?
The woman seems to beam with *see, he's not a total goner* radi-
ance, though maybe it's primitive relief that her husband hasn't
instigated another family crisis. Micah has explained how, for a
time, his grandfather was convinced that Mel was his wife. After
Birdie heard how that saga forced her in-laws to terminate a trip
to Paris, she began to call her mother-in-law to voice sympathy

and support, but got only as far as dialing the number. With Mel, she rarely finds the right words.

"I'm glad you're here," Veronika says. If she's still miffed about the glacial reception Birdie gave her in Iowa, it doesn't show—or she believes Birdie has belatedly followed the advice she dished out. "Micah tells me you're writing again," Veronika says. "You know you can always send me your manuscripts if you'd like an unbiased reader."

Would a vengeful Veronika skin her alive? Birdie reminds herself that if she wants to be a writer, she'd better grow a thicker skin. She'd be lucky to have this bookish woman as a beta reader. Mel, too, if she'd dare to ask her.

TONIGHT, IT IS the three of them together—Micah, Alice, and Birdie—in their Brooklyn apartment, which she is seeing with fresh eyes. After months of living in Iowa, where the rooms are ample and the view doesn't rudely terminate at a brick wall, their three and a half rooms look as if they were meant for a family of garden gnomes, not two rangy adults and a child who outgrows shoes every two months. Yet their home is not without charm. Whether Micah has hired a cleaner or given the place his own conscientious scrub, Birdie doesn't know, but the apartment gleams, and the kitchen table is set with supermarket roses and her favorite, softly worn cloth napkins. He has arranged a salad of tomatoes and fresh mozzarella, cooked a pot of spaghetti and meatballs, and bought black-and-white cookies and Birdie's favorite coffee ice cream.

Alice rediscovers her Magna-Tiles and rocker, hibernating dolls, and a green towel with a frog hood. Every time she stumbles on something familiar, she squeals like a survivor who learns that a tornado spared the family Bible. Alice insists that both parents put her to bed so she can be the filling in a Tobias sandwich.

It is late by the time Birdie and Micah collapse in their own bedroom. With no hesitation, they strip down for sleep and hold each other closely, arms and legs knowing exactly where they belong. "There's something I have to tell you," he says.

"Oh?" Birdie cocks her head toward Micah, and readies herself for an *I love you* that she's decided to return, depending on the answer to "Have you straightened out your mess with the accident?" She asks the question aloud.

With two fingers Micah lifts a shank of hair that has fallen over Birdie's face, shielding her eyes. "I think so, yes," he says. "But that isn't what I wanted to say."

Birdie's instincts have gone into remission. "What is it?" She doesn't realize she is holding her breath.

"I may have met someone."

He may have met someone.

That makes two of us. But while Micah tells a tangled, improbable story, Birdie shares hers only to the point where she announces that she has applied to MFA programs at the Writers' Workshop at the University of Iowa—again—as well as at the University of Wisconsin in Madison. Gwen Nordbeck has written a letter of recommendation for each that makes her blush. If accepted, she'll take out loans, apply for grants, and get a job.

CHAPTER 52

Mel

Though I have not thrown a child's birthday party for twenty years, I declare Alice's shindig an unmitigated success. She did not stop grinning for two hours, thanked every gift-giver, and only one kid had a meltdown, a boy who couldn't figure out how to slip pantyhose on a Barbie, causing Hazel and Tilda, daughters of staunch feminists, to call him a doodyhead. I have vacuumed up yesterday's balloon remnants, googled how to remove frosting mashed into a rug, and have devoured the last two cupcakes.

The best part was simply being with Alice. As soon as I saw my granddaughter, it felt as if we were starring in a new season of a binge-worthy television series, picking up where we'd left off months ago. When we are together, it's the only time I am able to live entirely in the present tense. After Micah and Birdie—polite, reserved, and vague—took Alice and her swag back to Brooklyn, Jake and I collapsed in blissed-out exhaustion.

Today I am up early for the therapeutic distraction of prepping for tomorrow's Seder. "I'll sleep when I'm dead," was my mother's mantra, which I take to heart. Considering that Maxine Glazer was only fifty-eight when she died, I am glad she tried to jam as much into her shortchanged life as her imagination and energy allowed. She was no bold soul—climbing Mount Everest did not merit her bucket list; not even Moose Mountain, overlooking Lake Superior, made the cut. Yet at the end, my mother assured me that she felt she'd lived a full, regret-free life. I quoted this in the eulogy I sobbed through before hundreds of her friends, distant family members, and congregants at her synagogue in Saint Paul. I hope I will have half the turnout at my own funeral. (Note to self: join synagogue, now.)

I review my to-do list. Homemade chicken soup? Remember to defrost and strain again, lest a guest chokes on a bone. Gefilte fish? Ordered, because I am not my great-grandmother, who kept a live pike in her bathtub until it was time to clobber and behead the beast and poach him into dumplings. Cornish hens? In the fridge. Salmon? Marinating. Matzoh balls? On the stove. I have added seltzer so they won't be as hard as grenades. If people request my recipe, I will imply that it's a family secret, though the directions are plainly on the matzoh meal box.

In case Steven Spielberg crashes her Seder, Veronika fancies-up her table with china and crystal that mimic treasures her mother owned until the SS came to call. She revels in ironing her ivory damask cloth and fanning its monogrammed napkins to geometric perfection before slipping them into sterling-silver napkin rings. I am a low-maintenance, stainless-steel-and-pottery hostess who feels life's too short to own silver polish, though this year I blew myself to a new tablecloth. After considering French cotton jacquard and weighty Italian linen, I got real and went for stain-and-wrinkle-resistant machine-washable polyester. But I do fuss over a centerpiece. At six this morning I made a pilgrimage to the flower district. Dogwood, roses, calla lilies, and freesia stand by in a sink full of cool water, waiting for me to charm them into an artful display.

I am making lists, checking them twice. My notes have notes

of their own. I have hired two helpers from Barnard College's party service, and for their edification, I plan to label each platter and bowl with Post-its to indicate what they will serve: horseradish, saltwater, sweet and sour carrots, prune *tzimmes*, green beans with almonds, and much more. Every place will have its own homemade Haggadah, amended and edited to my liking.

Spotify is blasting Nina Simone. Nina's feeling good and so am I. Even when peeling potatoes, my efforts feel like a labor of Tobias love. Why will tomorrow night be different from all other nights? On all other nights my family is scattered, but tomorrow night those dearest to me will unite around my Seder table.

Despite my efforts, I'm nervous. I recognize that we Tobiases are privileged, and our problems could be far worse. But they are still our problems, festering. There wouldn't be therapists like me or shrinks like Veronika if whatever mars people's joy didn't feel like a two-hundred-pound, four-foot-wide roll-top desk filling the mini-storage of our psyches. I want tomorrow to be mellow, inspiring, loving. Hence: my agitation.

JORDAN IS THE first to arrive, bearing her baking debut, a flourless chocolate cake studded with raspberries as big as five-carat rubies.

"The cake stand is for you, too," she says, presenting her peace offering on an exquisite orange glass pedestal plate. I ooh. I aah. We kiss and I thank her profusely for both the dessert and the gift. I have not seen my daughter in too long.

Last night she failed to attend her grandparents' Seder, claiming a twenty-four-hour virus, though today she looks robustly healthy, with cheeks as pink as dawn. I size up Jordan. She may have gained a pound.

"Feeling better?" I ask.

"Much. Thanks."

"Where's Kit?"

"Who?"

Oh my. "Your girlfriend? Who you live with?"

"Ah, Kit." Jordan enunciates her name as if I'd mispronounced it, which is hard to do. "She won't be coming."

"Did she catch the bug you had?"

"I wouldn't know."

We lock eyes and wait for the other to speak. I give in first because a mother should. "Care to tell me more?"

Jordan shifts from one foot to the other. "Kit moved out last week."

I restrain myself from wailing, "And this is the first I'm hearing about it?" in favor of, "Honey, you must be miserable."

"I'll live," she says, her cynicism hardened into a barrier I don't expect to penetrate.

It's still early enough in the evening for me to say, "Do you want to sit down, please, and tell me what happened?" though I doubt Jordan will.

"It's not that complicated."

If true, I am a size two and have a Ph.D. in astrophysics. "That may be, but let's go into the kitchen." I find space on the counter for the cake I am still holding, clear off two stools piled with serving pieces, and we sit.

"Kit took offense at all the butting-in and the family push-back about her carrying our child."

Who could blame her? Am I supposed to feel guilty? If I had a do-over, I wouldn't change a thing I said or did.

"She felt manipulated, unwanted, and unappreciated. We Tobiases scare her shitless."

By *we* I suspect my daughter means *me*. Jordan and Kit's breakup is the fault of the bitchy mother and possibly the sister-in-law I expect to arrive soon, who made it clear to one and all that she was not on board with her husband fathering his sister's child, a baby that would be her daughter's cousin and half sister. I practically needed a map to follow this potholed plan.

But where's the anger that contributes to the resentment I'd expect Jordan to display? Her arms are tightly crossed over her substantial chest, yet her voice is calm—which renders me suspicious. Jordan is nothing less than strategic. Will she seek revenge? Since it's too late to hire a food taster to sample her cake for toxins, maybe I should accidentally dump it in the trash.

"My intention was never to break you two up," I say. That may sound disingenuous. It's mostly true.

"Relax, Mom. You may have done me a favor."

Jordan called me *Mom*. Jordan may have paid me a compliment. Still, two and two are not making four. "I thought you love Kit," I say, as baffled as I would be had I walked into a Hitchcock movie twenty minutes before the end and was required to unravel the plot. "What am I missing here?"

"Kit was up for pregnancy, but not for motherhood."

I am eager to hear everything Jordan cares to share, but in twenty minutes all my guests should be here and they'll want to start the Seder immediately so they'll be fed sooner. I hug Jordan long and hard and remove Kit's plate.

CHAPTER 53

Mel

"CHOPPED LIVER FOR THE LADY," DAVID SAYS WHEN I OPEN THE door, handing over a fastidiously wrapped bowl. This is not a delicacy I attempt to make. To do it right, as Veronika does, you sauté chicken livers in *schmaltz*—chicken fat—which for me, is a bridge too far, like wearing my college bikini to a beach populated exclusively by my clients.

"These are for you, too." Veronika hands me a box from a Depression-era candy shop that has hung on so long its Lower East Side neighborhood has become whatever the current hip word for *hip* is. I thank her and find dishes for the dried fruit, *halvah*, and glossy chocolates, big as checkers. The cashews, my favorite, which I believe I have earned, I hide to savor in private.

I am putting out chocolate-dipped dried apricots when Jake returns from the liquor store. Seder-goers are expected to drink four cups of wine, each symbolizing a reason why God redeemed the Jewish people when they were enslaved in Egypt. While we Tobiases are not oenophiles—except for my urbane Jordan, who owns a small share of a Napa vineyard—Manischewitz Concord Grape wine won't cut it for Passover, not even for the prophet Elijah. As tradition goes, he makes a worldwide pub crawl in order to announce that the eternally procrastinating Messiah has decided to show. At each Seder, he gets his own goblet of wine.

Jake hauls a carton to the kitchen and, one by one, lifts out three varieties of wine—a dozen bottles in all. "California Chardonnay reputed to pair with matzoh balls," he announces as he puts the first four bottles on the table. "For the salmon and Cornish hens, some bubbly from the Golan Heights"—he retrieves four bottles that look like Prosecco—"and for those who prefer the taste of their childhoods"—Veronika and David—"a classic, hearty red."

If she drains all four glasses maybe even Birdie will have a loose tongue, I think. My daughter-in-law drinks in extreme moderation, as I imagine I would, too, if my father were a lush.

Jake surveys the overcrowded kitchen and asks, "Anything I can do to help in here?"

"We've got it under control," I say, though it appears otherwise. The Barnard students have arrived. One is filling water glasses and the other, as if she will be graded on her performance, is arranging parsley and cherry tomatoes on a platter in an intricate pattern. She might be spelling out *Happy Passover.* "Go be a host and hang with your family," I say to Jake.

Since on a holiday I always feel gripped by sentimentality, I am serving my mother's matzoh kugel, trying to time the baking so it will be airy and soufflé-ish when served, not a dense, sagging morass. As I put the dish in the oven, Alice, who I hadn't heard arrive, sprints into the kitchen wearing frilly white anklets, patent-leather Mary Janes, and a flowery smock dress that I suspect Joy-Ellen has produced on her sewing machine.

"Gran," she shouts, "freeze."

I freeze.

"Close your eyes tight and turn around."

I follow Alice's command, hands up like a perp.

"Open now and look!"

Alice is sporting giant waxy, cherry-red lips. She, too, has been visited by Veronika's candy fairy. I'm surprised—and frankly, touched—to see this glimpse of whimsy generated by my mother-in-law. When I walk into the living room to start a wild rumpus about the lips I see that David, Jake, Micah, and Jordan are wearing them, too.

"Photo op," I shriek. "This absolutely needs to be documented for posterity." Since God created smartphones with cameras, the first great invention of the twenty-first century, if an experience in my life isn't photographed, I'm not sure it took place. But my phone is MIA. "Damn, where is it?"

"Use mine," Jordan says. She grabs it from her bag parked nearby and corrals Alice. "C'mon, kiddo. Stand by your daddy."

Alice does and I notice how long-legged she's gotten in just a few months. She looks like a blossom in a bud vase.

"Veronika, you're not going to be in the picture?" I shout as Jordan art directs the shot.

"I'll pass," she says, sitting ramrod straight on a living room ottoman. "David will represent me."

"And Birdie. We need Birdie." I look around. No Birdie. In fact, only now do I realize she hasn't even arrived. "Hey, Micah, where's Birdie? We need her in the picture." For starters.

I haven't seen Micah in a tie and jacket since . . . I can't remember. He shrugs and speaks in a tone I cannot parse. "Birdie's not coming."

"She's went to 'sconsin," Alice adds, not helpfully.

Veronika corrects Alice. "She's *gone* to *Wis-con-sin*."

Wisconsin, 'sconsin, went, gone?

"Birdie's checking out an MFA program in Madison," Micah says, as if that explains anything.

My mind spins as I take in all his statement implies. I know a master's degree in fine arts is a long commitment, usually dragged out by writing a thesis, which is often a novel. There are excellent programs nearby, and Birdie's plan to stay in the Midwest can't mean anything good, not for tonight, not for this visit, not for the future. "Damn, she won't get to hear the special prayer I found for non-Jews at the Seder," I say. "I spent four hours online until I came across the right one." I realize I sound whiny and don't care.

"I'm sorry, too," Micah says. "It was her decision." Still not helpful.

Jake speaks up. "It's time to start, almost sundown," he says, as if he and I care about the religious fine print.

I notice Alice taking in the conversation, and grasp what Jake doesn't say: this isn't the moment to ask Micah if his marriage is truly over. "Dad's right," I say. "Let me remove Birdie's plate, and we'll get going."

"Mom, leave her place setting, please."

Now I'm more baffled.

"I may have a guest."

Jake's raised eyebrows and slight head shake say, *Don't even.*

CHAPTER 54

Mel

LIKE EXCLAMATION POINTS, DAVID STANDS AT ONE END OF THE
Seder table and Jake, the other. Jordan and Micah choose adjacent seats, as if they require one another's moral support. Alice
sits between Veronika and me.

"Welcome," says my husband, his yarmulke slipping off his
head. "Thank you, family, for joining us tonight." He takes a deep,
audible breath. "Now, if you'll turn to page one, we'll start with
Mel lighting the candles." Those of us who are sitting, rise.

I feel embraced by my snug city home with its rugs from a
long-ago trip to Morocco, objets d'art worth nothing and everything, and shelves crowded with literary giants glowering at trashy
beach books. Dusk shadows my small family until with my third
strike of the match and a slight sizzle, I kindle white tapers. They
rise from unadorned silver candlesticks given to my mother when
she married, and passed on to me. The memory of her singsongy
diction, Minnesota cadence intact, prompts me in prayer. We chant
a short blessing in a duet only I can hear.

"Amen," the Tobias family says in unison.

Amen.

"Tonight, we open doors long closed, lifting our voices in songs of praise," Jake reads, rabbinically.

The language of the Haggadah floats past me, invoking no emotion. What triggers tears I blink to suppress is knowing that despite grumbles and gripes, irritation and incompatibility, I believe we are a family united in optimism. Yet despite that hopeful anticipation, I find it impossible not to look back as I consider—and in my own way, pray—for the future.

Last year at this time, Alice was still my sidekick, David sailed through life steady as a Viking ship, and Micah had celebrated the first anniversary of starting his business. That and his marriage both seemed secure, or so Jake and I thought, nor had Micah's truck struck a woman—in my mind, it's always been a woman, not a man or a dog—from whom he fled. David and Veronika were an institution as sound as a New England stone wall, or they pretended to be. I sprinted through my days ricocheting between ruminations on clients' issues while, say, trying to remember the lyrics of "Sgt. Pepper's Lonely Hearts Club Band." But to echo a Yiddish proverb Veronika quotes (too) often, *Der mensch tracht, un Gott lacht.* Man plans and God laughs.

Jake asks his father if he'll lead the service, which is divided into two parts. The first half lasts no longer than thirty minutes, when dinner is served. As he never used to, David turns to Veronika for approval. I try to hide my worry that he isn't up to the job.

When Veronika says, "Go ahead," blessing him with a nod of her head as a mother might a timid child, he lifts a generously filled wineglass, belts out the Kiddush, and we are off to the races. He calls on family members, one by one, to recite portions of the Haggadah. Alice remembers her coaching and when The Four Questions arrive, asks, "Why is this night different from all other nights?"

See above, I think, considering my list. But an additional answer is that tonight, at the end of one of his "good" days, David's bearing is patrician and commanding. After a few prayers down the road he leads us in the song that's topped every Jewish chart for the last twenty-two centuries, "Dayenu." Its refrain translates to, "It would have been enough." *Had He brought us out of Egypt, dayenu. It would have been enough,* and so on, for numerous, rousing, off-key choruses.

The ballad prompts me to have a word with God, who has had His good, long chuckle at our family's expense. Going forward, would it be too much to beg You to please turn your attention elsewhere, Lord? Just asking.

If David hadn't started losing his marbles, it would have been enough. *Dayenu.*

If Micah had hauled ass to the police, it would have been enough. *Dayenu.*

If Birdie hadn't decamped to Iowa, Alice in tow, it would have been enough. *Dayenu.* Though if she and Alice returned home, it would be even better, much better. *Dayenu.*

I am continuing to improvise when I hear a soft rap at the door.

"Elijah must want the early-bird special," Jake says. We are more than an hour away from the prophet's cameo, which comes after the Seder meal is served. "Micah, will you open the door, please?"

It's got to be Birdie. I remind myself to overlook the past few months and treat my daughter-in-law with loving kindness. When she enters, she'll spew apologies for being late, announce that she's scrapped the idea of moving to Wisconsin or staying in Iowa, and wave an acceptance to a local MFA program.

My premonition, however, has been misinformed by wishful thinking. No prophet disguised as a blond Midwestern yoga instructor is knock-knock-knocking straight from heaven's door. Micah lets in a distinctly non-Elijah-like woman, short and slender with dark auburn hair hanging below her shoulders and a bashful smile that reveals a dimple. She is wearing a severe, high-necked

navy dress and black leather flats. Despite her youth—I'm guessing twenty—she is leaning on a cane. Micah steadies her as she
slips out of her coat. He offers his arm and escorts her, unhurried,
to the table.

"I'd like you to meet Delia Hemmings," he says, stern, and
turns toward the woman. As a smile slowly emerges, her face
turns delicately pretty.

Goose bumps cover my arms. A spectral shiver creeps down
my back. What is Micah doing with this woman? Why has he
brought her here? I don't dare look at Jake to see if he is putting
the pieces together.

Starting with Veronika—"My grandmother, Dr. Tobias"—
Micah introduces each of us. As if it's the first day of summer
camp and a counselor is leading an ice breaker game, Delia repeats every name.

When Micah reaches "Alice, my daughter," my granddaughter asks, in her high squeak, "Do you know my mommy?"
To this Delia replies with twice the poise I would expect, "No,
but I hope to meet her someday."

Does this timid woman plan to stay in our lives? In what
role? My shiver has turned clammy.

Micah gets to "My grandfather, David Tobias," who nods
cordially. "Pleased to meet you, Miss Hemmings," he says, but
unfortunately, that's not all. "Are you two a couple?" David
asks, ornamented by, "How did you meet?"

How indeed? Delia lifts her chin, blinks her deep-set dark
brown eyes, and peers at Micah, apparently waiting for him to
respond. He says nothing. Then the corners of her pale lips—no
lipstick—lift and Delia answers with, "We ran into one another."

I am afraid to look at Jake.

"Are you dating?" David continues, burning through his
filter.

"Grandpa, nobody 'dates' anymore," Jordan says, air quotes

flying like drones. Veronika shields Alice's ears and loudly whispers to David, "Darling, are you forgetting Micah is a married man?" This terminates an auspicious conversation that I imagine every Tobias adult except Micah would like to continue, some more than others.

I feel the pull of marital mental telepathy, and eye Jake. He catches my glance, lifts his eyebrows, and transmits a silent message. *Micah's story will unfold in good time. Chill, chill, chill.*

Completing introductions, Micah says, "My mother, Mel Glazer" and I respond with, "Welcome, Delia," nothing more. "Jake Tobias" receives an equally brief introduction. The silence that follows Micah's preliminaries stands between us like a moat. Nor will my son meet my eye.

I know an impasse when I see it, hop up, and, along with my Barnard helpers, busy myself with clearing the table, then serving dessert and coffee. Along with a plate of coconut macaroons I baked myself, Jordan's masterpiece disappears and I add *pastry chef* to my daughter's resume.

As my exasperation takes its grip, the second half of the Seder drags, and I am able to concentrate even less than usual, though it contains what my children used to refer to as the fun parts. Blurry-eyed, we drain our last cups of wine. Once again, Elijah the prophet is a no-show, but Alice finds the hidden matzoh, the *afikomen*, and Jake rewards her with a silver dollar. Minutes later, she curls up on the couch like a comma, and crashes.

The Seder ends, and the Barnard students shift into high gear along with Jordan and Delia, helping to put the kitchen in order. I would like to corner Micah, but he has escaped to the family room with his father and grandparents, and is comatose—or pretending to be—in front of TV news.

In a post-Seder ballet, while I circle again and again from the dining table to the kitchen, loading the dishwasher and wrapping leftovers, I overhear Delia tell Jordan what I already

know, that she grew up near Salt Lake City but has been working here as an au pair until she was in an accident.

"That's awful," Jordan says. "What kind of accident?"

Delia winces and answers, "I'd rather not talk about it."

I am a guided missile, ready to strike. I'd like to get Delia
and Micah together and interrogate them on how they found
each other and what the hell is going on. I can't help but worry
that my son has not only banged into this woman, causing her
physical and emotional harm, but is playing her, too.

"I hope whatever happened to you hasn't turned you off to
living here," Jordan, a New York City fangirl, says, "because—
well, it takes some getting used to, but it can be—"

"Are you kidding?" Delia interrupts as she dries a bowl.
"I'm thinking of applying to college here—Hunter for social
work or Baruch for business. I can't decide." Jordan hands off a
large platter. "Any advice?"

"With respect to social work school you'd be better off asking
my mother," Jordan says, switching on her serious face. "But Baruch's reputation has grown," Jordan adds, "and it's not expensive,
because it's a city school. They both are. You should absolutely
check them out," says the privileged white graduate whose parents spent megabucks on her two degrees from private colleges.
How entitled she is, my lovely daughter, failing to consider that
a city school is an excellent value but not free, and that to attend,
Delia would most likely need to also hold down a job.

My frustration flames. I'd like to join their conversation,
with a different set of questions, questions I know I shouldn't
ask, not even when Micah and I silently move snoozing Alice to
the guest room. She will stay with us for three days and I have
outlined an ambitious agenda—a children's play, a visit to the
carousel in Central Park, the Statue of Liberty, the knights in
shining armor at the Met—Micah's favorite—and craft projects.

Many craft projects. We'll start in the morning, when Jake will make *matzoh brei*, our Tobias family tradition. "You're coming for breakfast, right?" I ask my son.

He nods yes but conveniently shushes me with "I better get Delia home." In the kitchen, he offers copious thanks—more than I would expect—for the Seder meal. Delia is standing nearby, all eyes on Micah. Is his gratitude intended for her benefit, to demonstrate what a fine guy he is?

After Delia thanks Jake and me and the two of them depart, I ask myself, what kind of mother attributes questionable motives to her son? Mel Glazer, mother of Micah Tobias.

The cleanup speeds along. I overpay and dismiss the Barnard squad and except for our granddaughter and David—vociferously snoring—we are down to Jake, Jordan, Veronika, me, and the seldom-used fleet of crystal, once belonging to my parents, that I prefer to wash and dry myself. When I get to Jordan's seat, on the opposite end of the table from where I was sitting, I notice that her glass of the California white remains full.

How did I manage to raise an undeniable wine snob? As I carry the full glass to the kitchen, I snipe, "Was the Chardonnay not up to your standard?"

"*Au contraire.* I took a sip. It was outstanding."

Maybe Jordan was actually ill this week. "Are you on meds, honey?"

"No, Mother. Just not drinking."

I feel eyes on my back and turn. Veronika, shock in her gaze, looks past me, at Jordan, and asks, "Dare I imagine what I'd like to imagine?"

Jordan hesitates, then unlocks a sly smile. Veronika reaches out to my daughter, and they rock back and forth, arms entwined. Despite the awkwardness—my little girl has eight inches on her grandmother, who is not known to break out in physical joy—

I see the fierceness of their bond, the same titanium connection I feel toward Alice. Jordan lights up like a shooting star, and nods wordlessly to her grandmother, whose eyes mist.

"I'm thrilled." Veronika flicks away a genuine tear as it drips down her cheek. "How are you feeling?"

"Ready to puke all day long." Jordan's words rush out. "*Morning* sickness? But I'm flabbergasted and thrilled. Is there a German word for all that?"

Veronika tilts back her head and laughs. *"Gluckenwomit?"*

"Barffreude?" Jordan says.

When Jordan was about twelve, after Veronika defined *schadenfreude* for her, inventing German words became their game, which I haven't heard them play in at least a decade. Rightfully, Veronika detests anything to do with Nazis, but she has never lost her love of the German language.

This is not the first time when I have required more than a seven-second delay to keep up, but it may be the first time I've been speechless.

CHAPTER 55

Birdie

MADISON, WISCONSIN, MAY BE ONLY A FEW HOURS' DRIVE from her hometown, but Birdie knows the University strictly by reputation. That its population is nearly as big as San Francisco. That half of its freshmen enter with 4.0's. That while it's left of center, a hell-for-leather football-fetish prevails featuring a marching band that performs the "Chicken Dance" and *Friends* theme song postgame.

Not that this rah-rah culture was always so. Joy-Ellen has recounted her sole visit to the campus, when it was the People's Republic of Madison and nobody gave—and here she quotes— a "flying fuck" that its football team couldn't win a game. This was when students in bell-bottoms majored in Vietnam War protest, shouting, *Hey, hey, LBJ, how many boys did you kill today?* and *Don't trust anyone over thirty,* a slogan Joy-Ellen regards as the stupidest thing she ever heard.

Birdie can't imagine herself in either incarnation of the school.

Leif couldn't meet her at the airport because he was on call at the hospital. The Union is where she is waiting for him, not in its shadowy, cavernous Rathskeller but toward the back. Birdie checks her phone for the fourth time to make sure she hasn't just imagined that her messages from the Iowa Writers' Workshop and the Wisconsin MFA program have both arrived. But yes, they're there, one landing in her inbox two days ago and the other, this morning. They remain unopened, as if they carried a virus. If she's rejected at both schools, Birdie tells herself, life will be simpler, because if she is accepted, she'll need to make a major decision. The path of least resistance is to postpone reading the verdicts, which is what she, a self-appointed wimp, has decided to do.

From behind, she feels a tap on the shoulder. "Hey, you," Leif says. "You made it." He bends down for a tight hug followed by a kiss that Birdie doesn't rush to end. Leif smells fresh and cold. With wind whipping off its lakes, Madison makes Iowa feel temperate and New York, tropical. "Brave enough to sit outside?" he asks. Beyond tall glass windows he points to a broad terrace furnished with circus-hued iron tables and chairs, mostly empty. Birdie would describe the scene as enchantingly Parisian if the lake on the far side of the tables didn't look like an endless, icy cookie tin. She tightens the scarf around her neck, lifts her hands to show Leif she hasn't removed her fingerless gloves, smiles, and says, "No, thanks."

"Didn't think so," Leif says, "and I'm guessing you're not going to be tempted by an ice cream cone made by the ag students, either?"

Feeling very Anna Karenina, she says, "I might be tempted by you." As the words spill out, Birdie becomes intoxicated by the possibilities being far from home suggests.

"You hussy, you." Leif extends his hand. "Let's get the hell out of here."

"As soon as I look at some email." Her heart hammering, Birdie scrolls through her inbox, points out the two that might change her life, and hands Leif her phone. "Could you open and read them for me?"

He sees the senders and laughs. "You don't want to do this yourself?"

Feeling a sharp stomach cramp, Birdie balls her fists and winces. "I can't."

"Positive?"

"Doctor, just read, please."

Leif scans both messages, wipes all expression from his face, and says nothing.

"Well?"

"Oh, you wanted to know what the schools *say*?"

"You dick." Birdie holds her breath.

"'It is with great pleasure . . .'" Leif says, reading the first email, followed by the second, which begins, "'I am pleased to inform you that you have been admitted . . .'" He pumps a fist in the air. "Congratulations. Everyone wants you, babe. I'm not surprised, but—"

She hushes Leif with a finger placed on his lips. It takes a moment for her to think, *What now?*

Hand in hand, they walk through the maze of the Union, out the door, into the darkness of the setting sun. Snow has started to fall, and flakes soon stick to their noses, their eyelashes, and Birdie's bangs. Down the block and across the street, students start a snowball fight. Someone is tossing a Frisbee to a dog. A girl is making snow angels.

The sidewalk is icy. Birdie takes one slow, careful step at a time. But her strides get longer, to match Leif's, and soon the two of them are laughing and running, then sliding in the snow.

CHAPTER 56

Mel

I PULL JORDAN TOWARD ME, OUR TEARS MINGLING, AS I FEEL A dizzying whoosh of love. "You're having a baby," I say, stupidly and jubilantly. I will leave it to Veronika to invent a German compound noun for that emotion.

"I am."

"When?"

"End of fall."

I don't know what questions to ask first. Fortunately, Jordan keeps talking.

"Micah and I chewed through the whole situation over several beers and we agreed he had enough on his plate without becoming my child's baby daddy and infuriating Birdie. That left me with the professor's super-sperm. Did you know you can inseminate yourself? There's not any more to it than putting in a tampon."

"But what about Kit? Was this before or after she left?"

"This was why she left. She was feeling marginalized, blah, blah. I began to feel I'd made a mistake in everything except wanting a baby."

"But—" I am shut down by Veronika's glare.

"You're dying to ask how I'll ever manage alone," Jordan says.

This wasn't what I was thinking, but it's a fair question, that and many more.

"I'll be looking for a nanny—or an au pair."

"I hope you don't mean Delia."

Jordan throws back her head. "What are you smoking? We just met. Who is she, anyway?" There is nothing but curiosity in her voice. "And what's going on with Micah and Birdie?"

"You'd best ask them. I wouldn't know." I face my daughter in companionable silence until Jordan's words spill out.

"I realize you'll be spending a lot of time with Grandpa and I don't want to horn in on that, and there's your practice, obviously. But I'm hoping you'll be able to help me with the baby." She fixes me with the same blinding intensity I saw on her face as an infant. At the time I thought it was constipation. Now I see it is determination. "Please."

Every one of my emotions are caught in my throat. "Oh, honey."

Jordan looks sincere. Jordan rarely looks sincere. "I can't wait to be a mother," she says.

I admire this woman who is my daughter. At her age—or any age—I doubt I'd have wielded the grit to assume the double-decker responsibility of single motherhood along with a big job, but without a doubt, I know Jordan Tobias can handle it. Of course, I will help, along with many others, to shape this new life. It will be an honor. In months, I am going to meet someone new to love, and be able to see what kind of human being my daughter will raise. I already believe this child will be remarkable.

"You don't have to ask, Jordan. Your baby and David and Alice will all have first dibs on my time. I can't think of a better use of it."

"It's not just that I need the support—I want her to know you." Jordan's hands are on her taut tummy, not yet a baby bump.

"Her?"

"So they say."

I take the full glass of wine, pour half of it in another glass for Veronika, who has been quietly standing by—and I only now realize has heard our complete conversation—and dribble a few drops into a shot glass for Jordan. "To Tobias women!" I say, raising my glass and pulling Jordan and Veronika toward me. "Long may we be strong."

We clink. We hug. We grin. Jordan leaves the kitchen to share her news with Jake and, should he be awake, David. Veronika and I sit across from one another at the table.

"Did you see this coming?" I ask.

"I did not," Veronika admits. "But I am delighted. Are you?"

"Very. Still shocked and processing the news, but yes, thrilled." I am thinking out loud. "Jordan will make an excellent mother."

"Because she's had a good example."

Who might that be?

As if it's an indisputable fact, like night being dark and sugar being sweet, Veronika extends the highest compliment she's ever given me. "You."

I restrain myself from shrieking, and simply thank her.

"No need for that." Veronika sets her hands on the table and twists her diamond wedding band. "I should be thanking you, for all you're doing for David."

"No need for that, either. I'm glad we have a rapport."

"It's more than that. You have a gift, Melanie. Hardly anyone does."

Veronika's behavior is completely unlike her, and since David's onset of dementia, major personality mutations make me leery. I cross my legs, then uncross them and ask, "Do you realize Delia is most likely the person Micah hit?"

Veronika narrows her eyes. "I do only because Micah shared

the news with me a few days ago. He also wondered if he should tell Birdie about her."

Micah told Veronika about Delia, but he didn't tell me. I bristle but plunge ahead, and ask Veronika how she responded.

"I urged him to be transparent."

"I'm worried that Micah tracked down Delia to dupe her in some way," I admit.

"When did you become so cynical?"

When I married your son.

"And you've got it backward," Veronika adds. "Delia tracked down Micah. She spotted his truck parked somewhere, and it stirred a memory. She told Micah that she stalked the truck for weeks until she worked up the nerve to approach him and ask if it had hit a woman. As Micah tells it, he apologized, genuinely and extensively. Together, they decided they wouldn't involve the police as long as he helped pay her medical bills, which he has been doing."

Was this the honorable way for Micah to respond? I wish I could phone 1-800-Ethics and get a consultation. I have a raft of questions, beginning with, "Do you think Micah and Delia have feelings for each other?"

"I do. But that's pure conjecture. Micah doesn't tell me everything."

Thank God. "And Birdie—do you think she and Micah are finished?"

"Probably. But again, it's a hunch." Veronika sighs heavily. "I'm not happy about it."

We sit silently. I like talking to Veronika, woman to woman and, dare I say, equals? Perhaps the moment we are sharing is an aberration, but tonight at least, I find her insightful and kind. Will she ever fill the black hole left by my own mother's passing? Never. But perhaps the two of us could evolve into something almost like friends. There should be a word for this alliance between a daughter-in-law and her mother-in-law. Perhaps there is, in German.

"If Birdie goes back to school away from here and she and Micah do split up, maybe he can get custody." My head is spinning with ideas.

Veronika places her hand on mine. "Melanie, try not to get ahead of your skis. No good will come of that."

Minutes later, Jake is downstairs with his parents, walking them home. I check on Alice, clutching her monkey, deeply asleep. Her eyelids slightly flutter. She must be dreaming. I bend down to softly kiss my granddaughter. In doing so, for a brief moment, I feel my small world vibrate with possibility. I snuggle next to Alice on top of the duvet, and circle her with my arm.

I, too, can dream, of watching Alice—my *oldest* granddaughter—grow up, even if I must do it enabled by technology and partly from a distance. I dream of meeting Jordan's baby, and feel the early stirrings of love. I dream of being the kind of mother needed by the complicated adults my children have become. Of being a better wife and therapist and daughter-in-law. Of having the resolve to handle whatever hassles and hardships and health scares life hands me. Of getting the chance to become not just older, but wiser.

I am Mel Glazer, a lucky woman. I am filled with love and gratitude and matzoh.

Author Note

WHEN WE MARRY, WE TYPICALLY RECEIVE A GIFT-WITH-purchase, that punch line to a thousand bad jokes, a mother-in-law. Ditto for mothers whose child marries and a daughter-in-law becomes part of the package. Over time, these relationships may become the trickiest—or most rewarding—one(s) in our lives, yet I've rarely seen them addressed in a novel. I wanted to write *The Real Mrs. Tobias* to put such ties front and center.

For far longer than I had a mother, I've had a MIL. At this writing, she is ninety-eight. Still driving. Still "replenishing"—as she might say—her chic wardrobe, although she recently down-graded to flats. (We wear the same size, and I inherited far more gently worn party shoes than I expect to have parties to attend for the rest of my life.) Still playing killer bridge. Still reading the *Times* and tuned in to news when she's not watching golf tournaments and the movies of her youth or giving excellent advice. As the unquestioned matriarch of a big, blended family, she is actively involved in the lives of three children and eight grandchildren, plus partners for each, and twenty-one great-grandchildren ranging in age from four to twenty-one.

When I married my MIL's son I doubt I was the DIL she'd pictured. I was a North Dakota bumpkin relocated to her town,

Manhattan, hellbent on a career, which wasn't on her bucket list. I couldn't be the daughter she always wanted because she already had two. Yet while it didn't happen overnight, we've bonded. I adore and admire my MIL

Now that I am a MIL myself—with two strong, intelligent daughters-in-law—I've gotten an up-close-and-personal look at how challenging this role is, and how easily you can become toast. Each of the young wives of my sons has a mother to whom they are close, so to expect either one to become the daughter I never had is out for me, too. I plead guilty to having irked both DILs on occasion, feeding their children Skippy instead of organic peanut butter and posting too many photos of my grandchildren, whom I sometimes forget are *their kids*. I expect to spend the rest of my life fine-tuning this family collaboration. But imperfect as it may be, I also wanted to bring some of my own experience to this book, and I see parts of myself in all of the Tobias wives: Veronika, Mel, and Birdie.

Reader, if we were to meet, I imagine we'd find a great deal to talk about on the subject of MILs/DILs. Certainly, it's a topic that comes up with my own friends. This leads to another reason I wrote *The Real Mrs. Tobias*. Should the book be embraced by book clubs, which I hope it does, after members discuss Mel's, Veronika's, and Birdie's behavior, I imagine the conversation segueing into personal territory—as book club discussions tend to do—with tales about the MILs/DILs in real people's lives. So, with my blessing, please go forth and unload. Consider it my personal gift-with-purchase to you. I only wish I could hear what all of you have to say.

Book Club
Discussion Guide

1. Micah's accident kickstarts *The Real Mrs. Tobias*'s action. How might he have responded differently to this event? Do you feel any character gives him good advice?
2. Who is the better mother-in-law, Veronika or Mel? The better daughter-in-law, Mel or Birdie? Would you suggest that either one modify her behavior? Who do you think is the best mother in the book: Veronika, Mel, Birdie, Luanne, or Joy-Ellen?
3. Culture clash is an underlying issue in the marriage of Birdie and Micah. Have you observed that this is a common problem in intermarriages? How is it best resolved?
4. Which relationship do you feel is trickier: mothers and sons or mothers and daughters?
5. Does Mel's relationship with her daughter, Jordan, differ from the one she maintains with her son, Micah? Who seems closer to her daughter, Mel or Luanne?
6. Is Mel an effective psychotherapist?

7. Both Mel and Birdie had children at what currently is considered to be a young age in the United States. What do you think are the advantages and disadvantages to early parenthood versus later parenthood?

8. The Tobias and Peterson families illustrate different approaches to involvement in the lives of adult children. Which approach is most like your own? Which family strikes you as closer, the Tobiases or the Petersons?

9. When Delia suffers injuries from an accident, Norah, her employer, assumes support—financial and emotional—for her care. Do you agree with Norah's husband and mother-in-law that she oversteps boundaries?

10. For which family, Tobias or Peterson, does religion strike you as being more central to identity?

11. In Veronika's position, would you share a difficult medical diagnosis with your spouse?

12. Mel agrees to meet with Dr. T. What is her motivation?

13. Do you agree with Mel that it's preferable for Jordan and her baby to share a biological connection?

14. Which role do you think women find more rewarding, grandmother or mother?

15. Which role do you think is the trickiest, being a mother-in-law or a daughter-in-law?

16. Do you think that expectations for the roles of mothers-in-law and daughters-in-law have changed over time?

17. In your experience, do you believe that mothers-in-law are unfairly criticized?

18. Describe the lives of the characters a year after *The Real Mrs. Tobias* ends.

Acknowledgments

Dᴜʀɪɴɢ ᴛʜᴇ ᴇɴᴅʟᴇss COVID ʟᴏᴄᴋᴅᴏᴡɴ, Nᴇᴡ Yᴏʀᴋ Cɪᴛʏ, the early epicenter, became quiet. Very quiet. Except for hourly church bells I'd never before noticed, the seven o'clock clanging of pots for healthcare workers, and relentless ambulance sirens, an eerie calm settled over my neighborhood. With our sons grown and flown, my husband and I found ways to deal with the pandemic's confinement. For me, it meant a souped-up version of what I usually do—write. Every day, I escaped into this novel, whose characters became almost as real to me as the friends and family members I was missing during our obedient isolation. Now, as I consider the many people I wish to thank for help in writing this book, I'm amazed at how odd it is to have seen most of them only virtually during the pandemic, if that.

One person I have seen—and wish to thank—is my own mother-in-law, Helen Sweig, who would have made as excellent a shrink as the imaginary Veronika but overlaps with her only in that both have great style, explore New York City as if it were a village, and are blessed with sons who adore them. Many thanks go to Anne Hoberg and Kimberly Weaver Koslow, my beautiful daughters-in-law who each have their own darling daughter (and son). This is where their resemblance to Birdie ends!

I am grateful for the inspiration I received from real-life therapists in my family. Our resident psychiatrist, my sister-in-law Dr. Rochelle Caplan could not be prouder—nor can I—of her daughter, Leah Platkin Dallasheh, who, like my niece Nomi Teutsch, has become a social worker. Their grandmother, my mom, Fritzie Hertz Platkin, was a social worker, as well. How I wish she'd lived to see her legacy continue.

Dale Berger and Vicki Kriser, thank you not just for being—along with Rochelle—the best sisters-in-law anyone could have, but for sustaining the publishing industry with your enthusiasm for contemporary fiction. I wish everyone bought as many books as you do.

A big shout-out goes to the *Betsy*s: to my sister, Betsy Teutsch, now a writer as well as an artist, who is my energetic cheerleader; to the Betsy Hotel in Miami Beach, for providing a writer's residence that allowed me to jumpstart this book several years ago; and to Betsy Carter, a member of one of two book clubs I am fortunate to belong to along with Lauren Belfer, Catherine Cavender, Meenakshi Chakraverti, Janet Chan, Alexandra Horowitz, Elizabeth Kadetsky, Aryn Kyle, Patricia Morrisroe, Evelyn Reynold, Judith Roth, Patrice Samuels, Jennifer Vanderbes, and Susan Ungaro. If some of these names sound familiar it's because almost every one is an author or, like me, a recovering magazine editor. I'm grateful for these friendships as well as what I've learned from the authors of the novels and memoirs we've read.

On the subject of friends, I am blessed with many of long standing whose company I cherish and encouragement is high-octane fuel that often leads to laughter. Thanks Marlena Baraf, Jane Greenberg, Lisa Kroll, Janeen Johnson Ringuette, Patricia Stack, Carol Tannenhauser, Dan Vogel, Susy Madson Wester-holm, and Michele Willens, who I forgive for saying, after reading my first novel, that "this is very funny, but you're not funny." Michele, you're correct.

A special thanks goes to my indefatigable walking buddies, Patty Dann, Lisa Gornick, Ellen Oppenheim, and Barbara Fisher, who even in nasty weather have joined me in the parks that bracket my corner of Manhattan. Our conversations kept me sane during the quarantine, and, as my social media feed attests, I can now name check many a flowering tree.

My deepest debt goes to my stellar editor, Sara Nelson. What a pleasure to work with you again. I am grateful for your sharp insights, good humor, and ability to keep a thousand balls in the air while you and your colleagues work remotely. Every player at Harper Perennial is a class act: Mary Gaule, Lisa Erickson, Heather Drucker, Kelly Doyle, Viviana Moreno, Emi Battaglia, Jamie Lynn Kerner, Suzette Lam, Courtney W. Vincento, Amy Baker, Olivia McGiff, and Joanne O'Neill. My deep appreciation to one and all.

I am equally grateful for the continued professional guidance of Christy Fletcher, the editorial judgement of Sarah Fuentes, and the support of new-to-the-team Sally Wilcox.

Thanks always to Charles Salzberg, the first person who thought I, an editor and author of magazine articles on subjects like incest, loveless marriage, and how not to be fat after forty, might be able to write fiction. Were it not for you I wouldn't know Vivian Conan, Chaya Deitsch, and Sally Hoskins, whose feedback has been of tremendous value not only on this novel but several others. I loved reading your memoirs as they took shape in our ad hoc writing workshop.

Much appreciation to Johanna Resnick Rosen for my author photo, and to Ruth Feldman for her technical talent.

Publishing tribe, how terrific to witness and benefit from the support emanating from others in our world. Thelma Adams,

Lisa Barr, Jenna Blum, Jamie Brenner, Fiona Davis, Karen Dukess, Elyssa Friedland, Jacqueline Friedland, Alexis Gelber, Jane Green, Mindy Greenstein, Robin Kall Homonoff, Andrea Peskind Katz, Christina Baker Kline, Caroline Leavitt, Suzanne Leopold, Lynda Cohen Loigman, Camille Di Maio, Mary Morris, Amy Poeppel, Ann-Marie Nieves, Geneva Overholser, Pamela Redmond, Alyson Richman, Marilyn Simon Rothstein, Susie Orman Schnall, Susan Barash Shapiro, Rochelle Weinstein, Lauren Willig, Hilma Wolitzer, and Linda Yellin—all of you have my admiration and thanks.

Warm gratitude to Pastor Fred Melton for advice about a Lutheran Christmas Eve church service.

Last, thank you doesn't begin to cut it when I consider my partner in every way, Robert Koslow, who is unfailingly supportive, astute in his observations, big-hearted, and always one step ahead of me in plot development. You have my love forever. I am also deeply appreciative of our sons, Jed and Rory, who give excellent feedback, even better hugs, and are raising four bookworms. I never could have completed this book throughout the prolonged pandemic without all of you . . . you and streaming TV dramas.